'This is such a friendly ⟨...⟩ honesty and occasional ⟨...⟩ struggles many of us h⟨...⟩ reality of children's part⟨...⟩ other children's perfect parents while desperately trying to follow Jesus.'

Bridget Plass, writer and speaker

'What an engaging novel! Friendly, chaotic Becky is a busy mother with a strong urge to do something incredible for God. Her efforts appear to be frustrated as she tries to rise above the constant stream of distractions and everyday "disasters" perpetuated by her wonderful creative children. With realistic acuity, Fiona Lloyd's sensitive, humorous writing captures Becky's struggles, causing me to recollect similar instances from my own child-rearing years. A wonderful, thought-provoking read – I wanted more!'

Angela Hobday, MA, Chair of the Association of Christian Writers

The Diary of a
(Trying to be Holy)
Mum

FIONA LLOYD

instant
apostle

First published in Great Britain in 2018

Instant Apostle
The Barn
1 Watford House Lane
Watford
Herts
WD17 1BJ

British Library Cataloguing-in-Publication Data

A catalogue record for this book is available from the British Library

This book and all other Instant Apostle books are available from Instant Apostle:

Website: www.instantapostle.com

E-mail: info@instantapostle.com

ISBN 978-1-909728-78-3

Printed in Great Britain

For Andy, who believes in me even when I forget to believe in myself.

Contents

Chapter One

Tuesday 9th September

OK, so today I am officially the world's meanest mummy. Ellie screamed at me all the way round the supermarket because I wouldn't let her eat an entire packet of chocolate biscuits, Adam had a massive sulk when I told him off for dropping his book-bag in a puddle, and Jennifer shouted at me for almost barging into her bedroom when she was doing 'something secret'.

I prodded at the trail of paper offcuts she had left on the landing. 'It would be easier to keep it secret if you didn't leave rubbish all over the floor.'

'Ugh, Mum!' For a moment, I thought an enraged bull elephant in hobnailed boots was charging across the room, and I jumped backwards as she slammed the door in my face. 'I'm trying to do something important.'

Wednesday 10th September

Thirty-nine today. *Thirty-nine!* Spent an extra ten minutes in the bathroom this morning plucking out a fistful of grey hairs I'm convinced weren't there yesterday. Dave dropped a few points in the 'good husband' stakes by reminding me that tomorrow I'll be less than a year away from forty. Whose side is he on? Anyway, quite a good day otherwise. Adam, who's five, had made me a card with a picture of a racing car on the front. Inside he'd written *I loev you mumy* in letters that wobbled across the page like a spider with concussion. I almost forgave him for producing it at 6am. Jennifer (nine going on fifteen) had done something much more sophisticated with bows and flowers. Ellie's card looked like a random collection of scribbles, but she assured me it was a cat. Still, she is only two.

'Is it my birthday next?' said Adam.

Dave nodded. 'Yep. Four weeks on Saturday.'

Adam folded his arms, scowling. 'But that's *ages*.'

Meanwhile, Ellie had decided it was her birthday again (hers was last month) and was busy opening the presents for me. Not sure they were to her taste, but it looked like a good assortment to me:

- Socks, chocolates and flowers (from the children)
- Earrings and a jumper (Dave)
- Perfume (Mum and Dad)
- Book token (Dave's mum and dad)
- Smellies (my gran)

Thursday 11th September

Back down to earth with a bump today. Rang Dave's mum to thank her for the book token.

'Well, Rebecca,' she said, in clipped tones, 'we thought it was better that way seeing as the book we bought you last year doesn't appear to have been much help.'

Felt as if I'd been summoned to the head teacher's office for answering back in class. I replaced the receiver and searched for ten minutes before I found the book gathering dust on the top shelf of the bookcase in our bedroom. It was called *How to Run an Efficient Household*. Whoops!

Caught Ellie scoffing my chocolates this afternoon ... she had a huge tantrum when I confiscated them. By the time she had calmed down and I had scrubbed the chocolatey deposits off the sofa I was exhausted. Never mind thirty-nine, I feel like 109.

Friday 12th September

My best friend, Debbie, came over today to take me out for a belated birthday lunch. Told her about the phone call to Dave's mum, and she laughed. Her mother always buys her clothes for her birthday, in a size ten. Debbie is a delightful woman, but she has two children and the stretch marks to prove it. She hasn't worn anything in a size ten since she was eighteen.

Debbie said that there are more important things in life than whether the door hinges get dusted or not. Agreed with her out loud, but couldn't quite get rid of the image of Linda fainting away in horror at such heresy. Debbie always makes me feel better about things.

She licked the last smudge of cheesecake off her spoon before waving it at me. 'So, have you had a good birthday week?'

I checked Ellie wasn't watching before dropping an extra sugar lump into my coffee. 'It's been OK, mostly ...'

'But?'

'I dunno, it just feels like something's hanging over me.'

'Sounds a bit melodramatic.'

'You know: the big four-oh. Dave kindly reminded me I've only a year to go.'

'Yeah, but it's only a number.'

'I know it shouldn't be that big a deal. I just feel like I should have more to show for it.'

'Like what?'

'Like ... when I became a Christian, I had all these plans about how I was going to do fantastic things for God. Then Dave and I got married, and I thought that maybe we could make big plans together.'

I paused. Ellie had turned her juice cup upside down, and was busy shaking water all over the floor, while a smartly dressed couple across the aisle from us tutted into their cappuccinos. They didn't seem any more impressed when I grabbed the cup off her, resulting in a five-star demonstration of theatrical screaming.

Debbie passed me a napkin. 'And then you had kids.'

'Precisely. I mean, I do love them – most of the time – but these days the most exciting plans I have are about deciding what on earth I can cook for tea that everybody will eat without moaning.'

Debbie groaned. 'Well, if you ever work it out, please let me know.'

Saturday 13th September

Should've known better than to take all the children shopping with me this morning. Jennifer moaned all the way round the supermarket because she was missing her favourite TV programme, and Adam ran up and down the aisles pretending to be a Ferrari. Ellie 'helped' by grabbing things off the shelves when I wasn't looking. I ended up with a tin of butter beans and a packet of expensive biscuits I didn't mean to buy. Still, at least I can eat the biscuits (does anybody actually eat butter beans?). Dave – who teaches science at the local comprehensive – took the sensible option and stayed at home to do some marking.

My parents came to visit this afternoon. Mum spent most of the time telling me about the difficulties they were having with their paperboy always turning up late. Discovered this meant he didn't come till 7.30am some days. Tried to suggest that this wasn't too unreasonable given that they often don't get up before eight o'clock, but she wasn't convinced. Dave says my mother's happiest when she's got something to moan about.

'Mum,' said Adam, as I went to say goodnight, 'can I have a Formula One party this year?'

Hmm, possibly … if I knew what that meant.

Sunday 14th September

Usual mad rush to get ready for church today. Spent ages searching for Ellie's shoes, which turned out to be buried in the bottom of a toy box. Last week she hid them behind the settee. Tried to explain it wasn't very helpful, and she giggled. Dave reckons that in years to come she'll be able to twist any potential suitors around her little finger with that smile.

Interesting visitors at church this morning. Rupert and Elizabeth Strachan are in their late fifties. She was a GP and he's an ex-head teacher, and, five years ago, they were counting down the years to retirement. They now work for a missionary organisation in Guatemala. I'm always in awe of people like that. When I get to that age I think I'll still be busy enjoying the fact that I can have a bath without having to clear a stack of toys out of the way first. Even better, I'll be able to come into church without first having to stop and check for snot-marks on my coat.

Saw Helen and Brendan McKay having a protracted conversation with them at the end of the service. Helen makes the lady of Proverbs 31 look like the archetypal slovenly housewife. I sometimes wonder if she's the secret author of *How to Run an Efficient Household*, written one afternoon in between dusting the door hinges and rustling up a nutritious and appetising meal for her family. I don't understand what Brendan does for a living, but I know it's something terribly, terribly important. They're exactly the sort of people I could see going off to preach the gospel somewhere in the back of beyond. And no doubt Helen could have her own special ministry to any homes that didn't come up to her exacting standards of housekeeping. Cleanliness may be next to godliness for some people, but I don't think Helen would attempt to distinguish between the two.

On the plus side, this gave me the opportunity to sneak past them on my way out without having to stop and say 'hello' properly. I'm sure they're very nice people, but I'm concerned that missionary-itis might be contagious. (Yes, I know I ought to be more spiritual and be open to whatever God wants, but it's not always that simple when you're running around after three kids.)

Still – on reflection – it would be nice to do something of significance for God. Maybe I should try getting up earlier in future so I can have a proper quiet time. It shouldn't be difficult if I really put my mind to it.

Monday 15th September

Was determined to get up this morning and spend some quality time with God. Set the alarm for 6.30am. At 6.20, Adam climbed into our bed with a Thomas the Tank Engine book. Suggested he went back to bed because it was very early and I wanted to talk to Jesus, but he made such a noise he woke Ellie up as well. Her choice was *The Cat in the Hat*. Couldn't help wishing my children were more accommodating when I'm trying to be spiritual …

Had an enjoyable time with Ellie after taking the other two to school: playdough and painting. Even managed to get some tidying up done while Ellie was producing a rather original portrait of Dave. (Blue hair quite suits him, I think.) She went to sleep after lunch, so I thought I would sit and pray for ten minutes before getting a few jobs done. Woke up an hour later and ended up running up the road to fetch the other two. After that it was the usual chaos till they were all in bed. I'll try to do better tomorrow.

Tuesday 16th September

Forced myself out of bed when the alarm went off and made my way downstairs with my Bible. I'd just found the right page in my Bible notes and was looking up the passage (where on earth is Habakkuk, anyway?) when Dave appeared and said a button had come off his suit and was there any chance I could sew it back on again, as his other suit was at the cleaners'? It took me five minutes to find the right colour thread and another ten minutes to sew the button on. Dave reappeared downstairs two minutes later, looking puzzled.

He dropped the jacket onto the sofa. 'How do you propose I get into it?'

Turned out I'd somehow attached the front of the jacket to the back lining, so spent another fifteen minutes unpicking the stitches and redoing it. After that it was breakfast time.

Tuesday is Jelly-Tots (our mums and toddlers' morning) in the church hall. Ellie loves it as long as she can get control of one of the sit-and-ride cars: the red one is her favourite. Got talking to a new lady this morning, called Annie. She has a three-month-old baby called Ben, and the haggard look of someone who has averaged four hours sleep a night for the last week.

'Oh no,' she said when I asked her, 'it must be at least five!'

Annie became a Christian about six months ago, on an Alpha course, but hasn't been able to settle into a church yet, what with having Ben and things. Invited her round for a cup of tea tomorrow.

Wednesday 17th September

I promise I meant to get up for my quiet time this morning. Set the alarm for 6.30. Woke up at five to seven to a sharp pain in my right-hand side.

Dave dug his elbow into my ribs a second time. 'For goodness' sake! Are you planning to leave that going all day?'

'Oof, that hurt.' I prodded at the alarm clock until the beeping stopped. 'It can't be getting-up time already?'

'Clearly not, for some people.' He tossed the duvet aside and stomped off to the bathroom.

Annie came round this morning. The circles under her eyes were two shades darker than yesterday. Ben cried for the whole time they were here, except when he was feeding.

Annie sighed. 'He's been very colicky, especially in the evenings.'

Got the impression she's worried about bringing him to church on a Sunday morning in case he disrupts the service. Tried to persuade her that nobody would mind – there are so many kids at church now that one more won't make any difference – but she didn't seem convinced.

Ellie decided Ben was some sort of new toy. 'Baby sad!' she said, squatting next to his carry seat. 'Aah.'

Explained that Ben had a bad tummy-ache.

'Poor baby!' she said, and toddled off to find him a soft toy. She reappeared clutching her current favourite, a large giraffe which is such a virulent shade of orange that Dave reckons it's had an unfortunate altercation with a bottle of fake-tan lotion.

'Look, baby,' she said. 'My got a gwaffe for you.'

She rather spoiled her cute impression of an attentive mum later by having a tantrum when I wouldn't let her give Ben one of Adam's toy cars to play with.

Thursday 18th September

Woke up with a start at 6.30am from a dream in which Ellie was emptying all the toy boxes over Ben, while Annie was sobbing in a corner and I was trying to reassure her that Ben wasn't hurt. Staggered downstairs and tried to pray, but found it hard to get rid of the image of Annie in tears. Looked up the passage for my Bible reading, but the words wouldn't keep still on the page.

It didn't help my concentration when I remembered that Adam had a friend coming to tea. Spent the next ten minutes agonising over what to feed them, till Jennifer came downstairs and announced that she needed to read her school book or she would be in trouble with Miss Slater. (Miss Slater's word is law in our house.)

Discovered in the playground this morning that Jordan (Adam's friend) survives almost entirely on a diet of chicken nuggets and chips. At least that's straightforward. He's even more car-mad than Adam, so the two of them spent a happy hour after school charging up and down the garden pretending to be racing drivers.

'I'm acksherly having a Formula One party this year,' said Adam, when they paused for a pit stop.

'Cool!' said Jordan. 'Can I come?'

'So, what do you want to do at this party?' I said.

Adam shrugged. 'Jus' Formula One stuff.'

Well, I'm glad that's cleared up …

Ellie loved running round after them until she fell face down in the mud and had to go for an impromptu bath. Jennifer sniffed in disgust and went up to her room to listen to her music. Dread to think what she'll be like when she's a real teenager.

Sought Dave's advice as we climbed into bed. 'What do you think Adam means by a Formula One party?'

He yawned. 'No idea. If you watch it on the telly, all they do is go round and round in circles for two hours, and then throw their drinks all over the place.'

Hmm, sounds like any normal children's party to me ...

Friday 19th September

Couldn't face getting out of bed at 6.30, as Ellie was awake for a while in the night. Funny, it's not like her these days. She didn't want much breakfast, either. Didn't give it too much thought because Jennifer was in one of her argumentative moods.

'Mum, can I have a mobile phone?'

'Not till you're a bit older.'

'But you said that when I was eight, and I'm nine now. And Megan-at-trampolining has had one since she was five!'

I always get a sinking feeling when Megan-at-trampolining comes into the conversation. From the way Jennifer talks about her you'd think that Megan-at-trampolining had done most of the things one might expect to achieve in a lifetime while she was still in the womb.

Put on the most authoritative tone I could muster. 'Well, you're not having one yet, and that's final.'

Jennifer stomped off to her room and didn't re-emerge until it was time for school. I suspect I am the cruellest mother ever to have walked the earth. Felt guilty and confused all morning. Was I being too hard on her?

This evening was an entirely different story. Jennifer appeared to have undergone a personality transplant over the course of the day, and emerged from school this afternoon full of smiles as though nothing had happened. Made a cake together when we got home, and then I let her lick the bowl out.

When I tucked her up tonight she gave me a big squeeze and whispered 'I love you, Mum!'

Maybe I'm not such a terrible mother after all?

Saturday 20th September

Dave came to help with the shopping this morning, although it meant that he had to spend the afternoon doing schoolwork. Jennifer chattered at him the whole time until we got to the freezer section.

Dave reached over and passed her a bag of frozen prawns. 'Hey, Jennifer: why didn't the prawn and his brother have any friends?'

Jennifer dropped the bag into the trolley. 'What do you mean?'

He winked and leaned closer to her. 'Because they were two shellfish.'

'Dad!' She retrieved the packet from the trolley and pressed it against his cheek.

Groaned. 'Come on, you two: those won't be fit to eat by the time you've finished.'

Ellie whimpered at his mock-shrieks, but made no move to clamber out of the trolley: I hoped she wasn't coming down with something. Still, at least we didn't end up with any extra purchases this week.

This afternoon passed in (relative) peace. Ellie went to sleep for three hours, and woke up more like her normal self. Jennifer had a friend over and they spent most of the time in her room, making pom-poms. Dave hid himself away with his marking which left Adam and me, so we went and played football in the garden for a while. I was instructed to go in goal, which was fine by me, as it didn't require too much energy. Had to make sure I let a few in, though, otherwise Adam would have been frustrated.

This evening was rather strained. Thought perhaps Dave and I could have a relaxing evening together after the children had gone to bed, but it turned out he had some assessments to prepare. I wish he didn't bring so much work home all the time. Being a gracious, forgiving and godly woman, I hid myself in our bedroom and sulked.

Sunday 21st September

Dreadful, dreadful day! Up with Ellie three times in the night, while Dave managed to sleep through it all. He was very apologetic, but I still felt cross with him about yesterday evening, which didn't help matters. Dosed Ellie with infant paracetamol and hoped she'd settle down. Ended up being late for church because the car wouldn't start. Adam suggested we should buy a Mercedes instead. Jennifer said could we have a black car, because 'black's dead cool, and Megan-at-trampolining's mother has a black car'. (I might have known.) Our car is a charming shade of sludge-green.

Dave snorted. 'Given the current state of our bank account, I think we'd better get praying this car stops messing about.'

By the time we got there, the congregation was halfway through the first song. Looked around for Annie, but couldn't see her. Ellie refused to go into crèche without me, so I ended up missing most of the service. I can't understand what's going on. Last week I felt fired up to do great things for God: this week I feel like a disaster area. So much for making Jesus my top priority.

Got caught by Maggie Henderson at the end of the service. Every mother should know someone like Maggie. She's in her early sixties, with two grown-up children, and has better shoulders for crying on than anyone else I've met.

She elbowed her way into the coffee queue. 'How are you?'

'Oh, fine!' I put on my best full-of-the-joy-of-the-Lord smile.

Should've known better than to try to pull the wool over Maggie's eyes. She gave me a hug, and then offered me a tissue when I burst into tears. Honestly, how am I meant to persuade the world around me that Jesus makes a difference if I can't even convince my fellow believers?

Dave spent the rest of the day fixing the car. It's been making a few peculiar noises recently – a trip to town sounds like we have the entire percussion section of the BBC Symphony Orchestra stowed in our boot – so I was relieved when Dave came back inside smiling.

Meanwhile, Ellie continued to cling onto me, giving the other two space to try to break the world record for the number of arguments in one afternoon. Packed them all off to bed as soon as tea was finished. Maybe I should take Ellie to the doctor's in the morning?

Monday 22nd September

Remembered at ten past seven this morning that Jennifer hadn't learned her spellings over the weekend. However, I am a past master at supervising homework while making breakfast and preparing packed lunches … perhaps I've discovered a new spiritual gift. Had to look up 'necessary' in the dictionary to check she had the correct spelling (wasn't sure if it was 'neccesary'). Ellie seemed more settled, although she still had a slight temperature. Think I'll give it another day before I ring the doctor's.

Debbie popped in to say hello. Told her about my new 'spiritual gift'.

She laughed. 'That's not new. It comes as a package with childbirth.'

She suggested I ring the health visitor about Ellie. Now, why didn't I think of that?

Tuesday 23rd September

Managed to get hold of the health visitor on my third attempt. I'm sure she has a special *I-can't-believe-you-haven't-thought-of-this-yourself* voice reserved for clueless mothers like me.

'Probably teething. Has she got all her teeth yet?'

'Mmm … not sure.' Racked my brain in an effort to recall when Jennifer and Adam finished teething. 'You don't think she needs to see the doctor?'

The condescending tone was more pronounced. 'Not unless he's moonlighting as a dentist.'

Felt about six inches tall when I came off the phone. Persuaded Ellie to let me look in her mouth by bribing her with a jelly baby. There was no mistaking the white line forcing its way up through her gum at the back. Better make that three inches.

Ellie had perked up again by the time we arrived (late) at Jelly-Tots, and spent the remainder of the morning trying to climb the wrong way up the slide. Saw Annie again.

She grimaced. 'I did so want to be there on Sunday,' she said, 'but Ben was awake most of the night.'

Promised I'd pray for them both this Saturday. Didn't let on to her that my track record in answered prayer is pretty rubbish when it comes to children and sleep. I wish I had more faith.

Wednesday 24th September

Bad night with Ellie again. Don't remember it being this hard with the other two.

Thursday 25th September

3pm. Still feel exhausted. Ellie awake for an hour in the night. Think I'll try to go to bed early tonight.

11.30pm. Can't believe the things I end up doing for my children sometimes. Jennifer informed me as she got into bed tonight that she'd agreed to take buns into school tomorrow.

'I knew you wouldn't mind, Mum,' she whispered, yawning, 'because you don't have to go out to work like some of the other mums do, so you've got lots of time.'

I must have been speechless for a full thirty seconds (pretty impressive for me). What does she think I do all day? And why on earth hadn't she told me earlier?

I could feel myself about to explode when she added, 'Anyway, it's for charity, and you're always telling us how important it is to remember people who aren't as well off as we are.'

Trudged downstairs with the distinct impression that I'd been conned. Should I have put my foot down and insisted it was far too late to do anything about it now? I could almost hear Linda's voice ringing in my ears: *You need to be much firmer with your children, Rebecca.* On the other hand, that might give Jennifer the message that giving to charity wasn't important after all. Besides, I couldn't face the humiliation of Miss Slater noting me down as a mother-who-doesn't-care-about-her-children's-education. Aargh! I wish motherhood wasn't so complicated.

Scraped together enough ingredients to produce twenty-nine buns. Felt quite smug until I realised that they wouldn't all fit in the oven at once, and so had to cook them in two lots. Rather overdid the food colouring so the icing went bright blue, but I know from bitter experience that children are always drawn to things that look unfit for human consumption, so they should be fine.

Friday 26th September

Got the children to school twenty seconds before the bell rang. Miss Slater beamed as I handed her the buns. Felt rather pleased with myself, as though I were one of her pupils instead of a grown woman. Floated off into an agreeable daydream where my name was passed around the staffroom as an example of a mother-who-can-be-relied-upon. Got as far as my name being given a special mention in the school newsletter when my reverie was shattered by Adam's teacher reminding me that his school library book was now two weeks overdue. Oh well, back to reality ...

Remembered when I got home that I needed to ring Helen from church about the crèche rota. Had to make a cup of tea first to fortify myself. I'm sure she means well, but she always makes me feel like I'm about twelve rather than pushing forty. Last time I went to her house she apologised for the mess. Turned out she'd left the book she was reading on the coffee table instead of putting it back on the bookshelf. (It must be nice to be able to find space on your coffee table to put a book down in the first place!)

She answered the phone straight away. Asked if she could do a swap with Anita Draycott (our pastor's wife) for a week on Sunday.

Helen's voice always sounds as if life is one joyous adventure after another. 'Yes, that'll be fine,' she trilled. 'And how are all your little ones today?'

Started to tell her about the bun saga. Knew it was a mistake as soon as the words left my mouth: I could sense her revving up into 'inspirational mother' mode.

'We took ours in the other day,' she said, 'but I let the children do them. Hephzibah's a natural at that sort of thing.'

(Helen's children are called Hephzibah, Keziah and Elijah, and between them they could give Einstein a run for his money.)

Put the phone down with as much grace as I could muster. Surely it can't be natural for one's children to be quite so perfect?

Chapter Two

Saturday 27th September

Woke up in a stew this morning. Perhaps it *is* natural (having perfect children, I mean). Maybe it's me that's doing it wrong, and my children will turn into rebellious adolescents with green hair and body piercings in unmentionable places. Then they'll be dysfunctional adults who spend most of their spare time in therapy, and it'll all be my fault. Must try to do something before it's too late and they end up permanently scarred.

Tried to explain my feelings to Dave over breakfast.

He paused, butter knife in mid-air. 'Don't you think you might be overreacting a bit?'

Overreacting? Me? I slammed my coffee cup down on the table. 'Dave, I'm serious. I don't want our kids turning into juvenile delinquents.'

Dave sighed. 'Have it your own way. But can I just make a suggestion?'

Felt pleased he was listening. 'Go on, then.'

'If you want somebody to beat you up, why don't you give my mother a ring and get her to do it for you?'

Hmph! How am I supposed keep our children on the straight and narrow if that's all the help I get?

Worried all the way round the supermarket about what I should do. Kept imagining that people were watching my children for any hint of delinquent tendencies. Didn't notice at first when Jennifer and Adam waited to hold the door open for the woman behind us.

She stopped and smiled. 'Thank you, my dears, what beautiful manners.' She looked at me in approval. 'You must be very proud of them.'

Felt flustered. 'Er, yes ... I mean, no ... er, they're not perfect, you know.'

The woman's smile stretched into an enormous grin as she leaned towards me. 'None of us are, dear,' she whispered, before pushing her trolley out into the car park.

Wasn't quite sure what to make of this exchange. Does that mean it's all right *not* to be perfect ... or is that only for non-Christians? (And isn't pride a sin, anyway?)

Nipped into our local Christian bookshop on the way home, to see if they had anything that could help. The assistant pulled out something called *Stress-Free Child-Rearing for Faith-Filled Christians*. The authors, Shannon and Randy Hinkelberger, have seventeen children, so I guess they must know what they're talking about.

8.30pm. The kids are in bed, Dave's doing some marking, so I think I'll sit in the bath and have a look at my new book. Can't wait to find out where I've been going wrong.

10.30pm. I don't believe it! I knew I wasn't perfect, but didn't think I was that bad. The Hinkelberger children appear to have more spiritual giftings than the early Church. Four of them are regular preachers, two are gifted songwriters, and the youngest often disrupts the church crèche with her prophetic utterances. They never fall out and their bedrooms are immaculate. Shannon and Randy attribute their offspring's spiritual maturity to the fact that they themselves get up at 4am every day to pray for three hours. I've no chance. The last time I tried getting up earlier to pray, I gave up after less than a week. What am I going to do?

11.55pm. Can't get to sleep – I feel a complete failure.

1.30am. Still worrying. *Jesus, You've got to help me!*

1.50am. Still worryi ...

Sunday 28th September

Woke up determined to be a fair – but firm – mother. It shouldn't be so difficult to introduce a little more discipline into our routine.

Went downstairs to discover that Adam was already up and had made his own breakfast. There were as many flakes of chocolate cereal on the floor as in his bowl. Embarked on a ten-minute lecture about the importance of being careful with things. Adam went quiet: I could tell he was thinking hard.

'Well,' I demanded, 'what do you need to say?'

He looked at me with wide-eyed innocence. 'Please can I put the telly on?'

Was trying to work out an appropriate reply when I heard Jennifer charging down the stairs.

'Mum, do you know where my new pink top is? I'm sure it was on the chair in my bedroom.'

I stared at her. 'It was filthy. I put it in the laundry basket yesterday.'

It appeared this was not the response she was hoping for. 'But Mum, I *need* to wear it for church. Laura Draycott wants to see it. Couldn't you have washed it last night?'

Gritted my teeth. 'Couldn't you have asked me a bit sooner?'

She sighed. It was clear it was my fault. 'Well, how was I supposed to know it needed washing?'

'There was a huge splodge of tomato ketchup across the front. You must have noticed it. You'll have to find something else to wear.'

She stormed back upstairs, crushing chocolate cereal underfoot. I rummaged in the cupboard for the dustpan, biting my lip. It would never have happened like this in the Hinkelberger household.

Was still worrying about my parenting skills – or lack of them – when we got to church. Jennifer stomped off to sit with Laura, muttering under her breath. Realised as we sat down that Adam was still sporting a chocolate moustache, so spent the first ten minutes of the service attempting to wipe it off, while Adam fidgeted and tried to escape.

Was pleased to see Annie there, although she was standing at the back, jiggling Ben, who was already fractious. Ellie was more cheerful than last week, but I could sense disapproving looks coming our way when she insisted on singing *The Wheels on the Bus* at the top of her voice during the prayer time.

Dave leaned over to put a finger on her lips. 'Shh! We're talking to Jesus.'

Ellie frowned and stopped, thank goodness. Closed my eyes to focus on the prayers. Opened them again with a start when a small voice beside me piped up: 'The Jesus on the bus goes beep, beep, beep!'

What must people think of me? Grabbed Ellie before she had chance to start on about the Jesus on the bus saying move along, please, and ran out to the crèche room. Couldn't help noticing that Hephzibah, Keziah and Elijah McKay were absorbed in prayer. Helen had gone bright red and was trying to appear sympathetic and censorious at the same time, which had the unfortunate effect of making her look like the world's ugliest gargoyle.

Found Annie in the crèche room, feeding Ben. She offered me a tired smile.

'They never tell you in the books what it's really like,' she said. 'All he ever does is feed, scream and poo!'

Plonked myself down beside her. Ellie, delighted at having the whole range of crèche toys to herself, ran from one car to another, trying them all out for size. Wondered idly if there's a special toddlers' corner in heaven with an unlimited supply of fluorescent plastic cars.

Ben glugged contentedly.

'He's still not sleeping, then?' I said.

Annie shook her head. 'No ... well, that's not quite true. He does sleep sometimes, just not for very long. And when he's awake, he wants me.'

'Would he take a bottle? Maybe John could take over for a bit, give you a break.'

'We've tried that,' said Annie, 'but he just keeps spitting it out. I think John feels a bit helpless.'

She sniffled, and a tear trickled down the side of her nose. Found a tissue in my pocket that was almost clean, and passed it across.

'It's silly,' she continued. 'Before he was born, I was determined I was going to feed him myself. I was so pleased at first that it all seemed to be working well. But now I'm so exhausted, all my principles have gone out of the window. I'd be quite happy for him to have the odd bottle if it meant I could get a decent night's sleep.'

Didn't know what to say, so put my arm around her instead. Ellie came shooting past astride a vivid green bus. She was singing again, but (phew) she'd reverted to the traditional words.

Annie smiled. 'She's so cute.'

Cute? *Cute?* Not the word on the tip of my tongue.

I shook my head. 'Well, she was being a right pain in church.'

Explained about the alternative lyrics.

'I don't suppose anybody minded much,' said Annie. 'She's only two.'

Wasn't so sure. Remembered the look on Helen's face as we ran out of the service. Then I remembered Jennifer shouting at me earlier, and Adam decorating the kitchen floor with chocolate cereal. Could feel myself crumpling into a heap.

'What must people think of me?' I sobbed. 'I try to be a better Christian – and a good mum – but the harder I try, the more I seem to mess it all up.'

Annie gave me a hug. 'Poor you!' she said. 'I felt awkward when Ben was crying in church. There ought to be a noisy service, for mums like us.'

Sounded appealing, in a chaotic kind of way.

'Good idea,' I said, rooting around for another tissue. 'We could give out ear-plugs with the notice sheets.'

'And cushions, in case we wanted a nap halfway through,' said Annie, her eyes lighting up at the thought.

'There'd be oodles of tea ... and nice biscuits.'

'And it wouldn't matter if Ben cried, or Ellie was singing in the prayer time. Nobody would mind.'

Resisted the urge to say I thought Helen would mind very much indeed.

'Like that's going to happen,' I said.

Monday 29th September

Woke up to the strains of *The Jesus on the Bus Makes Too Much Noise*. Ellie was still singing it when we went out to school, attracting puzzled glances from passers-by. We'd just got home when the phone rang. It was Maggie. Whenever I'm feeling like a disaster area and the phone rings, it's always Maggie. How does she *know*?

We have a standard opening conversation for such occasions, which goes along the lines of:

'How are you today?'

'Fine.'

'Are you sure?'

'Yeah.'

'Really?'

'Well ... a bit rubbish, actually.'

After we'd gone through this routine and Maggie had prayed for me she said, 'Anita and I have been wondering about starting up a women's Bible study group for mums who have young children – would you like to come?'

Hesitated. It sounded good, but on the other hand …

'I'd like to,' I said, cautiously, 'but it's a bit difficult with Ellie – I'd have to bring her with me, and she's a bit loud sometimes.'

Maggie laughed.

'Don't be daft,' she said, 'that's the point. Everybody in the group will have small children with them, apart from me and Anita. We'll keep it very informal. Hopefully it'll give us all chance to support each other, as well as reading the Bible and praying together.'

Wondered whether Jesus would be able to hear us over all the tears and tantrums. (*Sorry, Jesus, I know You can hear us really.*)

Decided it was worth giving it a go.

'When is it?'

'We thought Thursday mornings, at my house. Around ten-ish. We're going to borrow some of the church toys for the little ones to play with. We've been praying about it for a while, but we both felt yesterday that it was time to get on with it.'

Had a lengthy discussion with Adam re: party invitations at teatime.

'Who do you want to invite to your party?' I said.

Adam pushed a lump of pasta round his plate. 'Jordan.'

'Anyone else? You can't just ask Jordan.'

'Dunno.'

'Do I have to come?' said Jennifer. 'It'll be well boring.'

Adam stabbed at the pasta with his fork. 'It won't!' he said. 'Mum, tell her!'

Jennifer scowled. 'Who wants a Formula One party?'

Waded in before World War Three broke out. 'Jennifer! If that's what Adam wants, it's up to him.'

'Don't want *her* to come, acksherly,' said Adam.

Defused the situation by agreeing with Jennifer that she could maybe go to Laura's for the afternoon. It then took a further twenty minutes of complex negotiations with Adam to come up with a list of thirteen names. I must be mad.

Tuesday 30th September

Had another go at the Hinkelbergers' book this afternoon while Ellie was having a nap, but got distracted by their cover photo. Shannon Hinkelberger looks as if she's walked off a photoshoot in some exotic and glamorous location. Hair, nails, make-up: they're all immaculate. Clothes that could feature in any catwalk show. And given that she's had seventeen children, how come she's as thin as a vaulting pole? For me, a good day is when I can zip up my size sixteen jeans without having to lie down on the bed and suck my tummy in. (Can't remember the last time I wore anything other than jeans or leggings.) Make-up? Nails? Huh! When would I have time for that sort of stuff?

Thought I'd better check Dave's opinion. Waited until the children were out of earshot after tea.

'Mmm ... Darling, do you mind that I'm not as slim as I used to be?'

His eyes widened. 'Why would I mind?'

'You don't think my bum's too big, then?'

Dave patted my backside. 'More for me to get hold of.' He took a huge swig of coffee.

Hadn't realised Adam had come back into the kitchen. His face looked as if he'd caught Lewis Hamilton driving the wrong way up a one-way street, and his forefinger wagged in indignation: 'Daddy, don't hit Mummy – it's not kind.'

Dave spluttered, showering me with coffee and biscuit crumbs. 'I wasn't really hurting Mummy – just pretending.'

Adam's disapproval was etched on his forehead. 'Hones'ly, Daddy, you shouldn't even pretend to hit people.' He turned and stalked out of the room.

Tried to keep a straight face until I was sure he'd gone.

Dave winked at me. 'Well, perhaps I should be sent straight to bed, without any supper.'

Threw the tea towel at him. 'Nice try – but you're not getting out of the washing-up that easily.'

Wednesday 1st October

Found a message on the church Facebook page this morning about the Bible study group. Pleased to see Annie's planning to be there. There was already a list of comments from several others.

Annie: I'm coming – just prod me if I start nodding off!
Debbie: Sounds good to me.
Blessing: I'll be there – I've threatened the boys with all sorts if they don't behave, but I'm not sure it'll make any difference – sorry!
Anita: Looking forward to seeing you all on tomorrow – just about to make chocolate fudge cake!!

Helen: Trusting that God will mightily bless our special times of fellowship.

Had forgotten that Helen would be there. I mean, there's no reason why she shouldn't be, and I'm sure (hope?) she's right about God blessing us; I just wish she didn't make me feel like a spiritual lightweight. And Blessing's lovely, but I'm somewhat in awe of her. Her ex-husband was – and presumably still is – cricket-mad, so the three boys are named after his sporting heroes. Debbie says Blessing put her foot down after their fifth (a girl) was born and said that no way was she going to supply him with a full team; at which point Granville took off with the lady from the butcher's.

Spent most of this afternoon praying hard that Ellie won't misbehave tomorrow.

10pm. *Honestly, Jesus, I'm so thick sometimes. Wasn't till I was getting ready for bed that I remembered my conversation with Annie on Sunday. What was it we said about a service for women?*

Duh!

Thursday 2nd October

9.30am. Feeling quite nervous this morning. I mean, it's a good idea to have an informal group for mums, it's just that everyone else is so ... *competent*.

1pm. Well, that was interesting! More relaxed than I thought ... apart from when Ellie tipped her juice all over the carpet. Maggie didn't seem to mind, though. There were eight adults and nine children:

Maggie and Anita (leaders)
Me and Ellie
Annie and Ben
Debbie and Sophie
Helen and Elijah
Blessing Robinson with WG and Brian (twins), and Lily
Gillian Taylor with Susie and Oscar

Because it was the first meeting, we spent some time introducing ourselves and talking about what we wanted from the group, and then Maggie led a short Bible study based on Psalm 23. Mmm ... lying down in green pastures (or anywhere else, come to think of it) sounds appealing. Although I'm not sure King David had to contend with an energetic toddler clambering all over him when he was resting in God's presence.

Then it was prayer time.

'Well,' said Anita, fishing out a pen, 'has anyone got anything they would like us to pray for?'

I've been around churches long enough to know that the appropriate response to this question is to look at the floor or out of the window. Helen, however, edged forward in her seat.

'Could we pray for our unbelieving neighbours?' she said.

'Good plan,' said Anita, making a note. 'It's always good to pray for people who don't know Jesus ... anything else?'

Racked my brains to try to think of something deep and meaningful to add to the list. Beside me, Annie started fidgeting.

'It sounds a bit selfish,' she whispered, 'but I'm really struggling with Ben ... he's still very colicky. Would it be OK to pray about that?'

A ripple of nods went round the room like a hands-free Mexican wave.

'Lily's being a right pain at the moment,' said Blessing, 'and when she screams in the night she wakes the boys up as well.'

'My husband's on nights,' said Gillian. 'Oscar's actually sleeping quite well, but Susie wakes up at five every morning, so I have to get up with her and take her downstairs, otherwise she'd wake him up too.'

Maggie nodded in sympathy. 'That's one of the reasons we wanted to set up this group,' she said, 'so we can support each other in prayer. After all, God's interested in all the things that concern us.'

Finished up having a good prayer time. It felt nice to think of God being bothered about things like sleepless nights. Wouldn't you think He'd be too busy sorting out the big stuff, like world peace?

Friday 3rd October

Isn't God amazing sometimes? Well, I know He's amazing all the time; it's just that there are times when His amazing-ness (if that's a word) jumps out at you without warning.

I was just sorting through the washing when my phone rang.

'Becky, it's me,' said an excited voice. 'Guess what? Ben slept through last night. I was so surprised when I woke up this morning, I had to go and check to make sure he was all right.'

Wished I could reach down the phone and hug her. 'That's brilliant! How long did he sleep for?'

'Eight and a half hours.' Annie sounded delirious. *'Eight and a half hours* – I can't believe it. He didn't settle down till half-ten, but then he didn't wake up till seven this morning. And I must have had just under eight hours. I feel almost human again.'

'Wow,' I said, 'I'm not sure I'll recognise you without the bags under your eyes.'

Annie giggled. 'It must be because we all prayed yesterday,' she said. 'And you know what else? I told John last night that you were all praying for Ben to sleep better.'

Annie's husband is – by all accounts – very nice, but he doesn't have much time for us 'Bible-bashers', as he calls us.

'What did he say to that?' I asked.

'Oh, you know John; he just grunted and muttered something about not getting my hopes up. He was taken aback this morning. I don't think he believed me at first when I said I hadn't had to get up at all in the night.'

Annie's giddiness was infectious. Caught myself singing *The Jesus on the Bus* while I was vacuuming the lounge. Ellie sighed and put her hands on her hips.

'Silly Mummy, that's not right.'

How come it's all right for her to sing it, but not me?

Saturday 4th October

Was still smiling when I got up this morning, thinking about Annie. Felt inspired to talk to God about some of the other things that wind me up. Started by asking for a car-parking space when I went to the supermarket. Ended up driving round the car park four times before I found one, at the furthest point from the store entrance. I suppose *technically* it's an answered prayer ... just not quite the answer I had in mind. Then I prayed that Ellie wouldn't need the loo while we were there. She went three times.

Sometimes, I don't understand this praying stuff.

Only a week till Adam's birthday. Negotiated with Dave to let me have the car on Friday, so I can shop for the party. The clincher was when I suggested the alternative was for him to go one evening after work.

'No, no,' he said, in a tone that implied I had suggested he go sky-diving without a parachute, 'it'll be fine. As long as you don't mind dropping me off at school.'

Had my usual internal debate about the merits of home-made cakes versus shop-bought. I hate forking out all that money for something ready-made. On the other hand, it's Adam's special day. I don't want his cake to look like something the cat sicked up.

Shared my dilemma via Facebook.

Anita: Home-made cakes taste so much nicer.
Annie: What sort of cake were you thinking of?
Debbie: Will Adam mind either way?
Maggie: Don't put yourself under too much pressure.

Helen: I have a recipe for a racing car birthday cake – it's very easy.

Me: Helen, that sounds great – could I borrow it?

Helen: Of course, I'll bring it to church tomorrow.

Sunday 5th October

Felt anxious about church this morning, given last week's performance. Managed to keep in Jennifer's good books by ironing the pink top while she was having breakfast. Ellie – thank goodness – had forgotten about Jesus' escapades on the bus.

She stood on her chair and sang at the top of her voice, about a beat and a half behind the rest of the congregation. She's quite sweet sometimes.

Annie looked more tired than I expected.

'How's Ben doing?' I asked her.

She smiled. 'Well, he's woken up the last two nights, but he's settled down again much quicker.'

I pulled a face. 'I was praying he'd keep on sleeping through.'

'Me too,' said Annie, 'but I don't mind too much. I feel like God's given me hope that he will grow out of this at some stage.'

George (our pastor) was talking about looking out for God's blessings, and how we can always choose to be thankful.

Dave grunted and leaned in closer to me. 'He's obviously never been stuck with Year Ten last thing on a Friday afternoon.'

Monday 6th October

Dave was late home as he'd had a staff meeting after school. He came in looking worse than when Wales beat England by scoring a winning try in the penultimate second of the match.

'You all right, love?' I said.

Dave pulled a face as he wrestled with his tie. 'We've got the spectre of Ofsted looming over us. We're well overdue for a visit.'

Tried to remember what had happened on the previous inspection. 'You did OK last time, didn't you?'

He nodded. 'We got a "Good", but the physics results weren't brilliant this year, so they might well choose to focus on our department.'

'Does that mean lots of extra work for you?'

'Yeah … in theory we should already have everything in place, but it's a case of making sure we have the right evidence to show them. They'll want to talk through the exam results, and we need to be able to say what strategies we have in place for improving things. Our head of department's asked me to tart up our development plan.'

Jennifer patted his arm. 'Silly Ofsted … hey, you could tell them a science joke, put them in a good mood. Miss Slater told us one this morning. D'you want to hear it?'

'Go on, then,' said Dave.

'Why was the battery feeling sad?'

Dave shook his head. 'No idea.'

'Because,' said Jennifer – pausing for dramatic effect – 'he was a little flat!'

Well, that should certainly give Dave a few bonus points with the inspection team.

Tuesday 7th October

Bit worried about Dave this morning: don't think he slept well. Gave him a prolonged kiss in the hall before he went off to work. Jennifer – who had picked that precise moment to come downstairs – recoiled in disgust.

'Ugh, gross!'

Got talking to a new lady at Jelly-Tots. Her son and daughter-in-law both work full-time, so she looks after their little boy for two days each week.

'Oh no, not Ofsted!' she said. 'My daughter-in-law was terribly, terribly stressed when they came into her school last year, she worked so awfully hard but they still picked her up on the tiniest of things. I thought she was going to make herself ill.'

Well, bless you for your encouragement, sister.

2.15pm. Just been on the internet to check the weather forecast for tomorrow. (Adam has a school trip.) 'Senior Ofsted inspector says schools aren't doing enough to improve pupils' prospects' was the main news story. Oh dear!

Dear Jesus, please help Dave with this development thingy. It sounds very complicated to me, but I'm sure You know all about it.

Wednesday 8th October

Adam was leaping around like a flea with an espresso habit this morning. Mrs Baxter was taking his class on a trip to a nearby castle, to fit in with their topic-work this term. Thought he might be disappointed when he found out there aren't any real knights living there these days. Jennifer did her best to put him off by describing the dungeons in nauseating detail. Turns out it's one of these places where they like to enhance the experience by adding grisly sound effects.

'It's mega scary,' said Jennifer. 'They turn all the lights out, and then you hear all the people screaming while they're being tortured.'

The colour drained from Adam's face. 'Are there acksherly people being torchured?'

'Yeah,' said Jennifer, 'and it's proper smelly in there as well. It's disgusting.'

'Don't be silly, Jennifer,' I said, 'it'll be a CD or something. Stop winding him up.'

Jennifer swung her foot against the table leg. 'I was only teasing.'

Ellie bounced up and down as if she was riding an invisible kangaroo. "Gusting, 'gusting, 'gusting.'

Needn't have worried about Adam. He emerged from school with a smile to rival the Laughing Cavalier's, and trousers which looked as if Mrs Baxter had decided to take a detour through a pig farm on the way home.

'Hey, Mum, it was awesome!' he said. 'The dunjun smelled like *poo*!'

'That doesn't sound very nice,' I said.

'And there was a real live skellington,' said Adam, his eyes shining at the thought. 'The man said it had been there for *hunjreds* of years. And Simran Banerjee got scared and Mrs Baxter had to take her outside so's she could be sick.'

'Oh, poor Simran ... what happened to your trousers?'

Adam scratched his head. It was obviously news to him that his trousers were no longer in pristine condition.

'I think I fell in a puddle. Me and Jordan were playing Formula One in the playground and then I fell over.'

'And did you find out lots of interesting facts?'

Adam sucked his cheeks in and bit his lower lip. 'Nah,' he said, after a few seconds' deliberation. 'It was just a castle.'

Dave came home smiling for the first time this week. 'I had Year Ten first thing,' he said, 'so I thought I'd tell them your joke, Jennifer.'

Jennifer giggled. 'Did they like it, Dad?'

'They all groaned, apart from Alice Winterbottom.'

'What did she say?' I asked.

'Don't geddit!'

Thursday 9th October

Good turnout again at Bible study group this morning. Quite encouraging, really. Started off by talking about answered prayers. Annie told everybody about Ben sleeping through the previous week.

'He hasn't done it any other night yet,' she said, 'but at least he hasn't been waking up as much as he was.'

Blessing pulled a face. 'Lily's not really any better,' she said. 'Although – thinking about it – it doesn't seem to have bothered the twins as much this week.'

There seemed to be a general consensus that things had gone a bit better this week, sleep-wise.

'Good stuff,' said Anita, 'but I think we'd better keep praying.'

Asked if people would pray for Dave: he's still worked up about this Ofsted business. Maggie said she'd had a verse from Proverbs going round in her head all week (that one about trusting God with all our heart instead of depending on our own wisdom).

This led onto a discussion about what it means to trust God. Everyone else nodded enthusiastically. Tried to join in, but was acutely aware of my own lack of spirituality. I could sense the colour rising in my cheeks.

'Erm, I understand what it says about trusting God,' I said. 'It just doesn't feel very easy sometimes.'

My voice sounded squeaky, and I knew how the little boy felt in the story of the emperor's new clothes. Waited for someone to stand up and denounce me as a heretic.

Beside me, Gillian cleared her throat. 'Actually, I struggle with trusting God sometimes, too. I mean, I know I should trust Him: it's just when I'm worried about something, it's easier to focus on the worry.'

'Yeah,' said Debbie. 'I do want to trust Him, but when I can't see what's going on, it's hard.'

Knew Helen was about to launch into one of her little homilies on the subject of why-I-never-have-any-problems-in-trusting-God-and-anyway-I-experienced-seventeen-miracles-on-the-way-here. Annie got in first.

'I was arguing about this with John the other day,' she said. 'He wanted to know how I could believe in someone without knowing the exact details of what I was letting myself in for.'

'What did you say to that?' asked Blessing.

Annie blushed. 'I felt a bit flustered, but I tried to talk about trust being a choice, and that faith wouldn't be faith if we knew all the answers.'

'Good point,' said Maggie. 'What did he make of that?'

There was a mischievous twinkle in Annie's eye. 'I don't think he was too convinced, but then I pointed out that it was a bit like a marriage, and that when he asked me to marry him he was choosing to trust me, even though he couldn't know how the future would turn out. He went a bit quiet after that.'

I'm not surprised. Wish I could think of responses like that when I'm talking to unbelievers.

Somehow, this was followed by a less helpful conversation about what we should call ourselves.

Maggie started it off. 'I've been wondering about whether we should have a name for this group. Any ideas?'

'Ooh, yes,' said Helen, 'like "Victorious Sisters"?'

(Oh please, no!)

Maggie should have gone for a career in international diplomacy. 'Well ... it's a possibility,' she said, 'but shall we see if anyone else has any other suggestions first?'

Caught Debbie winking at me across the room.

'Who's Victoria?' she said.

Reminded Dave at teatime that he'd promised I can have the car tomorrow.

He held out the keys. 'Are you still OK to drop me off at work?'

'No problem. I'll just set the alarm for half-six.'

Hurrah! I've got the day all planned out: party shopping, then nip into town to get Adam's present.

That'll still give me plenty of time to make the cake: I can't wait to see his face when I show it to him.

Chapter Three

Friday 10th October

Why is it always the days when you need everything to go right and run like clockwork that it all goes wrong instead?

Had today well planned out ... or so I thought! I'm convinced I set the alarm for half-past six this morning, but for some reason it didn't go off. Woke up with a start at 7.15 to find Dave was already banging around the bedroom.

I scrabbled through the washing pile in the hope of finding a top that looked half presentable, while snapping at Dave, 'Why didn't you wake me?'

Ellie – clutching her favourite orange giraffe – was hammering on the side of her cot, Adam was running around the lounge in his Brighton and Hove Albion football shirt, and Jennifer appeared to be fast asleep still. Dave muttered something about me and early starts being a contradiction in terms.

'What was that? I can't hear you because of Ellie.'

Dave sighed as he lifted her out of the cot. 'I thought perhaps you'd decided you didn't need the car after all.'

'But I've got a million things to do today, and I'm running late already.'

I grabbed a loaf of bread and some butter, and started making sandwiches as fast as I could. Cheese for Jennifer, tuna for Adam. Ellie followed me to the cupboard, in the hope of finding a chocolate biscuit for breakfast, but Dave caught her just in time.

He looked at his watch. 'I mustn't be late for work.'

I did some quick arithmetic. Fifteen minutes each way, then ten minutes' walk to school.

'We could leave at quarter to eight and you'd still be there on time. Can you sort out breakfast while I go and wake Jennifer up?'

Jennifer likes waking up even less than I do. Goodness knows what she'll be like when she hits puberty. She flung herself out of her room and down the stairs, fixing me with a malevolent stare as she did so.

Managed to drop Dave off by five past eight. Jennifer moaned all the way there because I said she was too young to wait at home on her own, and Adam asked why we didn't have two cars. He told me he's going to have at least six when he grows up. At least Ellie was content; sitting in her car seat in her pyjamas, chewing on a piece of toast.

Had a mad panic when we got home as Adam remembered (at the last minute) he needed his PE kit. Eventually found it stuffed under his bed. Dashed up the road to school ... only five minutes late in the end. Jennifer was in a grump again by this time. She hates being late for anything, although she hasn't yet managed to equate her desire to be punctual with the need to get out of bed earlier.

Decided I'd get the shopping out of the way with first. This was a mistake, as it seemed like everyone else had had the same idea: the supermarket was heaving when I got there. Filled the trolley with crisps, chocolate biscuits and various other items with minimum nutritional content. Ellie started screaming halfway round when she saw the crisps. Gave in after ten minutes and opened a packet for her, which she promptly emptied onto the floor. Aargh!

Made sure I selected the shortest queue at the checkout, only to discover that the bloke in front of me seemed to be paying in two-pence coins.

The woman on the till had just started scanning my shopping when Ellie announced in a loud voice, 'Need a wee, Mummy.'

Tried to placate her. 'Can't you hang on a few minutes?'

Her tone became more insistent. 'Need a wee *now*, Mummy!'

Could feel hostile eyes from the rest of the queue boring into me as I hustled her off to the loo. Typical!

Raced home and unpacked the shopping. Realised I'd forgotten to buy anything for the kids' tea. Never mind, they'd have to make do with cheese on toast. Bundled Ellie into the car and set off to buy Adam's present. I knew there was a particular remote-controlled car he'd set his heart on, and I'd seen it in a shop window the week before. Waltzed into the toy shop ... only to discover they'd sold out.

With a sinking feeling in the pit of my stomach I trawled round all the other shops I could think of, with Ellie's protestations at being confined to her buggy growing louder in each one. It was no use. I couldn't find the car anywhere, or even one remotely like it. In the end, I settled for some Lego and a remote-controlled robot. Why on earth didn't I buy the car last week? To make matters worse, I scraped our car on a bollard on the way out of the car park. Couldn't bear to think what Dave would say about it.

Plonked Ellie in front of her favourite DVD when I got home, then pulled out Helen's cake recipe. Managed to mix the ingredients together and put it in the oven without any interruptions, thank goodness. I was just going to check if it was ready when the phone rang. It was Linda. Told her about the plans for Adam's party.

'How many have you got coming?'

'We've ended up with about twelve, but we're having it in the church hall, so that should be OK.'

'Twelve?' Her disapproval levels were rocketing into the stratosphere. 'When David was younger we never had more than six. What on earth were you thinking of, inviting so many?'

Came off the phone feeling like an overindulgent mother who ought to know better. It's clear Linda thinks our children will grow up spoiled and selfish. I wish I could get the balance right once in a while.

Went back into the kitchen to be greeted by a nasty burning smell. The cake! When I got it out of the oven it was an unpalatable shade of black. No way could I use that for Adam's party: I would have to make another, and keep a closer eye on the time. Wrapped Adam's presents while the cake was cooking, then piled them on the coffee table while I went to get the cake out of the oven. It looked a bit flat, but at least it wasn't burnt. It would have to do. Went back into the lounge to find that Ellie had been having great fun opening the presents I had so carefully wrapped up.

Got to school only to find that I was in serious trouble. Jennifer's mood had not improved over the course of the day.

'Why didn't you pack my swimming stuff this morning?' she stormed. 'I had to borrow one from the office at the swimming pool and it was well gross. And you gave me Adam's sandwiches. I hate tuna.'

I must have mixed the sandwiches up this morning when I was in a rush, and I had forgotten it was her swimming day. Great! Now my mother-in-law thinks that I care too much, and my daughter thinks I don't care at all. (A more naïve parent might think that at nine she's old enough to sort her own swimming kit out ... if only!)

Dropped a few more brownie points when I had to drag the children out halfway through their favourite TV programme so we could go and pick Dave up. Slight sense of déjà vu when Jennifer complained that I wouldn't let her stay in the house on her own. Somehow got through teatime and eventually chased the kids into bed. Decided I would decorate Adam's cake before Dave and I had our tea.

When I had finished, it looked horrendous. I thought Helen said it was easy? I must have put half a bottle of red food colouring into the icing mixture, but it still came out a garish candyfloss pink. Whoever heard of a pink racing car? The wheels were not straight, either. (I bet Helen's car looked better than the picture.)

Dejected, I put it on the dining room table and went to get the casserole out of the oven for our tea. Still can't work out what happened next except that somehow the casserole pot caught on the edge of the cooker as I lifted it out, and chicken chasseur went in all directions. Dave came flying into the kitchen and found me sitting on the floor in floods of tears.

'Everything's gone wrong today,' I wailed. 'I wanted it to be so perfect for Adam's birthday, and it's all going to be a complete disaster. Why can't I be a better mother?'

Dave groped in his pocket for a hanky. 'Don't you think you're being a little hard on yourself?'

I blew my nose noisily. 'I try so hard to get it right, and yet I always end up feeling inadequate. If God wanted me to be a mother, why am I so useless at it?'

He put his arm around me. 'Stop beating yourself up. Adam will have a great time, you'll see. I'll go and get some fish and chips. You sit down and have a cup of tea. No more rushing round while I'm out, promise me.'

Did as he suggested, and sat down with a cup of tea. Couldn't stop my brain from whirring round, though. All I wanted was for Adam to have a nice birthday, and I can't even get that right. I'd love to be able to work out exactly where I'm going wrong.

Saturday 11th October

My not-so-little-any more boy is six! How did that happen? Feels like only yesterday I was pushing him round the park in his pram, with Jennifer moaning because I said she was too big to climb in next to him.

Dave had the bright idea of adapting traditional party games to feature as many Formula One references as possible. So, we had musical cars (with cut-out car shapes to stand on when the music stopped), pin the chequered flag on the racing circuit, and pass the Ferrari. Nobody was sick, and no one burst into tears; although I'm concerned that Adam's eyesight needs checking as he declared the fuchsia-pink cake complete with wonky wheels to be 'awesome'.

Needn't have worried about the presents, either: the robot was soon put to work exterminating everything in sight, bashing a few more lumps of paint off the skirting boards in the process. Dave went upstairs at bedtime to say goodnight, and came back down limping.

'What's the matter?' I asked.

He winced. 'You know that new Lego set we got him?'

'Uh-huh?'

'Well, it's all over his bedroom floor.'

Sunday 12th October

Lively service at church today. The student house group was leading the worship time. They take some getting used to, but you can't fault their enthusiasm. They're also very loud: Ellie sat with her fingers in her ears for the first ten minutes.

'Hey, guys, are you ready to do some hanging out with Jesus?' the leader bellowed. Most of us mumbled politely.

'Yes, yes, yes!' shouted Edith Mason, waving her stick in the air, and just missing Blessing, who was trying to pacify Lily. 'Go for it.'

I love Edith: she must be pushing ninety, but she has more energy than the rest of us put together.

Couldn't help staring at Blessing in the coffee queue after the service. She was jiggling Lily on her hip, while her twins clung onto her legs, meaning that she walked as if she was wading through jelly. Blessing's other two children kept bounding up to her, demanding biscuits. (Why do children never walk normally? They're always bouncing or running or somersaulting.)

Blessing didn't seem fazed.

'Leave those alone, you've had three already. You need to wait your turn.' She glanced down at her legs. 'And you two'll need to let go if you want a biscuit.'

She caught my eye and winked. 'Kids, eh! Who'd have 'em?'

Felt mesmerised. 'How on earth do you cope? It's hard enough with three.'

Blessing hefted Lily onto her shoulder. 'Not sure I do, most days,' she said. 'When I'm feeling desperate, I lock myself in the bathroom with a large glass of wine.'

Couldn't tell if she was being serious or not. 'But you always look as if you've got everything under control,' I said.

Blessing snorted. 'I wish! I'm afraid it's all an act ... *Brian*! Eat that biscuit nicely or I shall take it off you!' She thrust Lily at me. 'Here, Becky – will you hold Lily a minute while I find a tissue?'

Grabbed hold of Lily, who was not enamoured of the change in personnel. There was a noticeable crescendo in her whimpering, and Blessing grinned an apology. 'Told you it was just an act,' she said. 'WG! Stand still. You've got chocolate all over your face.'

Does that mean it's not just me, then?

Monday 13th October

Children fairly calm today after the excitement of a *birthday weekend*. Wish the same could be said for me, but I still feel exhausted after the stress of Friday.

Jennifer patted my shoulder in an attempt at sympathy when I explained I was feeling tired. 'I expect it's hard when you get old,' she said.

Huh! Think I almost prefer it when she's being stroppy ...

Tuesday 14th October

Elijah McKay's 'Intermediate French for Three-year-olds' class (or whatever it is he normally goes to on a Tuesday morning) must have been cancelled, as Helen pounced on me the minute we arrived at Jelly-Tots.

'So how was the cake?'

'It was OK,' I said. 'Adam seemed to like it, anyway.'

Helen beamed in the manner of a long-suffering teacher whose least able pupil has just read their first word. 'I said it was easy, didn't I? I was looking on Facebook in case you'd put any photographs.'

Laughed. 'Didn't want to frighten any of the parents. It wasn't exactly the world's best-looking racing car.'

The corners of Helen's mouth drooped a little. 'Oh, poor you! I could come and help you next time, if you like?'

Huh! Just what I need. Flipping Helen 'call-me-Mary-Berry' McKay breathing down my neck while I annihilate a perfectly good cake ...

Wednesday 15th October

Decided I'd better tackle the laundry basket this morning. It wasn't until I was transferring it to the tumble dryer that I discovered the crumpled letter in the pocket of Adam's school trousers. Tried prising it apart, but it disintegrated into a pile of soggy confetti. The school badge was still vaguely discernible, but everything else had turned to mush.

Rang the school to check whether it was anything important. The woman who works in the school office sounded as though she was used to this kind of call.

'Don't worry, dear, it happens all the time. Now, just let me check ...'

There was a pause, punctuated by a series of soft clicks as she studied her computer screen.

'Adam Hudson ... that's Mrs Baxter's class ... ah yes, here we are.'

'Was it anything important?'

'Well, it's a good job you rang when you did. It's his class assembly this afternoon. Two o'clock. Will you be able to make it?'

Attempted to match her unrelenting cheeriness. 'Of course, no problem. See you in a bit.'

Two o'clock! That gave me precisely forty-three minutes to have lunch and get to school; rather less if I wanted to be there soon enough to guarantee finding a seat. Grabbed some ham from the fridge and bodged together a couple of sandwiches. Ellie screamed when I turned off the telly and wrestled her into a bib.

'Come on, we need to get a move on: we're going to watch Adam's assembly at school.'

'Wha's a 'sembly, Mummy?'

'It's … it's …' Racked my brains. 'It's like a play. A bit like when we went to the pantomime.'

Oops. Realised too late what I'd done. We all went to see *Jack and the Beanstalk* a few months back, and Ellie was terrified of the giant.

She screwed up her face. 'Don't wanna go 'sembly,' she wailed.

I picked her up to try to calm her down just as the phone rang. It was George, our pastor.

'Hi, Becky.' He paused as Ellie grizzled on my shoulder. 'I'm sorry, is this a bad time?'

I twisted as far away from Ellie as I could manage without dislocating my neck. 'No, it's OK … you just caught us, actually.'

'I won't keep you … just wanted to ask a favour.'

'Sure.'

'D'you remember the Strachans? They came to preach a few weeks ago.'

'The missionary couple?'

'That's them. They're going to be with us again this Sunday. They're speaking at a conference at the university on Monday, and we've said they can stay over with us. The thing is ...'

He paused again, and I offered up a quick prayer that he wasn't going to ask if they could stay with us instead. We do have one of those blow-up mattress thingies, but last time we got it out Adam was using it as a trampoline, so I wouldn't like to vouch for its inflatability. Ellie snivelled dramatically, then proceeded to rub her nose into the shoulder of my cardigan: I could feel dampness seeping through the fabric. I cradled the receiver between my shoulder and my ear so that I could use my free hand to tackle Ellie's nose.

Almost missed the next part of George's request: ' ... so if you would be willing to host them at lunch time, we could pick them up about five ... it's only because we'd forgotten that Anita has to take Laura to a party.'

Phew. *Thank You, Jesus.* They're not staying over.

5pm. Glad I made it to the assembly. Ellie clung on to me the whole way through, but at least she wasn't running down to the front to try to join in. Adam looks very cute when he's concentrating. Wasn't quite sure what to make of his artwork, though: I thought they were supposed to be doing pictures about their castle trip. Jordan had done what I guessed was a knight on his charger, and there were various depictions of towering turrets and mediaeval princesses. Adam's looked more like fifty shades of black.

'That was an interesting painting you did,' I said, at teatime, 'but it was a bit hard to see from where we were ... what was it a picture of?'

Adam chased a bit of sausage round his plate, and frowned as though I'd just asked him the name of the world's best racing driver. 'It's a pikshur of the castle.'

'Mmm, I guessed that. Just wasn't sure what part.'

He stabbed at the sausage in frustration. 'Hones'ly, Mummy, it was the dunjun, when they put the lights out.'

Dave winked at me from across the table. 'Well, that was very illuminating.'

Beside me, Jennifer groaned. 'You're not funny, Dad.'

Thursday 16th October

I'm starting to regret agreeing to help George out.

Anita came to give me a hug when we arrived at Mums' Group this morning.

'Thanks so much for saying you'll look after the Strachans on Sunday,' she said. 'I hope we haven't caused you too much bother.'

Hugged her back. 'It'll be fine. I'm sure I can manage two more.'

Helen picked up on the conversation. 'I can lend you some of my recipe books, if you want,' she said. 'Have you decided on a menu yet?'

Hadn't realised this was supposed to be an *à la carte* experience.

'I thought I'd just do a casserole or something,' I said. 'They're not vegetarians, are they?'

Anita shook her head. 'Well, if they are then they can't have thought much of that beef bourguignon I gave them last time they were here.'

'I felt a bit in awe of them,' said Annie. 'I can't imagine giving up my nice cosy house to go and work somewhere abroad like that.'

'I take my hat off them,' said Blessing. 'Soon as my lot leave home, I'm planning to lie down for about a year; not tootle off to work somewhere where I can't even speak the language.'

'Brendan and I had such a special conversation with them,' said Helen. 'We could just sense the spirituality oozing out of them.'

Debbie leaned over so that her head brushed against mine. 'Sounds a bit messy to me,' she whispered.

Helen fixed me with an earnest stare: the one she uses whenever she's trying to encourage me to up my spiritual game. 'Poor Becky. You're going to have your work cut out for you this weekend. I'll pray.'

Hmph! I'm sure Helen was *trying* to help … so why do I feel even more inadequate than usual?

Friday 17th October

Spent this morning poring over recipe books. What was it Anita said she had done? Beef bourgui-wotsit? Hmm. I work on the principle that if I can't spell it, I won't be able to cook it. Eventually whittled the list down to about ten choices. Sole Véronique? Spinach and ricotta cannelloni? Duck à l'orange?

Rang Debbie to get some advice.

'They all sound yummy …' she said.

I could sense the hesitation in her voice. 'What? What is it?'

'It's just I'm not sure I'd persuade my kids to eat any of those.'

I sighed. 'You're probably right. I just feel a bit stuck. Maybe I should have said no to George. It's hardly going to be a relaxing afternoon for them.'

Debbie laughed. 'Hey, give yourself a break! Fill them up with nice lunch, then you can leave them to snooze with Dave in front of the telly.'

'Hmph! As long as I can think of an idea for a nice lunch.'

'Yeah …' She paused. 'Why don't you do a roast? You can shove it all in the oven before you come to church, and leave it on the timer.'

I love Debbie: she's so *practical*.

'Good idea,' I said. 'I'll do a chicken. All the kids will eat that, and it's pretty foolproof.'

'Sorted. Now, d'you fancy meeting me and Sophie in the park this afternoon?'

Saturday 18th October

Hurrah! For once in my life, I feel organised. Bathroom cleaned: tick. Shopping done: tick. Lounge vacuumed: tick. Hoover bag emptied so that I could retrieve three bits of Lego which apparently are a vital part of Adam's current building project: tick.

Dave – what a star! – volunteered to do the supermarket shop for me. He didn't even flinch when I wrote a list to rival the Declaration of Independence.

'I can take Ellie with me, if you want,' he said. 'That'll give you space to do the bathroom.'

What a wonderful man!

Came downstairs to discover he'd even unpacked it and put it all away. *Thank you, Jesus, for providing me with such a loving, helpful husband.* I feel truly blessed.

(Might even sit down and relax with a glass of wine this evening.)

Chapter Four

Sunday 19th October

Dear Jesus, about that husband of mine ...

Woke up later than planned, as Dave and I reckoned we deserved more than one glass of wine apiece last night. Hadn't intended to polish off the whole bottle, though. Staggered downstairs feeling groggily grateful I'd managed to get so much ready the day before. Peeled enough spuds to feed the 5,000 and left them soaking in water.

Dave poked his head around the kitchen door. 'I promised George I'd go down early to help set the chairs out, but I'll come back and get you all just after ten.'

Blew him a kiss. 'No problem. There's not much left to do, anyway. I'll just grab a quick shower, then my hair can be drying off while I finish sorting lunch out.'

Made an extra effort to look presentable: I know God looks on the heart and all that, but I don't want them to think they've wandered into the nearest homeless shelter by mistake. Made sure Ellie was dressed and that the other two were at least moving in that direction before I went to sort the chicken out.

You'd think that Dave, with his super-scientific brain, would be quite efficient when it comes to putting shopping away but, for some reason, any sense of logic evaporates as soon as he gets within three feet of the fridge door. The chicken wasn't on the shelf where I expected it to be. Started rummaging through piles of cheese and a month's supply of yoghurt. (No prizes for guessing what was on special offer this week.) Not there. Behind the fruit juice? Nope. In the salad drawer (a bit ridiculous, but I was getting desperate) … still no sign of it. *Dave!*

Grabbed my mobile, but he wasn't picking up. Reopened the fridge in the hope that the chicken might make a miraculous appearance from behind the mustard jar, but all that was there was a large packet of sausages. Hardly *Cordon Bleu*. I had two choices: I could be mature and spiritual, and pray about it … or I could take a leaf out of Ellie's book and sob histrionically. I flopped down on the nearest chair, and wailed.

Dave charged in through the front door at 10.14. 'Sorry I'm late.'

Jennifer forced her feet into her shoes without bothering to undo the laces. 'Mum's in a strop.'

'Becky?' He paused as I wiped a tear off the end of my nose. 'Is there a problem?'

I spat the words out. 'The problem is that I can't rely on you to do anything.'

'What d'you mean?'

'You said you'd take care of the shopping.'

'I did, didn't I?'

'Apart from the most important item, which was the chicken we were supposed to be giving our visitors for lunch today.'

'The chicken!' His face paled. 'I meant to go back and get it at the end so that it didn't get squashed under everything else.'

'A squashed chicken would have been a sight better than no chicken. What on earth am I supposed to do now?'

'I'm sorry … ' He checked his watch. 'Look, I need to get back to church. D'you want to drop us off and then nip to the supermarket?'

I was not in the mood to be appeased. 'I don't see why I should have to miss church because of your incompetence. Besides, I'm meant to be in crèche this morning.'

He reached for my hand. 'Look, I am sorry, Becky. Can we try to keep chilled? I'm sure we can sort something out.'

I snatched my hand away. 'Oh? Like what?'

'I dunno … what else have we got in?'

'A pack of sausages and about four gallons of yoghurt.'

'Couldn't we just do bangers and mash? I'm sure they'd be fine with that.'

I slammed the car door. 'Very sophisticated, I'm sure.'

Dave squealed the car out of the drive, and next-door's cat shot across the lawn. 'I'm trying to help here.'

'Yeah?' I snarled. 'Well, don't bother.'

In the back seat, Ellie started crying. 'Mummy not shout!'

Bit my lip and stared out of the window for the rest of the journey to church.

George was in energetic mode. 'Good morning, church,' he said, grinning. 'Are we ready to make a joyful noise to the Lord?'

We launched into one of those upbeat worship songs that require you to dance around and shout 'Hallelujah!' in between the verses. I don't mind jigging around a bit with Ellie, but today I wasn't in the mood. Good morning? Huh! *Joyful* noise? Pah!

Glancing around, it felt like being back at the school disco, when everybody else had paired up with someone while I hid in a corner. Even Dave was clapping determinedly, which is as close as he gets to dancing.

Sneaked out halfway through the second song on the pretext of going to check if the crèche room was set up. Ellie was still whimpering and clinging on like a human barnacle. Moments later the door opened, and Debbie came in.

'What's up, Becks? Did you forget to turn the oven on?'

'Not much point me turning the oven on.'

'Oh no! What's wrong?'

'Dave forgot to buy a chicken, and I didn't realise until just before we came out.'

Went through the whole story, with Ellie casting suspicious glances in case I lost my rag again.

Debbie tutted in sympathy. 'How frustrating. Haven't you got anything else you can give them?'

'Sausages. Not very exciting, is it? I wanted to do something special.'

Debbie fiddled with her hair. 'Mmm … I dunno … it's not supposed to be a competition.'

'I know: I just don't want them to think I haven't bothered.'

'It'll be fine. Who doesn't like sausages?'

I thought for a moment. 'Pigs?'

Debbie stretched. 'Well, I wish I was coming to yours. We've gotta go to Mum's for lunch.'

'You get on all right with your mum, don't you?'

'Yeah … it's just that she'll have done about twenty-seven varieties of vegetables and then be offended because the kids will only eat potatoes and peas.'

Left crèche feeling much calmer. Kissed and made up with Dave in the coffee queue, much to Jennifer's disgust. Ended up being some of the last to leave church, as Helen was having another intense conversation with Rupert and Elizabeth, so I guess it was a good thing we hadn't left a chicken in the oven.

'Thank you so much for taking the time to share that with us,' said Elizabeth, when they managed to extricate themselves. 'It's always so interesting to hear what God's doing in people's lives.'

Helen's eyes shone. 'You're welcome,' she gushed. 'I do hope you have a blessed time this afternoon. Becky always tries *so* hard.'

Hmm. Can't quite work out whether that's a compliment or not. Chose not to look at Helen's face as we went out of the door, just as Adam came running up.

'Are we having sausages, Mum?'

8pm. Well … that wasn't what I expected. (In a good way, though.) I always think of people like the Strachans

75

as being on a different plane. You know, spiritual giants who are so busy communing with the Almighty that they become detached from the real world. But it wasn't like that at all. Rupert and Elizabeth (*please call me Liz*) seem so ... *ordinary*. Dave and Rupert soon discovered a shared love of rugby, and got into an animated discussion regarding next year's world cup. (Yawn!) I had difficulty dragging them through to the kitchen when lunch was ready.

'Rupert!' said Liz, with mock severity. 'If you don't get a move on, you'll have to go without.'

Rupert rolled his eyes. 'Och, woman, will you quit nagging me?' He turned to Dave. 'Looks like I'm in trouble again.'

Adam's curiosity got the better of him. 'Are you having a row? Mummy and Daddy were shouting at each other this morning.'

Could feel the colour rising in my face, but Liz just laughed.

'Good to know it's not just us,' she said, looking at her husband. 'Thirty-six years we've been married, and he still forgets to put sugar in my tea.'

'Tsk!' said Rupert, winking at Adam. 'At least I don't keep leaving the lid off the toothpaste.'

I started serving out the sausages. 'I'm sorry it's not very imaginative. We had a bit of a disaster this morning.'

Rupert rubbed his hands together. 'Looks grand to me.'

Liz nodded. 'This is inspired. We don't get anything like this when we're in Guatemala.'

Rupert steered me away from the sink while I was running the hot water.

''Bout time I made myself useful,' he said. 'You and Liz go and have a sit-down.' He winked at Dave. 'That means we can get on with talking about the important stuff.'

Dave grabbed a tea towel. 'So: who d'you think they'll pull in to captain England now that thingy's gone?'

Liz groaned and took my arm. 'Come on, let's go and find somewhere to have an intelligent conversation.'

Ellie came prancing into the lounge to join us; stark naked, apart from a plastic tiara and her princess slippers from the dressing-up box.

'Ellie, what's happened to your clothes?' I asked.

Ellie performed an energetic pirouette, lost her balance, and sat down with a bump right in front of Liz. 'Look, Mummy, my nay-kid.'

'So I see. Don't you think you should put some clothes on?'

Ellie stretched out on the floor and began drumming her heels on the carpet. 'No clothes, Mummy,' she said. 'My nay-kid.'

'I don't think ...'

There was a muffled snorting noise, and I turned to Liz to find her clamping her lips together in an effort to suppress a smile. 'Don't worry on my account,' she said. 'Goodness, you forget what hard work they are at this age.'

'Do you have any children?'

'One of each, both grown up now. Our son is married with two daughters.'

'How old are they?'

'The eldest is six, and the little one's coming up to five.' She looked wistful. 'I do so miss my grandchildren when we're away.'

Was amazed how fast the time went. At quarter to five, Anita texted to say George would be with us in twenty minutes.

'You must let us have your email address,' I said. 'I can get our Mums' Group to pray for you.'

Liz nodded. 'That would be fantastic. And can we pray for you now, before we go?'

'Dear Jesus,' she said, 'thank you so much for this lovely couple, and their delightful children ...'

Can't remember the rest of what she said, but it was one of those prayers that leaves you feeling cosy and secure. She talks to Jesus as though He's her best friend. I mean, I know that we all say that He is, but Liz really believes it.

Felt bold enough to give her a hug as they left. She squeezed me back, then leaned in close. 'You know, Becky, I think God has something extra-special in store for you.'

Monday 20th October

God has something special for me! (Just wish He'd hurry up and show me what it is.)

One of those frustrating, bitty days today: you know, the ones where you feel you're rushing around all day, but nothing much gets done.

Couldn't find Jennifer's lunch box this morning. Discovered it after ten minutes of searching, on the chair in her bedroom, with half a cheese sandwich from Friday in it. Yuck! Made the mistake of asking what it was doing there.

Jennifer gave an exaggerated sigh. Clearly, *I* was a few sandwiches short of a picnic.

'I thought I might eat it after I came home from school,' she said.

'But you didn't,' I said, 'and it's all stinky and horrible now. Why didn't you bring it down on Friday teatime?'

Jennifer should have a degree in withering looks. 'Calm down, Mum,' she said. 'It's only a sandwich.'

Offered a few choice words about not wanting to be spoken to like that, which resulted in a sulky silence from Jennifer all the way to school. Miss Slater was standing in the playground.

'Good morning, Jennifer,' she said, 'and how are you today?'

Jennifer beamed. 'I'm fine, thanks,' she said. 'What are we going to be doing today?'

Miss Slater – serene as ever – smiled at me over the top of Jennifer's head. 'She's always so cheerful,' she said.

Are we talking about the same child?

Nipped into the supermarket on the way home to pick up a couple of things. Was just heading towards the checkout when I caught the basket against a display stand full of special offers. Three jars of jam crashed onto the floor.

'Oh ... fiddlesticks!' I said, in a voice that echoed across the aisle.

Ellie patted my arm. 'Calm down, Mummy,' she said, giggling.

Smiled at her through clenched teeth. I'm not sure I needed a two-year-old commenting on my behaviour with half a dozen complete strangers listening in.

(Thanks a bunch, Jennifer.)

Ellie seemed tired after lunch, so I put her down for a sleep. Thought I could be efficient and get a few jobs done. Started writing a list (it's very satisfying being able to tick things off):

- Ironing
- Clean bath (again! – Jennifer's into glittery bath bombs at the moment)
- Vacuum lounge
- Peel spuds for tea
- Plan crèche rota for after half-term

Thought I'd tackle the bathroom first until I discovered an enormous spider on the bath mat. Tried to catch it in a cup, but it scuttled off and hid under the radiator. Ugh! I don't do spiders.

Dear Jesus, I know George said we should choose to be thankful – but really, spiders? Are You sure? And please don't get me started on wasps, earwigs or those disgusting black slugs that ate all our marigolds this year.

Abandoned the bathroom in favour of vacuuming, till I realised the bag was full, and we hadn't any left in the cupboard. Ironing was more productive, but I'd only done four shirts when the phone rang. (Must be the third time in as many weeks someone's wanted to tell me I've been mis-sold PPI.) Ellie woke up with a start, then clung to me like a limpet every time I tried to put her back down.

The downside of making out a list is it's *so depressing* when you can't even cross one thing out.

Tuesday 21st October

Almost had a nervous breakdown this afternoon. Was just sitting down with a cup of tea when my phone beeped: Hi Becky, I've been sorting through Keziah's clothes, and there are quite a lot of things she's grown out of. I wondered if you might like them for Ellie. Love in Christ, Helen.

Helen's children are always immaculately turned out (of course).

Texted back: That would be great! Thanks. Love, B. xx

Helen: Super! Can I drop them off in about half an hour? I could go through them with you, and if there's anything you don't want, I'll take it to the charity shop.

Me (what I wanted to say): Helen, it's very kind of you, but I'd rather you didn't come today because there's Lego all across the lounge floor and a pile of dirty washing in the kitchen. Jennifer was in one of her creative moods last night, and I won't be able to vacuum up the glitter from the carpet until I get hold of some more bags. Plus Ellie thought she'd try on the potty this morning, but unfortunately didn't quite get there in time. I'd like to say you can come tomorrow instead, but the truth is I don't suppose it'll be any cleaner or tidier by then. Maybe sometime next year would be better – except by then Ellie will have grown out of Keziah's stuff as well.

Me (what I actually put): Sure – see you soon. B.

Aargh!

Pushed the Lego into one corner of the room, and crammed the washing into the machine. It could get sorted through once Helen was out of the way. Did my best with the glitter, but it's amazing how that stuff clings. I was discharging half a can of lavender spray in the hall when the doorbell rang.

Helen wrinkled her nose. 'These cheap air fresheners can be so overpowering.'

Was tempted to say it was better than being overpowered by the smell of wee, but decided I couldn't face one of Helen's little lectures on the best way to potty-train one's children. Went to put the kettle on. Came back into the lounge to find Helen brushing crumbs off the sofa cushion, which she then deposited carefully in the wastepaper basket. (Maybe I should have sent that text.)

'And how has God blessed you today, Becky?' she said.

Without thinking, I went into flippant mode. 'Well, I experienced a major miracle on the way to school this morning.'

Helen leaned forward, eyes shining. 'Isn't God good! What happened?'

'Well,' I said, 'we got all the way to school and back without any whingeing or arguments.'

Helen looked as though she had bitten into what she thought was a chocolate caramel, only to discover that it was full of horseradish. 'I don't understand,' she said. 'We so enjoy our walks to school – it gives us a chance to pray for all the children's friends.'

Just when I thought I couldn't sink any lower in the rubbish mothers' league table …

Wednesday 22nd October

(Note to self: need more bags for vacuum cleaner.)

Debbie had a doctor's appointment this morning, so promised I'd look after Sophie for her. She's a few months older than Ellie, but they get on quite well together. In fairness, it would be more accurate to say that they don't often fall out, probably because Sophie is quite placid and will sit and play with a jigsaw, whereas Ellie tends to be too busy climbing on the furniture to interfere.

It was lunchtime when Debbie got back, so she stayed for a sandwich and a cup of tea. Told her about my conversation with Helen. She laughed.

'I'd quite happily settle for that sort of miracle,' she said. 'Jack moaned all the way to school this morning because I insisted he had to wear his coat.'

'I just feel like I'm doing it all wrong,' I said. 'Name me one other person who has a carpet full of glitter.'

'You can borrow my vacuum cleaner, if you want,' said Debbie, 'although I quite like the sparkly effect. We could play at being princesses. Anyway, at least it's hygienic. I found a mouldy bread crust shoved under the settee this morning. Goodness knows how long it had been there.'

Dear Jesus, I know that Helen is hyper-spiritual – and mega-organised into the bargain – so why is it I feel more comfortable with Debbie, whose children are nearly as argumentative as mine, and who thinks that a glittery carpet is an excuse to play dressing-up?

Thursday 23rd October

Anita was in a creative mood and got the children to decorate biscuits with her at Mums' Group. At least, I think they were supposed to be decorating biscuits: most of them looked as though they'd been decorating themselves instead.

Had the prayer time at the beginning while the children were occupied. Maggie read a verse from Isaiah about God gently leading those who have young.

'I think we can put ourselves under too much pressure as mums,' she said. 'There's always so much to think about and, if we're not careful, we lose sight of what really matters.'

'My brain feels like it's about to burst sometimes,' said Blessing.

'My head's permanently foggy,' said Annie. 'I find it hard to focus on anything much.'

'That's why He leads us gently,' said Maggie. 'He knows all the things we have to face each day.'

'What I've found helpful,' said Anita, 'is to try to see each situation as an opportunity to learn more about Jesus, rather than as an excuse for ignoring Him. But it's not always easy.'

Hmm, sounds interesting ... though I'm not sure what a sparkly carpet can teach me about Jesus. (Really must get some more bags.) On the plus side, the glitter is now working its way from room to room, so if I don't get the vacuum cleaner sorted soon at least it'll look festive for Christmas.

Friday 24th October

Getting ready for school took ten times as long as it should have done, as school in their infinite wisdom had decreed that today was to be a non-uniform day. Well, I'll clarify that: Ellie doesn't mind what I put her in as long as she can wear her ladybird wellies and jump in all the puddles. Adam will put on the first thing he comes across, regardless of whether it's clean or not. Jennifer, on the other hand, could have been planning to spend the day on the catwalk.

'I don't know what to wear!' she moaned.

'Clothes!' said Dave.

Jennifer sighed. 'You're not funny, Dad.'

'What about your pink top?' I said.

'Too new,' said Jennifer. 'I don't want to get paint all down it.'

'Green jumper?'

'Too warm.'

'Flowery dress?'

'Too small.'

'Jeans and a T-shirt?'

'Dunno … if all my friends are wearing skirts, I'll just look stupid.'

'I don't think it matters if you're not wearing the same as your friends. What about that nice blue skirt Grandma bought you?'

Jennifer's eyebrows rose several millimetres. 'Oh, *Mum*, I can't wear *that*.'

Went upstairs when Ellie and I got back from the school run. There were enough clothes on Jennifer's bed to dress a hockey team. (And what did she choose? Jeans and her pink top!)

Saturday 25th October

8.30am. Hurray, it's half-term! No running up the road to school at the last minute for the next week. We can do lots of fun, family things together and enjoy each other's company. This is going to be a special week; I can feel it.

9.30am. Spoke too soon. Ellie has just broken Adam's favourite car. Adam retaliated by hitting her over the head with a plastic hammer. Tears all round, including me. Sent Adam to his room for five minutes to calm down, but I'm not sure it had the desired effect: he came down muttering something about wishing Ellie lived somewhere else, and why couldn't he have had a little brother instead? In the meantime, Dave got into Jennifer's bad books by telling her that no, she couldn't have eight of her closest friends round for a sleepover.

12pm. Left the kids with Dave while I went shopping. Came back to find the house in complete chaos. Ellie had forgotten to tell him she needed the potty, and was running up and down the hallway with a pair of dirty knickers in her hand. The contents appeared to have been shared equally between her clothes and the carpet. Ugh! Jennifer was busy making Christmas cards (in October?!) and had spread bits of coloured paper and glitter across the kitchen table, so that it looked like an exotic snowstorm. (More glitter!) Meanwhile, Dave and Adam were in the middle of some elaborate construction project, and had tipped Lego all over the lounge floor.

Tried to keep calm while I cleaned Ellie up. Barged back into the lounge to ask Dave why on earth he hadn't noticed the fragrant aroma coming from the hall.

He looked up from a multicolour version of the Empire State Building (at least, I think that's what it was meant to be). 'Sorry, darling, I forgot to tell you when you came in. My mum phoned to see if they could come and see us on Monday, so I said that would be OK.'

Stared at him, aghast. 'Dave! Have you seen the state of the house?'

He glanced round. 'It's not that bad, is it? I can help you tidy up tomorrow, if you want.'

I shook my head. 'I've got a better idea: you can take the kids out while I clean.'

His face fell. 'But there's rugby on the telly tomorrow afternoon.'

'Never mind. You can catch up on it later.'

Before we had children, I used to fantasise about what it would be like when we did: how we would be one big, happy family, and always get on with each other. Dave and I would be firm but fair parents, and our children would respond by being polite and obedient. Can't work out why the reality has been so different. Guess I must be doing it all wrong.

Chapter Five

Sunday 26th October

Spent this afternoon charging round with the vacuum cleaner (yes, I finally remembered to get some bags). Cleaned the bathroom, tidied the kitchen. Persuaded Adam to confine his Lego-building activities to one corner of the lounge. Phew! And I thought Sunday was supposed to be a day of rest.

Dear Jesus, you know that bit in the Bible where it talks about You blinding Paul on the road to Damascus? Well, if You could just blind Linda's eyes to the layer of dust on the mantelpiece, it would make my life so much easier.

Monday 27th October

Landed myself in trouble with all three children this morning. Jennifer got sulky when I wouldn't let her do more Christmas cards – complete with glitter snowstorms – and Ellie was cross because I said she couldn't pull all the cushions off the settee and jump on them. Then Adam tipped half his Lego over the floor because he was searching for a missing piece. He was most indignant when I insisted that he put it all away again at once.

Honestly, did they not notice I spent most of yesterday tidying up?

They'd all calmed down by the time Linda and Graham arrived on the dot of half-ten.

Linda ruffled Dave's hair as if he were a ten-year-old. 'David, Rebecca, how delightful to see you. And how are my beautiful grandchildren today?'

Beautiful? Good job she didn't see them earlier. I snorted derisively, then had to pretend I was having a coughing fit.

'Now, is there anything I can do to help while I'm here?' said Linda. She rummaged in her oversized handbag and produced a flowery apron and a pair of rubber gloves. 'Some hoovering, perhaps?'

'Mum did the hoovering yesterday,' said Jennifer. 'She was getting proper stressed about it.'

Linda missed the implications of this statement. 'I'm sure she was, dear,' she said. 'It's a big responsibility, having a home and family to look after. Now, Rebecca, would you like me to do the bits you didn't get round to?'

'It's OK, I got it all done yesterday, thanks.'

Linda's eyes widened in disbelief. 'But I thought I saw ...'

Dave came to my rescue. 'Actually, Mum, I know Becky won't say anything 'cos she doesn't like to put on people, but would you mind doing a bit of ironing?'

Linda smiled. 'My pleasure, dear, just show me what you want doing.'

Could hear her humming away to herself while I was in the kitchen sorting lunch. You'd think she'd won the lottery or something. Still, I did end up with an empty ironing basket. Linda irons everything, even Ellie's knickers.

Tuesday 28th October

Dave needed to get on with some work today, so I rang Debbie.

'Hi, d'you fancy going swimming? Jennifer's been nagging me about going to the new leisure centre.'

'Good plan,' said Debbie. 'Jack and Sophie have been winding each other up all morning.'

The new pool was impressive; lots of fancy slides and a wave machine. However, it appeared that everyone else had had the same idea. It looked like Ibiza in mid-August. Jennifer – who's a confident swimmer – must have queued for ten minutes before she got a turn on the slide. Spent most of my time carrying Ellie (who doesn't like being splashed), and trying to keep out of the way of a group of Olympic-style swimmers who were determined to race up and down the pool as if the rest of us had no right to be there.

Took the kids to a burger place for lunch, which they regarded as the pinnacle of fine dining. (Not quite sure why; all they wanted to do was to play with the toys.)

Dave was grinning when I got back.

'Work going well?' I asked.

He shrugged. 'So-so ... but I did make an interesting discovery.'

'What's that, then?'

'If I put Ofsted through the spellchecker, it suggests "offside".'

Wednesday 29th October

Maggie rang to suggest that as it was half-term we should meet in the church hall for Mums' Group tomorrow.

'That way, there'll be room for the older children,' she said.

Sounds like a recipe for chaos, although I don't suppose it can be any worse than the leisure centre.

Had to take the children into town on the bus this afternoon. Adam needed new school shoes (again). He and Jennifer sat without fussing, but Ellie fidgeted and whined most of the way there. The woman in front of us turned round every so often and glowered at us. She got off two stops before us, muttering as she did so.

'Mum,' said Adam, just as she reached the door, 'why's that lady so grumpy?'

Saw the woman pause and stiffen. Looked out of the window and pretended I hadn't heard anything, although anyone with access to a portable ultrasound would have seen my insides shrivelling with embarrassment.

Thursday 30th October

Well, who would have thought it? Our study group leaders shall henceforth be known as Marvellous Maggie and Amazing Anita.

Got to church just after ten to find a range of activities set out for the children. Maggie and Anita must have been there since goodness-knows-when setting it all up. In addition to the usual range of crèche toys there was a craft table, a painting area and water-play for the younger ones. Jennifer – who had been suspicious it would all be beneath her – brightened up when she saw Laura Draycott.

'C'mon,' said Laura, grabbing Jennifer's hand. 'Mum's asked if we can help look after the little ones while they're doing their sticking.'

Did a quick head-count while we were having a cup of tea. Twelve adults and twenty-two children. Oh, and one teenager. Emily Draycott (fourteen) made it clear she didn't mind coming to help, but under no circumstances was she to be counted as one of the children. Funny, though: despite it being so noisy, it felt remarkably peaceful. Twenty-two children (and one teenager), but very few squabbles. The children were pretty well-behaved, too …

Finished off with a Bible story from Maggie; the one about Jesus blessing the children. Quite appropriate, really, and good to be reminded about Jesus enjoying the children's company.

'And,' said Maggie, 'don't forget it says there were people there taking the children to Jesus. If we're seeking to bring our children closer to Him, we're doing something of vital importance. It doesn't matter if other people don't approve. Jesus knows what we're doing, and He's chuffed to bits about it.'

Hmm, was that for me? And if it was, how did Maggie know? Not sure what I think about Jesus being pleased with me. (Well, obviously, it's a nice thought … just not sure how much I can believe it when I think about all the other umpteen times I've messed up recently.)

Friday 31st October

Tonight didn't turn out as expected. Invited Debbie and family plus Laura Draycott round for a film and pizza night as an alternative to trick-or-treating. Hoped the foul weather might have discouraged the usual stream of children we get on Halloween, but just as I was about to put the pizzas in the oven, the doorbell rang. Opened the door to find a goblin, a ghost and a princess standing outside. I could see a woman (no costume) waiting for them by the garden gate.

The goblin waved a plastic tub under my nose. 'Trick or treat?'

'I'm sorry,' I said, 'but I don't think ...'

The ghost was peering past me into the hall.

'Hi, Jennifer, hi, Laura.'

Jennifer's face lit up. 'Hi, Chantelle.'

She turned to me. 'Chantelle's in my class at school. She's in the same maths group as me.'

'Mum,' shouted Chantelle-the-ghost. 'It's Jennifer's house. You know, Jennifer from school.'

As the woman came up the path, I recognised her as someone I'd seen waiting in the playground.

'Hello, Jennifer,' she said. 'Why aren't you out trick-or-treating?'

Gulped. Didn't want Chantelle's mum to think I was some sort of weirdo mum who never let her children have any fun. 'Well,' I said, 'we're Christians, and we think ...'

Jennifer interrupted me. 'Hey, Chantelle, we're having pizza and a film, and then Mum's going to get the chocolate fountain out. D'you want to join us?'

'Cool!' said Chantelle. 'Can I, Mum?'

'Is that all right?' said Chantelle's mum. 'I don't want her to intrude.'

The princess tugged on her mum's arm. 'Me have pizza?'

'They could all come in, couldn't they?' said Jennifer. 'We've got tons of pizza.'

Mentally ran through the contents of the freezer. 'Why not?' I said. 'I can put some chips in as well.'

'That's very kind,' said Chantelle's mum. 'If you're sure it's not too much trouble?'

I stood back to let them all in. 'I'll put the kettle on. Tea or coffee?'

'Ooh, coffee, please, it's horrible out there.'

Had a great evening after that. The goblin and the princess turned out to be Ethan (aged seven) and Maisie (aged three) respectively. The children between them demolished a mountain of pizza and chips, and smeared plenty of chocolate down themselves but (thank goodness) none on the furniture.

Carly (Chantelle's mum) seemed to enjoy herself, too. She's been looking for a toddler group to take Maisie to after her last one closed down, so she's going to give the church one a try.

Saturday 1st November

Can't believe half-term's almost over. Decided I'd be organised for a change. Ironed the school uniforms. Got Adam and Jennifer to pack their school bags, ready for Monday. Gave myself a mental pat on the back and put the kettle on for a well-earned cuppa.

Two minutes later Jennifer appeared, and plonked a pile of books on the kitchen table.

'What's that?' I asked.

Jennifer rummaged through her pencil case. 'It's my literacy work.'

'Your *what*?'

'My literacy work. Miss Slater said to do it over the holidays.'

She shook the pencil case, scattering the contents across the table.

I bent to retrieve a pen from the floor. 'Why didn't you say you had homework to do?'

'You didn't ask me.' She started testing gel-pens on a scrap of paper. 'What colour d'you think I should use?'

Plopped sugar into my tea and stirred it furiously. 'Never mind what colour. I can't believe you've left it this late to start your homework.'

Jennifer selected a lurid green gel-pen. 'Stop fussing, Mum, it'll only take me five minutes.'

Grrr! Retreated upstairs with my cup of tea. Why do I always end up feeling like it's me who's being unreasonable?

Sunday 2nd November

Another challenging talk from George this morning, all about when Samuel anointed David as king over Israel. I like George's sermons, but he does have an irritating tendency to ask too many rhetorical questions.

His opening gambit today was: 'Do you ever think that God's plans don't make any sense?'

Nearly got caught out: opened my mouth to shout 'Frequently!' but Dave nudged me just in time.

Did make me think, though (George's talk, I mean). He was going on about how David was one of the last people you might have expected God to choose, but God knew what He was doing.

'If we have a heart that wants to serve God, then He can use us,' said George. 'It doesn't matter what other people think: we just need to be ready to respond to God's call.'

Well, I admit it would be nice to be used by God; just not sure why He would pick me when lots of other Christians are so much more spiritual.

PS Not that I'm saying He wouldn't use me. In fact, going by George's theory about God choosing the most unlikely people, I should be high up the list.

PPS Still, it would be exciting to do something dramatic for God.

PPPS As long as there's no giant-slaying involved. Or spiders.

PPPPS …

Sorry, Jesus, I don't mean to put conditions on my serving You, but I would be ever so grateful if Your plans for me didn't include any spiders.

Monday 3rd November

It would be fair to say there was limited enthusiasm for getting up and going out to school in our house this morning. Dave checked and rechecked his development plan a dozen times before going out to work.

Jennifer began pouring herself some orange juice. 'What's that you're looking at, Dad?'

Dave attempted a smile. 'I suppose you could say it's my homework.'

Jennifer slammed the carton down on the table. 'S'not fair. How come grown-ups are allowed to do their homework at the last minute?'

Adam appeared at breakfast wearing his new Brighton shirt.

'Adam, where's your uniform?' I said.

Adam shrugged and chased a stray cornflake round his bowl. 'Dunno.'

'But it's a school day.'

Adam stuck his lower lip out, jabbing at the cornflake with his spoon. 'But I want to wear this.'

'Well, you can't,' I said. 'The school rules say that you have to wear uniform.'

'Why?'

'Because they do.'

'But *why*, Mummy?'

Gritted my teeth. 'I don't know. I don't make the rules.'

Adam dropped his spoon in his bowl, splattering milk across the table. 'Why not, Mummy?'

'Because Mrs Jenkins is in charge of the school, not me.'

Adam glared at me. 'Why?'

I know it's unlikely, but if I ever get to be editor of the Oxford English Dictionary, I shall take great pleasure in banning the word 'why'.

Tuesday 4th November

Was pleased to see Carly and Maisie at Jelly-Tots this morning. Hoped Maisie wouldn't feel fazed by lots of new faces. Needn't have worried.

'Pizza, pizza!' she shouted as soon as she saw me.

Carly smiled. 'Thanks so much for Friday,' she said. 'We had a great time. Much better than tramping round in the rain.'

Maisie was soon pedalling round after Ellie on a bright pink tricycle. 'Hello, Mrs Pizza-Lady,' she said, every time she came past where we were sitting.

Ellie found this hilarious (she would), and insisted on repeating my new name several times on the way home. Great! I can just imagine the scene when I get to heaven: everyone else will be rejoicing over their new names, while I'll be forever known as Mrs Pizza-Lady.

Linda rang when we got home. Passed the phone to Ellie.

'Would you like to talk to Grandma?'

Ellie danced round the lounge with the phone sticking out at right angles to her ear. ''Lo, Gan-ma.'

Linda's voice crackled in the receiver, and Ellie nodded. 'Mums ... tots,' she said. 'I dancing.'

She waved the phone above her head, and I could hear Linda's cultured tones. 'Is Mummy there?' she asked.

Ellie beamed. 'Mummy!' She brandished the phone under my nose, 'Mummy Mrs Pizza-Lady? Gan-ma wants you.'

'She seems very excitable today,' said Linda. 'What was it she called you?'

Explained about Halloween and the pizza party.

Linda sniffed. 'It doesn't sound very healthy,' she said. 'I do hope you're not encouraging them to eat too much junk food, Rebecca.'

One of these days, it'd be nice to have a conversation with Linda that doesn't include her criticising my parenting and/or housework skills.

Wednesday 5th November

Bonfire night has to be the biggest con ever. Spent £15 on a box of twelve fireworks. Two of them refused to light, while the others lasted an average of seventeen seconds each. I make that just under three minutes' worth of entertainment, which means that I spent the equivalent of £300 per hour. Ouch! The sparklers were more successful, although Ellie was so excited that she kept running up to the other two to show them her 'pikshers' … it's a miracle she didn't set Jennifer's hair alight in the process.

Thursday 6th November

Mums' Group was back to normal today. (Well, as normal as you can be when there are nine under-fives in the room.) Maggie said she thought it would be a good idea to discuss what George had said on Sunday morning.

'I love the idea of God doing something exciting through me,' said Annie.

'Yeah, but I always feel other people are better qualified,' said Debbie.

'Isn't that the whole point of what George was trying to say?' said Blessing. 'It isn't about how well qualified we are, but whether we're willing for God to use us.'

'That's true,' said Maggie. 'The Bible's full of people who were used by God, and mostly, they weren't the ones you'd have expected Him to pick.'

'Ooh, like Moses,' I said.

'And Ruth,' said Anita.

'Esther.'

'Peter.'

'Gideon.'

'Paul.'

'John Newton,' said Gillian.

We all turned and looked at her.

Gillian blushed. 'I do know he's not in the Bible,' she said. 'I was thinking he was somebody else that God used.'

'What bothers me,' said Blessing, 'is, how do we know when God's calling us to do something, anyway?'

Maggie said: 'I'm sure there must be times when we miss what God wants us to do because we're too busy thinking about how somebody else could do it better.'

Helen shuffled forward on her seat so she could sit up straighter. 'I always have an hour with God first thing,' she said, 'and He often talks to me about how I can serve Him more effectively. It's such a blessed time.'

Hmm. Don't always feel I can match up to Helen's exacting standards. On the other hand, maybe she has a point: I don't want to miss God's voice through a lack of commitment on my part. Perhaps I should try getting up early again?

Friday 7th November

God must have big plans for me!

Set the alarm for six this morning. Came downstairs to a deserted lounge. Good long quiet time. Felt a real sense of anticipation. Nothing specific from God, but I'm sure there will be before long. Can't wait to find out what He's got in store for me. Maintained my aura of composure even when Adam knocked apple juice all over the table at breakfast.

I snatched the dishcloth. 'Don't worry, dear, these things happen.'

Jennifer paused, spoon midway between bowl and mouth. 'Are you feeling OK, Mum?'

Amazing! People are already noticing the difference.

Saturday 8th November

Don't think Dave was impressed when the alarm went off again at six.

'Whash that?' he mumbled, burying his head under a pillow.

'I'm just going to have my quiet time.'

'Bu' ish Shaturday.'

'I know that. It's my new regime.'

No reply to this, just a muffled snorting.

Honestly, you'd think he'd have worked out by now that God doesn't have days off. Some people have no commitment.

Sunday 9th November

Up at six again this morning. That's three days in a row. It's easy when you put your mind to it ... can't think why people make such a fuss about getting up early to pray. I'm clearly more spiritual than I realised.

Felt quite weary after lunch (all this extra praying is hard work).

'Darling, I think I'll have a lie-down for an hour,' I said.

Dave dropped a pile of books on the table. 'But I've got a stack of marking. I could do with some help here.'

Guess he's challenged by my sacrificial lifestyle. Suggested he might benefit from spending more time in prayer and less time worrying about schoolwork.

Dave opened an exercise book and adjusted his glasses. 'Why, thank you, Barnabas.'

Adam came charging in. 'Mum, can you be goalie?'

I shook my head. 'Not now. I'm too tired. I was up at six, talking to Jesus.'

Adam looked bemused.

'I thought you said we could talk to Jesus anytime,' he said. 'Why don't you get up later? Then you can still talk to Him, and you can be goalie as well.'

'It's not quite as simple as that.'

Dave snorted. 'Isn't it?'

I dunno, I don't remember the disciples telling Jesus off for getting up too early. I suppose I'm bound to experience opposition if I'm taking a stand for Jesus, but hadn't expected it to come from such close quarters.

Monday 10th November

Getting up is a fierce battle, but I'm choosing to rejoice that I can be victorious. Had to have words with Jennifer when she started moaning about the fact she'd got a test at school this morning. (Having such a negative attitude is so ungodly.)

'OK, Mum, keep your hair on,' said Jennifer.

Ellie banged her spoon on the table. 'Hair on, Mummy, hair on.'

Naturally – or should that be supernaturally? – I forgive them for trying to stand in the way of God's purposes.

Tuesday 11th November

Jelly-Tots was a challenge this morning: all those women (and two men) fussing about minor details like teething and MMR jabs. I am a woman who listens to God. OK, I'm still waiting to hear something significant, but I expect that's the reality of being a true disciple: needing to have faith to keep going when others are caught up in the worries of the world.

Read some more of the Hinkelbergers' book this afternoon. Not sure I'm quite ready for getting up at four, but I'm heading in the right direction. If I wasn't so mature, I'd be feeling quite smug.

Wednesday 12th November

Found it tricky to focus this morning. I'm sure I was being tempted to succumb to sleep, but managed (on the whole) to resist. Have to say I'm surprised God hasn't spoken more clearly by now. A person of lesser faith might have given up.

Shared this with Dave over breakfast. (Thought it would be good to encourage him to be more committed to his relationship with God.)

'Actually,' said Dave, 'I think God's given me a word for you.'

Wasn't sure whether to be excited or disappointed. I mean, it's always good if God has something to say, but I did think He might have spoken to me directly, what with all the time I've been spending with Him this past week. Still, maybe that ties in with His plans not always making sense to us.

'Go on, then,' I said.

'He says you're bonkers.'

Huh! I had hoped that Dave would be a bit more supportive.

Thursday 13th November

Couldn't wait for Mums' Group as I wanted everyone to know just how seriously I had been taking last week's challenge.

'OK,' said Anita, 'has anyone got anything they'd like to share?'

Pulled myself up straight and rearranged my features into what I hoped was a spiritual-yet-humble look.

'Actually,' said Annie, 'I've had some brilliant conversations with John. I've been praying for ages that God would help me to talk to him about Jesus.'

'I've been asking God what he wanted me to do for Him,' said Blessing, 'and I had a sense that He wanted me to help my mother out a bit more. She's got bad arthritis, but she's quite stubborn about accepting help.'

'And?' said Maggie.

'Well, I prayed that God would give me an opportunity, and on Monday when I went round, she admitted she was struggling with the washing. I've offered to do it for her.'

'Haven't you got tons of washing, anyway?' said Gillian.

Blessing shrugged. 'Enough to keep a small launderette in business. A bit more won't make any difference.'

'I don't think God's given me anything specific,' said Debbie. 'I've just felt thankful that He loves me, anyway.'

Opened my mouth to tell them about my early morning prayer times, then shut it again.

'Are you all right, Becky?' said Anita. 'You're very quiet this morning.'

Was horrified to realise that tears were rolling down my cheeks.

'I've tried so hard to listen to God this week,' I said, 'and it doesn't seem to have made a scrap of difference.'

Felt foolish talking about my attempts to get up early when God had obviously done the sensible thing and had a lie-in so He could have normal conversations with normal people at a normal time of day.

'D'you think you might be pushing yourself too hard?' said Anita. 'You've got plenty on your plate as it is.'

Maggie shuffled up so she could give me a hug.

'You are daft,' she said. 'God already loves you to bits. You can't make Him love you any more by trying to get up before you've gone to bed.'

Wiped my eyes with the end of my sleeve.

'I've been reading this book,' I said, 'by this couple who get up at four every morning to pray for their kids. I thought maybe I could start at six, and then work back.'

'Huh!' said Blessing. 'I hate those books ... say they'll help you be a better Christian, but end up making you feel like a pile of poo.'

'Blessing!' said Helen.

'Oops, sorry,' said Blessing, looking as though she was anything but.

'Mummy said "Poo!"' shrieked Brian, dancing up and down in delight. 'Poo, poo, poo!'

Anita chortled. 'Good job the elders don't know what really goes on here. We'd all be excommunicated or something.'

'It's all right,' said Debbie, 'if George asks, you can say we were talking about being fertile ground.'

'Or how to get rid of the rubbish in our lives.' (Blessing)

'And not letting our gifts go to waste.' (Gillian)

'How about not being afraid to get our hands dirty?' (Debbie again)

'Ugh, gross!' (Annie)

Helen shook her head. 'I'm afraid I don't follow you.'

Suddenly saw the funny side. Tried to keep a straight face, but caught Debbie's eye at the wrong moment. Tears streamed down my face for the second time that morning as I collapsed in a fit of laughter.

There was no danger of the atmosphere getting too spiritual after that: the prayer time was punctuated by regular shouts of 'Poo!' (Brian), and outbreaks of giggling (me and Debbie). Anita read the verse about God taking great delight in us, and Annie prayed I'd be able to catch up on some sleep. Realised I felt more peaceful than I had done all week.

Had one of those (God?) inspired moments at the end of the meeting. Helen came across to give me a hug.

'You're in a battle, Becky,' she said. 'I'm sure God will equip you to stand firm: I just wish I could have done more to help.'

Recalled the puzzled expression on her face when we were responding to Blessing's comments. 'Actually, Helen,' I said, 'you were very helpful. You said just the right thing at exactly the right time.'

Chapter Six

Friday 14th November

Couldn't be bothered to get up at six this morning, although part of me felt a bit guilty. (Perhaps I'm not cut out to be spiritual.) Dragged myself out of bed at twenty-past seven when Jennifer started practising *While Shepherds Watched* on her recorder outside our bedroom door. Her life's ambition at the moment is to get picked to play in the school carol service.

My personal opinion is that twenty Year Five pupils shrilling away in supposed unison is a far more terrifying prospect than an angelic visitation. Dave got himself into bother the other day when Jennifer overheard him suggesting to me that perhaps we ought to take pity on Miss Slater and buy her a set of earplugs for Christmas. The situation was only defused when he agreed to listen to her playing through her entire repertoire. Still, I do feel sorry for her (Miss Slater, I mean). I'd love to know how she manages to deal with a class of thirty children every day when I struggle to cope with three.

Saturday 15th November

Didn't get up till half-past nine today!!

That's the longest I've slept in since the day Jennifer was born. Dave (bless him) had given the children breakfast before bringing me a large cup of tea and some toast. Ellie clambered onto the bed next to me.

'My had toast,' she said. 'Daddy maked it.'

I glanced at her hair. Her golden curls – unruly at the best of times – were clumped together at the back. I reached out a tentative finger.

'That sounds yummy,' I said. 'Did you have jam on it, by any chance?'

Sunday 16th November

Funny: last week when I was trying so hard to be spiritual and listen to God, church felt quite stressful. This week – when I wouldn't exactly come top in any international Bible-reading competition – I felt very aware of God's presence. How does that work?

Monday 17th November

Had a chatty email from Liz Strachan this morning. They've been up in Scotland with their son and his family:

Can't believe that we're into November again already. Only three days till we go back to Guatemala. It's hard leaving family and friends behind, but I'm sure God has a purpose for us in all this. Please would you mind praying for us? There's a couple of tricky situations we have to deal with when we get back. I'm trying to trust God in the midst of it all, but it doesn't feel very easy sometimes.

Lots of love to your delightful family – we're praying for you, too.

Blessings, Liz xx

Wrote straight back:

Really enjoyed our time with you the other week. We'll be praying for you – I can ask others to pray too, if you'd like. Please keep in touch, and let us know if there's anything specific we can be praying for.

Love, Becky x

Liz: Hi, Becky, we'd appreciate it if you could pass our prayer requests on – didn't you say you were involved in a women's Bible study group at church? We try to send a prayer update by email to our supporters about once a month, so we could add your name to the list. We've just put George and Anita on there, too. Xx

Made a mental note to ask Maggie if we could pray for them at Mums' Group this week – I'm hoping they might all have forgotten about the toilet jokes by then.

Tuesday 18th November

Felt much more chilled at Jelly-Tots today. Maybe God doesn't mind us chatting about the small stuff, like teething problems and potty training.

'Are you OK?' said Annie.

'Much better. Still wish I could hear God more clearly, though.'

'Mmm. I'm sure we had a discussion about this when I was doing Alpha. The guy who was leading it said that God tells us things at the right time, and that sometimes we have to wait.'

Sighed. 'Sometimes, I feel like I spend my whole life waiting. At the moment, I spend an inordinate amount of time waiting for Ellie while she sits on the potty. It wouldn't be so bad if she did something … but that tends to happen about ten seconds after she's climbed off.'

Annie wrinkled her nose at the thought. 'Not looking forward to that bit,' she said. 'Given the state of Ben's nappies recently, we might have to start calling this session *Smelly-Tots* instead.'

Wednesday 19th November

Spent the morning at Debbie's: she's been promising for ages that she'd cut my hair for me. Couldn't work out whether to just trim the ends or go for something a bit different.

'I could cut it up to here,' said Debbie, trapping about four inches of hair between her fingers. 'You'd have the same sort of style, but it might feel a bit more manageable.'

Couldn't believe the improvement when I looked in the mirror. The ends had thickened up beautifully, and now danced in a neat line just below my shoulders.

'Your hair looks nice, Mum,' said Jennifer, as we walked home from school.

'Thanks. Debbie did it for me.'

'She's well clever,' said Jennifer. 'D'you think she'd do mine?'

9.30pm. Dave's only just got in (Year Twelve parents' evening). He must be worn out, as he hasn't noticed my new, glamorous look.

Thursday 20th November

Arrived at Maggie's to a chorus of whistles.

'Fab hair,' said Blessing. 'It must feel strange.'

'Haven't quite got used to it yet,' I admitted, 'but I do like it.'

This week's discussion was on Mary and Martha.

'I feel sorry for Martha,' said Blessing. 'I mean, there she was, doing her best to make the house look nice, and then Mary's the one who gets the thumbs-up from Jesus.'

'Doesn't seem fair,' said Debbie.

Opened my mouth to agree, but Helen got there first.

'I've thought about this,' she said, 'and I think the problem is that Martha wasn't as organised as she could have been. If she'd had a more efficient timetable for cleaning the house, she'd have had time to sit down with Jesus, too.'

What???

Caught sight of my reflection in Maggie's telly. My mouth was still hanging open: I looked like a young blackbird waiting for a particularly succulent worm.

Anita laughed. 'I guess I'm too much like Martha,' she said. 'It's not that I don't want to spend time with Jesus. I just get too easily distracted.'

Maggie nodded. 'I don't think this story is about whether we should clean the house or not,' she said. 'Isn't it more about learning to recognise the things that distract us from developing our relationship with God?'

Ellie came pottering across with a plastic jam jar from the toy kitchen, which she dropped at my feet. 'Calm down, Mummy, calm down!' she said.

I groaned. 'Like children, you mean?'

Maggie lifted Ellie onto her lap and pulled out a book to show her. 'No, not necessarily,' she said. 'We all have busy lives, and it's not always possible to switch everything off so we can be on our own with God.'

'Yeah, but life'd be so much simpler if the kids had an on-and-off switch,' said Blessing. 'Even going to the loo on my own feels like a novelty these days.'

Spent a large proportion of this evening tossing my hair back over my shoulders to see if Dave noticed anything.

'Are you feeling OK?' he asked as we climbed into bed.

'I'm fine. Why?'

'Dunno, you just seem a bit restless this evening.'

Huh!

Friday 21st November

9am. Feel challenged by what Maggie said yesterday about being too easily distracted, especially as I forgot to ask if we could pray for the Strachans. Perhaps that's why my spiritual life often feels a bit flat. Maybe if I write a list of all the other things that get in the way of me spending time with Jesus, it'll help me do better with my quiet times.

5.30pm. I did intend to write that list today … honest! Thought I ought to check Facebook first to see if anyone else had commented on yesterday's meeting. Checked again at 11.05am (nothing), 12.57 (still nothing) and 3.46pm (just in case – people can be a bit slow to respond to things). Found a link to a hilarious clip of a kitten chasing a ping-pong ball across a wooden floor. Watched it again so I could tell Dave all about it. Then Adam wanted to know what I was laughing at, so showed it to him and Ellie. Not sure Ellie knew why it was funny but she screeched with laughter anyway, which caught Jennifer's attention. Played it again (twice).

This was a mistake, as it triggered off two of Jennifer's favourite arguments: 'Why can't we have a cat?' and 'Why can't I have my own Facebook account?'

Wouldn't you know it, Megan-at-trampolining has been on Facebook since she was three. (Really?) She also has a horse, two cats, three dogs, two rabbits, six terrapins, a guinea pig and a budgerigar (and presumably, her own private zoo to keep them all in).

Caught Dave watching me with a puzzled expression after tea.

'What's the matter, darling?'

He took his glasses off and cleaned them with his handkerchief. 'Just wondering. Have you coloured your hair or something?'

Sometimes, I wonder why I bother.

Saturday 22nd November

Didn't have much chance to think about that list this morning, as I needed to get the shopping done first thing so Dave could drop Adam off at a birthday party at lunchtime. Knew I wouldn't be able to concentrate till I'd put it all away. Discovered a furry tomato – yuck! – at the back of the salad drawer, so spent the next three-quarters of an hour emptying the fridge and wiping it down.

Remembered after lunch that I hadn't spoken to my mum for a few days. Came off the phone an hour later still not having spoken to her properly: Mum has never understood the concept that conversation is meant to be a two-way thing.

Me: Hi, Mum, it's me.

Mum: Oh, hello, dear, I was just talking to your father about you and saying I wonder if Becky will ring up today because she hasn't rung for a few days, do you think she's all right, but your father said I'm sure she's fine, why don't you ring her if you're feeling anxious about her, but I said no it's all right, I don't want to interrupt her if she's busy … you're not too busy, are you, dear?

Me: No, I'm fi …

Mum: Have you heard from our Katie recently? She rang up the other day, it was so nice to talk to her, but I think she's quite busy as well, of course she's just got the two kids to look after but it's still a big responsibility, isn't it? How are Jennifer and Adam and Ellie?

Me: They're all OK, Mu …

Mum: They're growing up so fast, aren't they, doesn't seem a minute since you were coming home from the hospital with Jennifer – how's she getting on at trampolining, has she done any badges recently …

I'd like to say that the conversation got better after that, but that would be a lie. Dave's often suggested I might as well ring up and then go and get on with something else, as she wouldn't notice for at least half an hour. It's tempting, I must admit.

Dave volunteered to supervise the kids before tea so I could have a bit of time to myself. Almost succumbed to Blessing's recommendation of a glass of wine, but decided to make do with an extra-large cup of tea. Took my Bible and hid in the bathroom. Managed a full four and a half minutes' peace and quiet before being interrupted by Adam, who was desperate for the loo. Typical!

As far as I'm aware, nowhere in the Bible does it say Jesus withdrew to spend time with His Father, only to give it up as a bad job five minutes later due to the toileting requirements of a nagging six-year-old.

Sunday 23rd November

Anita came to help me in crèche today. She's great with the kids: she told them the story of Jonah, with added sound effects. Not sure how much they understood, but the bigger ones all liked shouting 'Splash!' when Jonah was thrown overboard. Then we had prayers.

Anita said: 'Thank you, God, for looking after Jonah.'

WG said: 'Thank you for the whale.'

Brian (not to be outdone) said: 'Thank you for biscuits.'

'Ellie, is there anything you want to say thank you to Jesus for?' I asked.

She shook her head and ran off across the room. Moments later she rode back on a bright green tractor.

'Jesus ... cars,' she said, tapping the tractor.

Well, I suppose that counts.

Jennifer appeared after the service with Laura in tow. 'Hey, Mum, can Laura come for lunch?'

'I suppose so,' I said, 'if Anita doesn't mind dropping her off.'

Anita hesitated. 'What about your reading book for school? You need to finish that and write it up in your log.'

'Aww, *Mum*!' said Laura. 'Do I have to?'

'Sure do.'

'Can't I just leave it for this week – Miss Slater won't mind.'

A hint of tension crept into Anita's voice. 'If Miss Slater's asked you to do it, then you'll do it. I'll pick you up from Jennifer's at four, and you can do it then.'

'But that's hardly any time. It's not fair!'

'Well,' said Anita, folding her arms across her chest, 'that's my final offer. Take it or leave it.'

Laura gave an exaggerated sigh and flounced out of the room. Jennifer chased after her. I could hear them chuntering at each other in the corridor.

Anita shook her head. 'She's so *adolescent* sometimes,' she said. 'Whatever I do, it's the wrong thing.'

I nodded. 'I don't understand it. Jennifer can be charming, but then other times she's completely obnoxious. I thought hormones weren't supposed to kick in till they got to high school.'

'Oh, the joys of having children!' said Anita. 'See you Thursday?'

Monday 24th November

(Still haven't managed to write that list.)

Had Linda on the phone this morning.

'Hello, Rebecca,' she said. 'I was just wondering if you'd any ideas about what David might like for his birthday. You do *know* it's his birthday on Saturday, don't you?'

Resisted the impulse to say that it had been on the twenty-ninth of November for as long as I had known him, and I wasn't aware he had any plans to change it.

'Mmm ... I know there's a couple of CDs that he'd like, or you could get him a computer game.'

Could sense Linda's mouth settling into a line of disapproval.

'Oh, I don't know about that, dear. What about something practical? A nice jumper? Or a tie, perhaps?'

I know for a fact that Linda and Graham have bought Dave jumpers for at least the last three birthdays. I also know for a fact that they are all buried somewhere in the back of his wardrobe with the tags still attached. Last year's offering looked like one of Ellie's paintings: the ones where she gets bored and tips the paint tray across the paper.

Tried to be tactful. 'I think he's got quite a lot of jumpers already.'

'Oh, I'm sure he'd be pleased to have another,' said Linda. 'We'll see you on Saturday, then ... about twelve? So glad you invited us.'

Have I missed something? Exactly *when* did I invite them?

Tuesday 25th November

(Mustn't forget to get Dave's present before Saturday.)

Glad to see Carly was there again at Jelly-Tots. Had a good chat about the delights or otherwise of having a toddler in the family.

'I don't know how I cope some days,' said Carly. 'Yesterday Chantelle and Ethan had a huge argument over whose turn it was to have the toy from the cereal packet. I was so busy trying to sort them out that I didn't realise Maisie had found an old lipstick in my handbag, and was colouring in her bedroom walls with it.'

Well, that's one thing I don't have to worry about: it's so long since I had time to think about make-up that I don't even possess a lipstick any more. I threw my last mascara out over the summer on the grounds that having languished (opened) in the back of a drawer for five years, it was bound to be a health hazard.

Wednesday 26th November

(He's always so difficult to buy for.)

Texted Dave at lunchtime to try to get some inspiration.

Dave: No idea – haven't got the energy to think right now – we've just had word that Ofsted are coming in tomorrow.

Me: Sorry – that's a pain. Does that mean you'll be late back?

Dave: Should think so – my head of department's gone into overdrive.

Prayed hard this afternoon. I hope Dave's plan thingy is up to scratch. Wondered whether I should ask God for a verse, but all that came to mind was Isaiah 43:2: 'When you pass through the waters, I will be with you; and when you pass through the rivers, they will not sweep over you. When you walk through the fire, you will not be burned; the flames will not set you ablaze.'

Didn't know what to make of this. I mean, given my recent struggles with hearing from God, it could be my imagination playing tricks again. On the other hand, if by some minor miracle the Holy Spirit has got through to my addled brain, I do think He might have given me something a bit more understandable.

Dragged the kids out after school so they could choose presents. Ellie wanted to buy him a children's DVD, but was persuaded (after some debate) to go for something more grown-up. Adam chose a mug with a picture of a racing car, and Jennifer got him a glass beer tankard (he got severely chastised when she caught him drinking from a can the other day).

Thursday 27th November

Felt sorry for Dave this morning. I know he's quite organised when it comes to stuff like lesson plans, but even so, he must have checked his planner about twenty times over breakfast. Gave him an extra big squeezy hug as he set off, and slipped a packet of Jelly Babies into his pocket. They're his favourite; and if all else fails, he can use them to bribe the inspectors. (I'm not suggesting that

HMI are morally suspect; maybe bribing the pupils would be a better idea.)

Went back to the kitchen to find Adam studying Dave's (half-full) cereal bowl.

'Daddy hasn't finished his breakfast.'

'I don't think he felt very hungry this morning,' I said. 'He's got a lot on his mind.'

Adam tipped his head to one side for a moment, then shoved his bowl away from him. 'Acksherly, I'm not very hungry, Mummy,' he said. 'Can I go and watch the telly?'

Flippin' Ofsted: they've got a lot to answer for, if you ask me.

Got Mums' Group to pray for Dave. Felt blessed to have such a kind, supportive group of friends. Even Helen made sympathetic noises. Felt not-so-blessed when Ellie had a tantrum because I wouldn't let her have a third chocolate biscuit. She sat on my lap and wailed while I tried to talk over her about the weekend.

'I never know what to get Dave, and now he's got his head full of Ofsted, there's no chance of him coming up with any ideas, either.'

'I bought Brendan a gorgeous fountain pen for his birthday,' said Helen. 'I know he uses it all the time when he's signing stuff at work.'

Pulled a face. 'I'm not sure Dave'd want to use something like that at work,' I said. 'It'd just disappear.'

Helen raised her eyebrows so far that they vanished under her fringe. It made me think of the faces Emily Draycott pulls when she's taking selfies on her phone, and I had to smother a laugh.

'You don't mean the children steal things? I didn't realise it was *that* sort of school.'

'Well, not exactly *steal*,' I said. 'More like permanently borrow.'

At the start of every school year Dave buys one of those multipacks of fifty biros, on the grounds that it saves him wasting the first five minutes of every lesson trying to find a spare pen for students who hadn't realised they might be expected to do some work. He reckons he's doing well if the packet lasts till Christmas: according to him, there's probably at least ten hidden in the bottom of Alice Winterbottom's bag.

The conversation got rather stuck after that. Seems like everyone else has the same predicament when trying to shop for spouses/fathers-in-law/granddads: in fact, any male over the age of about twelve.

'And just to cap it all,' I said, 'I've got Dave's mum and dad coming for lunch on Saturday, which means I'll have to spend tomorrow scrubbing the house from top to bottom.'

Maggie caught my arm on the way out. 'I'll be thinking of you on Saturday, and I'll pray for some inspiration for a present.'

She's such a sweetie, although I couldn't quite get away from the notion of God scratching His head when it came to Dave's birthday.

(Just for the record: Dave doesn't teach in 'that sort of school'. Helen made it sound like he works in some sort of grim school where the pupils all carry knives, and the staff deal drugs in their spare time.)

9pm. Dave seemed more relaxed this evening when he (eventually) came home. He says he was observed today, which sounds horrendous, but at least it means he's off the hook for tomorrow.

Plonked myself down on the sofa next to him and patted his knee. 'I'm pleased it went well for you today. Did they look at that plan you've spent so much time on?'

'They've got a copy of it,' said Dave, yawning, 'but we'll have to wait for their written report to see what they have to say about it.'

'Are you anxious about it?'

He covered my hand with his own. 'A bit, but at least it's out of my hands now, and the boss seemed pleased with it, so I'm hoping it'll be OK.'

'That's good. Now – hope you don't mind me changing the subject – have you had any more thoughts about Saturday?'

'Mmm …'

He went quiet. Assumed he was about to come out with a brilliant suggestion till I heard the sound of snoring.

Friday 28th November

Aargh! What am I going to get Dave for his birthday? And how on earth am I supposed to get the house presentable for Linda and Graham coming?

Thought about the verse I read the other day about not being overwhelmed: shame it doesn't include a line about not being buried by an avalanche of plastic toys every time you enter your children's bedrooms. Ran round with the vacuum cleaner. Rushed round again with a damp cloth wiping jammy fingerprints off the paintwork. Ellie followed me with her toy vacuum, which makes a lot of noise but doesn't pick anything up. (Bit like Dave's Year Ten class.)

She bashed it against the skirting board. 'My like hoov'ing.'

Linda would be so proud (although I bet Ellie won't be so keen once she gets to the age where she can do it for real).

Whizzed to the supermarket: I've decided to do a buffet lunch tomorrow with lots of things I can either prepare in advance or shove in the oven. Not sure Linda will approve, but I can't stand the thought of her breathing down my neck while I'm trying to cook a posh dinner. Found a couple of CDs in the music section that I think Dave will like. It's hardly original, but let's face it: I'm desperate.

Had an edgy hour and a half with the kids after school, chivvying them to make cards and get their presents wrapped. Ellie used more sticky tape than paper, so it may well take Dave until next birthday to get into it. Was just sitting down with a well-earned cup of tea when Jennifer sauntered back into the kitchen.

'Can I have a look at Dad's cake?'

Cake? *Cake?* Looked at the clock and gulped. No way was I going to be able to bake a cake before Dave got home, never mind decorate it.

Jennifer patted my shoulder. 'Don't worry, Mum. Why don't you nip out in the morning and buy one? Dad won't mind.'

Groaned inwardly. Dave wouldn't mind at all, but Linda would take it as further incontrovertible evidence of my complete incompetence.

My phone buzzed in my pocket. I tapped the answer button, and Helen's voice gushed in my ear.

'Hi, Becky, hope you're having a blessed day.'

No, not really. Just stressing about my in-laws coming for lunch and criticising my parenting skills yet again.

Out loud, I said: 'Well, sort of. It's been, y'know, quite busy.'

Realised after I'd said it that this wasn't the sort of super-spiritual answer I guessed Helen was hoping for, but she appeared not to notice.

'I've had such a relaxing, peaceful, day.' (Well, she would do.)

'Anyway, I was just in a mood for doing some baking this afternoon.' (Honestly, does she have to rub it in?)

Gritted my teeth. 'That sounds nice.'

Good job Helen's immune to sarcasm.

'Oh, it was, but then I thought of you, having to do all that cleaning, and I know that baking's not your forte, so I wondered if you'd like one of these cakes for tomorrow?'

Decided I could ignore the veiled criticisms of my housewifely abilities. 'A cake? You've made a cake for us?'

'It's nothing fancy,' said Helen, 'just a coffee cake with butter icing and chocolate swirls on the top.'

As it was, I'd have settled for any cake, but Helen's 'nothing fancy' cakes regularly win first prize at the PTA bake-offs, and coffee cake is Dave's favourite.

'Helen, you're a saint!'

'I think you'll find we're all saints,' said Helen. 'I don't know if you've read that bit in Ephesians ...'

Couldn't think which bit she meant, but I was too chuffed to get dragged into some deep theological argument which I'd undoubtedly lose, anyway.

'I'm really grateful. Would you like me to come and pick it up?'

'No, no, it's fine. We have to take the children out to their orchestra rehearsal tomorrow morning, so we'll drop it off around ten.'

Perfect! That means there's less time for Ellie to swipe all the chocolate off the top when I'm not looking. Shame I couldn't think of anything more exciting to get for Dave, but it feels as if everything else is coming together.

10pm. Just wondering if we might have an early night when the phone rang. Dave was semi-comatose on the sofa by that point, so I got up to answer it.

'Hi Becky,' said Maggie. 'I've had this brilliant idea.'

Chapter Seven

Saturday 29th November

I think what Dave would have liked best for his birthday was a long lie-in, followed by a lazy afternoon in front of the telly with a bottle of beer for company. What he actually got was three giddy children jumping on top of him at five past seven.

Ellie – and Ginger Giraffe – wriggled into the space between us. 'Wake up, Daddy, wake up!'

'I can play *Happy Birthday* on my recorder,' said Jennifer.

She proceeded to demonstrate; a performance which took three times longer than necessary due to her insistence on stopping to correct herself every time she went wrong.

'Did you like it, Dad? I can play you something else if you'd like.'

Dave pulled himself upright. 'Er ... no ... that was very good, though. I think I should open some of these lovely presents.'

'How old are you, Daddy?' said Adam.

'He's well old,' said Jennifer. 'He's forty-one.'

'Wo-ow!' said Adam. 'Are you forty-one, Mummy?'

Shook my head. 'I'm much younger than Daddy. I'm only thirty-nine.'

Adam thought for a moment. 'Jordan's mum is twenty-two.'

Jordan's mum is like a human tornado: large and lively. I know she's always full of energy, but I didn't think she was so much younger than me. Still …

'How d'you know?' said Jennifer.

'She was sorting some clothes out when I went to Jordan's for tea,' said Adam. 'I saw the label in the back of her jumper.'

Dave ooh-ed and aah-ed over the kids presents.

'That's perfect. I can sit and watch the film with a glass of beer, and then I can have a cup of tea before I go to bed.'

I held out a large white envelope. 'Happy birthday, darling.'

Dave edged the sheet of paper out of the envelope. 'Ooh!' His eyes lit up.

'What is it, Dad?' said Jennifer.

Dave turned it round so she could see it. 'Thank you, that'll be fantastic. Just what I need after the hassle of Her Majesty's Inspectors.'

'It was Maggie's idea.'

'Well done, Maggie … though I think she's got the thin end of the deal.'

Jennifer had been scrutinising the document. 'You're going out for tea. Can we come?'

'Uh-uh,' I said. 'This is a grown-ups only meal. Maggie's going to come and look after you.'

'Anyway,' said Dave, 'I think we'll go for a curry.'

There was a simultaneous 'Yuck!' from all three children. Some people would view it as a failure on my part to have produced offspring who refuse to eat curry. I'd say it's a distinct advantage.

Helen's cake arrived – as promised – mid-morning, and looked so scrummy it took me a full month's worth of willpower not to stick my finger in the icing when I was carrying it through to the kitchen. Ellie trailed behind me like a forlorn spaniel.

'Cake, peease, Mummy?' she said, straining on tiptoe to see where I had pushed it to the back of the worktop.

Scooped her up and marched firmly out of the kitchen. 'No way, José. You can have some later when we've all sung *Happy Birthday* to Daddy.'

Ellie wriggled in protest, then stuck her fingers in her ears as I pulled the door shut. 'Don' like the noise, Mummy!'

Tickled her tummy. 'I think the hinges need oiling. Maybe I'll have a look later.'

Waited till she was safely absorbed in a game of 'Connect 4' with Dave before heading back to the kitchen to set the table out. By half-eleven, most of the food was ready, apart from the sausage rolls and a pizza which I could shove in the oven once Graham and Linda arrived.

Dave appeared just as I was finishing off. 'This looks grand – thanks for organising it all.'

'Mmm. Sorry it's not all home-made.'

'Who cares?' He nodded towards the worktop. 'Is that one of Helen's creations?'

'Certainly is – and if you're a good boy and eat all your main course, you might be able to have a piece later.'

'Spoilsport.'

'So your children keep telling me. Speaking of which: would you mind checking they've left enough space in the lounge for your parents to sit down? I'll go and put the kettle on.'

By ten to twelve we were – miraculously – all ready. The lounge was almost clear of debris, the oven was heating up, and Adam had been persuaded to exchange his mud-spattered Brighton shirt for a clean jumper. My stomach was still turning somersaults at the notion of entertaining Dave's parents, but at least I wasn't running round the house with the oven gloves in one hand and a duster in the other, praying that Linda and Graham would be late for once in their lives.

Ellie – who had been climbing on and off the sofa for several minutes – suddenly paused, an intense look of concentration on her face.

'Ellie, do you need your potty?'

She nodded, her face reddening. 'My get it.' She ran off to find it, just as the doorbell jangled.

Linda thrust a large, squishy parcel at Dave. 'Happy birthday, David. Rebecca thought you might like something practical.'

Dave leaned forward to hug Linda, raising his eyebrows towards me at the same time.

'Nothing to do with me,' I mouthed. Honestly, it's bad enough that she invites herself round for lunch, without blaming me for her appalling lack of taste in knitwear.

Jennifer and Adam allowed themselves to be fussed over and kissed, although from the expression on Adam's face, I guess Linda might not get away with it by this time next year.

Linda shook out her scarf and folded it neatly before hanging it carefully on the coat peg with her raincoat. 'Now, where's my other favourite granddaughter got to? Ellie?'

'Gan-ma!' Ellie toddled into the hallway, naked from the waist down. In her hands was a steaming, pungent potty. She held it out for Linda's approval. 'Look what my done, Gan-ma!'

Had to admit that things went pretty well after that, although Linda's lips formed a perfect straight line when I let slip that I hadn't actually made my sausage rolls from scratch. We still managed to scoff a mountain of food between us; so much so that Dave suggested we have a coffee break before tackling the cake. Graham frowned as the kitchen door squealed shut behind us. 'You want to put some oil on that.'

Sighed. 'It's on my list of jobs to do. Not sure whether we've got any left, though.'

Dave nodded towards the hallway. 'Isn't there some in the under-stairs cupboard?'

'Maybe. I'll have a look later.'

I was half-comatose by the time Linda disappeared off to the bathroom, closing the lounge door carefully behind her. Moments later, the kitchen door squeaked. 'Only me,' called Linda. 'Just thought I'd put the kettle on again.' She reappeared a few minutes later with a fresh pot of tea and a jug of milk on a tray.

'Aren't you going to open your present, Dad?' said Jennifer, patting the carefully ironed wrapping paper.

'Good idea,' said Dave, doing his best to remove the sticky tape without tearing the paper. 'I wonder what it is?'

The jumper was garish, even by Linda's standards. She leaned forward expectantly. 'Do you like it? I thought the colours would suit you.'

Dave attempted a smile. 'It's very ... striking,' he said. 'Shall I try it on?'

I really think Linda's presents should come with a health warning. If he's ever foolish enough to venture outside wearing the latest monstrosity, we'll have to issue free sunglasses to all our neighbours first.

Dave peeled the jumper off again, leaving fluorescent-coloured fluff dotted about his shirt. 'It's lovely and warm,' he said, by way of an apology. 'It'll come in handy when the weather gets colder, but I don't want to risk it getting covered in cake crumbs.'

Manoeuvred myself out of the armchair. 'Is that a hint? I'm surprised Ellie's been able to wait this long.'

'Where is Ellie, anyway?'

'Good question – I'll give her a shout.'

There was a muffled bump from the direction of the kitchen, followed by the patter of footsteps. Ellie charged into the lounge, her index finger pointing aloft.

'My had choc-lit, Mummy.' She licked the end of her finger and sighed appreciatively. 'Yours want some, Mummy?'

I snatched a tissue and started scrubbing at her hands and face. 'Ellie! That was Daddy's special cake.'

Dave passed me his hanky. 'I thought you shut the kitchen door?'

'I'm sure I did – and we'd have heard if she'd opened it again.'

He turned to Graham. 'That's one advantage to having squeaky hin ...' He stopped. Linda's face was almost as bright as Dave's new jumper.

'I'm sure I didn't mean to cause any trouble,' she said.

'Ee, love, what have you done now?' said Graham.

Turned out Linda – not wanting to pass up the opportunity to help/interfere/generally poke her nose in – had decided to attend to the door hinges when she nipped upstairs to the bathroom, and had retrieved the oil from the cupboard in the hall. Unfortunately, this disarmed our 'Ellie-alert' system, leaving her free to sneak into the kitchen, drag a chair across to the worktop and snaffle an early helping of cake.

'Still, it's not all bad news,' I said to Dave as we waved goodbye to Linda and Graham. 'I don't think your mum's ever apologised to me before.'

Dave tucked his arm around my waist. 'Let's face it: the expression on her face when she realised what she'd done more than compensated for the offering of another dodgy jumper to add to my collection.'

Sunday 30th November

The kids obviously felt they'd had enough of being nice for this year as they insisted on making up for their (reportedly) angelic behaviour with Maggie last night by having a mega bust-up at breakfast time when it transpired that Adam had helped himself to the last of the chocolate cereal before the girls had had a chance to gazump him.

George was talking about preparing for Christmas. Christmas! It sneaks up on me every year, even though the telly adverts have been full of it since late August. Wondered whether it was worth being organised and starting the Christmas cake before we hit December, for a change.

'My help?' said Ellie, eyeing up the packets of fruit and cherries as I lined them up on the kitchen worktop.

'Sure. I'll put them in the scales, and then you can tip them into the bowl for me.'

Much to my surprise, most of them ended up in the bowl rather than on the floor.

'Oh dear!' said Ellie, retrieving a stray raisin from the worktop, and popping it in her mouth.

'Was that yummy?'

She reached her hand towards the bowl. 'More raisin?'

'Just one, or there'll be none left to go in the cake.'

'T'anks, Mummy.'

She clambered off the stool and ran off to find the others, while I tipped a generous slug of sherry over the fruit.

'Mum!' shouted Jennifer. 'Can you help me with my literacy?'

Found her lying on her stomach on the lounge floor with her book spread out in front of her.

'Why don't you sit at the table and do it?'

Jennifer scowled. 'It's more comfortable like this.'

'Surely you can't write neatly when you're lying like that?'

She flipped through the pages till she found the right one. 'What's wrong with doing it like this?'

Squinted over her shoulder. 'Well, you're not concentrating, are you? You've spelled *believe* wrong.'

Jennifer prodded at the page. 'I thought that's how you spelled it.'

'No, it's B-E-L-I-E-V-E. Haven't you learned about *I before E, except after C*?'

'Dunno.'

She grabbed the nearest pen (raspberry pink) and tried to transpose the fourth and fifth letters. 'That doesn't make sense, anyway.'

'What doesn't?'

'That rule. *I* before *E*. What about science?'

'Mmm, works for everything else, though.'

Jennifer sat up indignantly. 'No, it doesn't. What about *weird*? Or ...'

Our edifying and intellectual discussion was interrupted by a frustrated wail from the kitchen. Ran through to find that Ellie had pulled a chair across to the worktop and was dipping her fingers into the alcohol-soaked fruit. A pile of discarded raisins was clustered like sheep droppings on the floor.

Snatched the bowl. 'Ellie! What are you doing?'

Ellie fished in her mouth and extracted another raisin, which she deposited on the floor with the others. She turned to me, her eyes brimming with tears. 'Raisins all nasty, Mummy.'

Her mood was not improved by me grabbing a cloth and trying to remove the gunk from between her fingers.

'Look on the bright side,' said Dave, who had come to find out the cause of the commotion. 'It'd have been worse if she'd been enjoying them.'

Monday 1st December

Woke up in the middle of the night and realised I'd forgotten to buy advent calendars for the kids (again!). Panicked. Had to send Dave down to the newsagents first thing before he went off to work. Fortunately, they still had a few, and a major crisis was averted. So now we have three calendars depicting princesses (Jennifer), Formula One (Adam) and dinosaurs (Ellie – it was all they had left). Funny, I thought Christmas was supposed to be about Jesus. Jennifer wasn't sure about having princesses till she discovered that hers was the only one with chocolates. She was less pleased when I told her she'd have to share them with the other two.

Helen rang up this afternoon. Somehow ended up telling her about my near disaster with the advent calendars. (I should've known better.)

'Oh dear, you did cut it a bit fine, didn't you! The children and I made ours last week using egg boxes and cereal packets. They look absolutely stunning, I promise you. It's amazing what you can achieve with a bit of imagination. You ought to try it next year. You can copy ours, if you like.'

I'm sure she was trying to be kind, but I couldn't help feeling discouraged as I put the phone down. Asked Dave later on what he thought God was doing putting me in a Bible study group with Helen.

'Helping you grow in grace?'

If that's the case, why does she make me feel so ungracious?

Tuesday 2nd December

Discovered a new dimension to the Christmas story this afternoon. Mrs Baxter appeared in the playground as Adam's class came out after school, and started working her way around the groups of adults sheltering under the covered walkway.

'Just wanted to let you know there's an important letter in Adam's book-bag,' she said, as she approached me. 'I've told all the children to make sure it doesn't get forgotten about, but you know what they're like sometimes.'

Made sure I rescued it as soon as we got home.

Dear Parent/Carer,

I'm sure you will be delighted to hear that Adam has been chosen to be an alien in the Key Stage 1 nativity play this year.

Please could you send a named bag into school by Monday 8th December containing:

long T-shirt, pale blue or green; blue or green tights; silver deely boppers (if possible).

Performances will take place on Wednesday 10th December and Thursday 11th December, starting at 1.45pm. Tickets are available from the school office, price £2 – please order using the slip on the reverse of this sheet.

Best wishes, Mrs Baxter and Mr Greenwood

'Adam,' I called, 'is this right? Mrs Baxter says you're going to be an alien in the school play.'

Adam stomped through from the lounge. 'S'not fair. I wanted to be a cowboy, but Mrs Baxter said we had too many already.'

An alien? Cowboys? Whatever happened to traditional nativity plays?

'Never mind,' I said. 'I'm sure you'll do a fantastic job.'

Told Dave all about it later.

'Actually,' he said, 'I think you'll find the aliens are scripturally sound.'

'I must have missed that bit.'

'Are you doubting me?' He grabbed his Bible from the coffee table. 'I remember George reading it out the other week.'

'Sure you weren't snoozing again?'

'Oh, ye of little faith.' He pushed his glasses up a centimetre or so. 'Here it is: Isaiah 61:5: "Aliens will shepherd your flocks; foreigners will work your fields and vineyards."' He snapped the Bible shut. 'Satisfied?'

'Mmm.' Tried hard to resist the image of sheep being chased around the desert by little green men. 'I'm not sure that's quite what it means.'

Wednesday 3rd December

Debbie offered to have Ellie today so I could go Christmas shopping. We've ordered loads of stuff online, but I'm struggling for inspiration with Linda and Graham, and my mum and dad. Needed to get some odds and ends for the kids' stockings, too. Oh, and something for Dave ...

Three hours later, I was losing the will to live. The shops were teeming with harassed-looking shoppers carrying mountains of carrier bags, and fraught assistants with forced smiles. Every other shop appeared to be playing *Fairytale of New York* on repeat, while, at the far end of the high street, a Salvation Army band was doggedly working through a more traditional selection. After much dithering, I finally settled on a posh tea and coffee hamper for my parents, then queued for about a week to pay for it. Purchased an assortment of tat for the stockings in the pound shop, including – much against my better judgement – a tube of pink glitter for Jennifer to add to her craft box.

Thought I might treat myself to a cup of tea and a mince pie in my favourite department store, but the line for the café was so long you needed a telescope to see the other end.

It was well past lunchtime when I staggered up the path to Debbie's front door. She thrust a super-sized mug of tea into my hands.

'Successful trip?'

I took a satisfying slurp. 'Sort of. I'm doing quite well with the kids' stuff, but I still don't know what to get for Dave, or his parents. They're a nightmare to buy for.'

'What did you get them last year?'

'A voucher for afternoon tea at that fancy hotel next to the station.'

'Isn't it dead posh there?'

'Mmm. I thought it was a good idea, but apparently, they don't starch their tablecloths properly.'

Debbie opened her mouth wide in mock horror. 'I'm surprised they haven't been closed down.'

Giggled. 'I'm amazed Linda didn't suggest it.'

Thursday 4th December

Don't think Christmas is very good for my spirituality; a bit of a worry, given that it's one of our key festivals. My desire to have a cosy family time celebrating the birth of Jesus somehow gets muddled up with the world of retail's plan for me to spend more than I can afford on things I don't need. Attempts to meditate on the wonder of the incarnation are derailed by my ongoing internal debates about whether it was wise to cave in to Adam's demands for more Lego, and why you can never find that mint-flavoured Turkish delight these days.

This morning's Mums' Group didn't help, either.

'Are we all ready for Christmas, then?' said Anita.

Blessing groaned. 'You must be joking.'

'I've written three cards so far,' said Annie.

'That's two more than me, then,' said Debbie.

I nodded. 'Every year I have this big plan to be organised, for a change, and every year I get to the middle of December and realise I've still got tons of stuff to do.'

'I always do all my shopping in October,' said … (no surprises there, then).

'Well,' said Anita, 'I know most of us have still got plenty of things to do, but I thought it'd be good to spend time thinking about what we could give to Jesus.'

'What, like giving to charity?' said Blessing.

Anita nodded. 'That's one way. Anything else?'

Helen put on her most beatific smile. 'Ourselves.'

Closed my eyes in the hope it would make me feel inspired.

Ellie tugged at my arm. 'Yours all right, Mummy?'

Gave her a squeezy cuddle. 'I'm fine ... just trying to think what to give Jesus for Christmas.'

Ellie cocked her head on one side, then started beaming from ear to ear.

'Choc-lit!'

Well, I guess it'd make a nice change from gold, frankincense and myrrh.

Friday 5th December

Feel exercised by this notion of giving something back to Jesus this Christmas ... just don't know what. Feel equally exercised by the number of presents I still need to buy. (OK, I know that makes me sound completely unspiritual.)

Tried praying, but couldn't really focus as that verse was whizzing round in my head again; that one from Proverbs about trusting God. Can't see what that has to do with Christmas.

Saturday 6th December

Chickened out and asked Dave if there was anything particular he'd like to find under the tree.

He leaned over to plant a kiss on the top of my head. 'Only you, my sweet.'

I shook my head. 'You'll have to do better than that. Don't think I fancy being unwrapped in front of your mother.'

'Shame.' He pulled me in closer. 'We could always lock her in the kitchen with a mountain of Brussels sprouts.'

Adam marched into the kitchen. A look of horror spread across his face. 'Yuck! I'm never gonna get married.'

Sunday 7th December

Jennifer bounded up to us after the service. 'Mum, Dad, I'm going to be an angel in the Sunday school play. I've got to be one of those people who tells the story.'

'A narrator?' I said.

'Yeah, one of them.'

'Better make sure you learn your lines, then,' said Dave.

Jennifer gave an exaggerated sigh. 'I will, Dad, don't worry.'

'That's good,' said Dave. 'Otherwise, you'd have to wing it.'

Monday 8th December

Remembered to put the bag containing Adam's outfit by the front door last night so there was no chance of us forgetting it this morning.

Dave waved the bag in front of me. 'What on earth's this?'

'It's Adam's costume. Don't think he's too impressed with having to wear tights, though.'

'Well ...' Dave peered into the bag and grimaced, 'I expect it's a bit of an alien concept for him.'

I'm sure he's getting worse.

Tuesday 9th December

Annie arrived at Jelly-Tots with a stack of envelopes.

I tucked the card she offered me into my bag. 'Have you done them all, then?'

'Most of them. How about you?'

Sighed. 'It feels like I've spent a fortune already, but I'm always left with one or two people who are impossible to buy for.'

'Dave, by any chance?'

I nodded. 'Love him to bits, but he's a right pain this time of year. I've only just recovered from the stress of finding him a birthday present.'

'Does he read much?'

'Mmm, there's a couple of books I might get him. And I've ordered him a goat.'

'A what?'

'You know, one of those charity gifts. Dave gets a card, and the goat goes to a family in Ethiopia.'

Annie's eyes lit up. 'That's a good idea. Maybe I could do that for my present to Jesus. I don't think John could object to that.'

Groaned. 'That's another thing. I've tried praying, but all I get is that verse about trusting God.'

'Well, maybe … maybe God's saying He wants you to trust Him more.'

Squirmed. 'Yeah – but what does that mean, exactly?' I looked up gratefully as Anita appeared with the urn. 'Hey, are you ready for a cuppa?'

Wednesday 10th December

Asked Dave this evening for his opinion on Annie's suggestion.

He frowned. 'I think trust's one of those funny things: you've got to use it for it to grow.'

'How d'you mean?'

'Like when I think I need to be more patient, and God reminds me I have Year Ten last thing on a Friday afternoon. I can't be patient in a vacuum. I guess it's the same with trust.'

'So, what I need to help me is a bunch of argumentative fifteen-year-olds?'

Dave smiled. 'You're welcome to them, but I think it's more about looking out for opportunities to trust God.'

Sounds scary ... but maybe that's the point.

Thursday 11th December

Anita started off Mums' Group by reopening the discussion on: 'What can we give to Jesus this year?'

'It doesn't have to be something huge,' she said. 'It might be as simple as committing to praying for someone more regularly.'

Offered up a silent apology to God as I felt the colour rising in my face. 'Um, actually, that reminds me: I was wondering if we could spend some time as a group praying for Liz and Rupert?'

Anita picked up her notepad. 'Good idea. And it's nice to know God's been speaking to you this week. Is there anything in particular we could pray for?'

Couldn't quite bring myself to explain that even if it was God's idea I'd been sitting on it for more than three weeks ... then agonised all the way home about whether I'd been dishonest. Guess I'd better add 'lack of humility' to my list of spiritual failings.

Left Ellie with Maggie after Mums' Group so I could go and watch Adam's Christmas performance. I didn't realise that along with several shepherds and five wise men, the infant Jesus was also visited by three cowboys, two aliens, Elvis Presley and Doctor Who. Shame they didn't have photo albums back then.

Friday 12th December

Can't wait till I'm old enough and incontinent enough to embarrass my kids.

Decided that seeing as our cupboards looked as though *The Tiger Who Came to Tea* had been for an extended visit, I'd better come home via the supermarket after dropping the kids off at school. Was just standing by the meat cabinet debating the merits of chicken chasseur versus spaghetti Bolognese when I felt Ellie tug at my leggings.

She pointed to the floor. 'Look, Mummy!'

I followed the direction of her finger. 'Oh dear, looks like somebody's spilled something.'

'Oh dear!' said Ellie, poking at the puddle with the toe of her welly.

'Don't ...' I stopped as an acrid aroma hit my nostrils. 'Ellie? *Ellie?*'

She buried her face in the hem of my coat. 'Oh dear, Mummy!'

The supervisor was unfazed when I went to find him, although I'm sure my face must have been redder than Santa's trousers. (Maybe I'll have to start shopping online instead.)

Dave made appropriately sympathetic noises when I told him all about it. He patted my shoulder. 'Still, could have been worse.'

'Really?'

'Yeah. Could have been my mum's new carpet.'

Saturday 13th December

Finally gave into the barrage of nagging from the kids and bought our Christmas tree today. Took Dave and I three attempts to fit it into the stand, and it still looked as though it'd be more at home in Pisa.

'Can we help decorate it, Mum?' said Jennifer. 'We'll be careful.'

Left her in charge; not that the other two took much notice. Adam – working on the principle that you can't have too much of a good thing – put about ten ornaments on the same branch. Ellie thought that the tinsel had escaped from the dressing-up box, and insisted on modelling it around the house. In the meantime, Jennifer had established a pecking order for the various baubles and other decorations, so that the ones she liked best (anything pink or sparkly) were clustered together at the front, with the also-rans (knitted angels and the like) skulking in a group somewhere at the back of the tree.

Jennifer glowed with pride. 'D'you like it, Mum?'

Couldn't bring myself to tell her it looked as if they'd been playing a festive version of 'Pin the Tail on the Donkey'.

'It's very ... Christmassy,' I said.

For the sake of international peace and harmony, I waited until they were all fast asleep before taking everything off the tree and starting again. If I tell them I had to move a few things to make room for the chocolates, I should get away with it.

Sunday 14th December

Had a musical journey to church as the kids thought it necessary to run through their Christmas repertoire. Just as well Jennifer had left her recorder at home, otherwise we'd all have been deafened. Took the opportunity to pick Dave's brains.

'D'you think your parents would like something for the garden this year? They're having a 20 per cent off weekend at the garden centre.'

'What's that?'

'Your mum and dad. We could get them a flowering cherry or something.'

He didn't answer.

'What d'you think?'

'Uh-huh?'

'Dave! Are you even listening to me? We need to get something sorted.'

He snapped to attention. 'Sorry. Can you hear something rattling?'

Tipped my head to one side. It was difficult to be sure with the carol concert going on in the back, but there seemed to be an indistinct clattering somewhere.

'Maybe ... d'you need to stop and have a look?'

He shook his head. 'I'll check when we get home. It's probably nothing.'

'What did you do in Sunday school this morning?' I asked as we pulled out of the car park later on.

'We were doing stuff for the nativity service,' said Jennifer. 'Anita says we've got to learn the songs by next week.'

'Better get practising, then.'

We were onto the fifth repeat of *Away in a Manger* when there was an ominous bang. A wisp of smoke escaped from under the bonnet, then the whole car juddered to a halt.

'What was that?' said Jennifer.

Dave was already halfway out of the car. 'Don't know, but it doesn't sound good.'

He fiddled around under the bonnet for a few minutes, then knocked on the passenger window.

'Can you try the ignition?'

I reached across and turned the key. The engine gave a feeble cough, then subsided back into silence. Dave mimed at me to try again, resulting in an even more pathetic whimper. By the tenth attempt, even the whimpering had stopped.

Dave slid back into his seat, wiping grubby hands down his new trousers. 'It's no good. I'll have to get George to tow us to the garage.'

Chapter Eight

Monday 15th December

As if I didn't have enough to do ...

Rang the garage at lunchtime to ask how long it would take to fix the car.

The mechanic inhaled for several seconds. 'It's not looking good, love.'

'But you can fix it?'

'Well ...' He paused so long I thought we'd lost the connection. 'It's like this, you see ...'

'Did you get the car mended?' said Jennifer, pushing her peas around the rim of her plate.

Grabbed at a pea as it rolled towards the edge of the table. 'The man at the garage said we'd be better off getting a new one.'

Adam looked up from hacking at his fish finger. 'Yay! Can we get a Porsche?'

Jennifer stopped toying with her food and gave me a fixed stare. 'Can I choose what colour we have? If you and Dad choose it'll be well boring.'

I often worry that as far as Jennifer's concerned, life is one long fashion parade.

Tuesday 16th December

Dropped the kids off with Debbie after school so I could meet Dave in town as soon as he'd finished work. Trawled round two or three places till we found a car that we liked at a price we could (just about) afford.

'Won't that use up all our savings?' I asked.

'We'll have a little bit left over. And I'd rather us spend a bit more and get something reliable.'

Arranged to pick the car up on Saturday. Dave's head of department has offered to give him a lift for the rest of this week.

'Kind of her to help us out,' I said.

Dave looked a bit glum. 'S'pose I should be grateful. It's just that she thinks she's running late if she's not in school by seven.'

Ouch!

Wednesday 17th December

Hope none of our kids ever consider a career in economics. Adam and Jennifer looked at me as if I'd blown our savings on the adult equivalent of Ellie's favourite sit-and-ride car.

Jennifer wagged her forefinger at me. 'Orange? You bought an *orange* car?'

Adam looked glum. 'I wanted a Porsche. I told Jordan he could have a ride in it.'

Tried to explain that having a limited amount of money available rather restricted our choice of make and colour.

Jennifer sighed. 'You're so boring, Mum.'

Thursday 18th December

While I'm generally in awe of anyone who's brave enough to take up teaching for a living, I have to say that they don't make my life any easier at this time of year. Apart from the fact that the school staff started the Christmas preparations in mid-October, and have consequently been winding my children up to a complete frenzy ever since, it's also taken me most of the last ten days to convince Adam there isn't a corner of heaven where angels, aliens and cowboys coexist in perfect harmony. Then there's the question of their presents ...

I have no problem – in principle – with buying small gifts for Adam and Jennifer to pass on to their respective teachers and classroom assistants. In many ways, it's the least they deserve (the teachers, I mean), having coped with my stroppy offspring for a whole term and still being able to smile at the end of it. What I find difficult is the length of time it takes to come to any sense of agreement with said offspring about what constitutes a suitable present.

Adam's suggestions centred around items featuring racing cars: calendars, mugs and the like. Jennifer's ideas were more tasteful – but also very expensive. I'm sure Miss Slater would love a cut-glass vase or a pair of diamond earrings, but I was rather hoping to have enough money left over to buy us a turkey.

Friday 19th December

Hope Adam's not planning a career in international espionage when he's older. He came out of school with his book-bag clutched tightly against his chest.

'You mustn't look in here, Mummy,' he said, lowering his eyebrows and glaring at me. 'It's got somefink secret in it.'

Well, at least he's remembered to bring it home. The card he made last Christmas didn't appear until late March when his teacher was sorting through her class trays.

Saturday 20th December

Hallelujah, we have a car again!

Jennifer wrinkled her nose up as Dave turned into the driveway. 'Why didn't you go for black? Or silver ... silver's nice.'

Adam's shoulders sagged. 'Can we get a Porsche when this car breaks?'

Hoped he hadn't developed a prophetic gifting.

'It's not going to break,' I said. 'Let's just be thankful we were able to find a new one so quickly.'

Ellie reached out and patted the door with sticky fingers. 'Nice car!' she said.

Sunday 21st December

Well, we made it to the year's biggest performance: the children's nativity play, at church. This one at least can be relied upon to more or less follow the biblical narrative. There were lots of *oohs* and *aahs* as Mary and Joseph skipped down the aisle, although their progress was somewhat hampered by the fact that Mary kept dropping the cushion which was supposed to be secreted under her cloak.

Debbie leaned forward to whisper in my ear: 'Wish I'd felt that energetic when I was nine months pregnant.'

Jennifer was ecstatic because she'd been chosen to play an angel-cum-narrator; a role she carried out with dignity and confidence (even if she did have to pause every now and then to adjust her halo). But, all-in-all, it was a good show. Mary remembered to remove the cushion before she put baby Jesus in the manger, and sat sucking her thumb while the shepherds and wise men came to pay their respects. One of the three wise men got stage fright, and refused to hand over the frankincense, while WG Robinson (a sheep) started fiddling with the baubles on the Christmas tree. His twin – ignoring the urgent whispers from Blessing – spent most of his time on the stage excavating his nose with his little finger.

'That was fantastic!' said George, when they had finished. 'Thanks to the children for reminding us so beautifully of the real reason we celebrate Christmas.'

Jennifer rushed up to me after the service. 'Did you see me, Mum? Did I do well?'

Reassured her that she was brilliant. 'You too, Adam,' I said. 'The best sheep I've seen in a long time.'

Glanced behind me to see Ellie trying to force-feed the infant Jesus with a chocolate biscuit. He was still smiling, but there was now a chocolate ring around His lips. Sophie tried to join in, but Ellie snatched the doll out of the way.

'No, no!' she shouted. 'My Jesus!'

'Oh dear,' said Dave, 'another church schism.'

Monday 22nd December

The spirit of peace and goodwill continued to elude Ellie.

'Mum!' shouted Jennifer. 'Ellie's eaten the rest of the chocolates from the calendar, and it was my turn today.'

Rushed into the lounge to find Ellie with a chocolatey grin.

'More choc-lit?'

'No, Ellie, that wasn't kind. You need to say sorry to Jennifer.'

Ellie grabbed Jennifer's legs by way of an apology. 'Sor-ree.' She turned back to me. '*Now* more choc-lit?'

Appeased Jennifer and Adam by promising I'd replace their goodies when I went out to the shops later.

Sat everyone down at the breakfast table, then produced a notebook and pen.

'Right,' I said, 'there's loads to do before Thursday, so I want you all to be as helpful as possible.'

'Why?' said Dave. 'What's happening on Thursday?'

There was a collective groan.

'Hones'ly, Daddy, it's Christmas,' said Adam.

Dave's eyes widened in mock-surprise. 'I wish you'd told me earlier. I haven't written my letter to Santa yet.'

'Ugh, Dad!' said Jennifer. She turned to Adam. 'He's trying to be funny.'

'Not sure you've been a good boy this year, anyway,' I said. 'Now, about this list …'

'Can I ice the cake, Mum?' said Jennifer.

'That would be good, but we also need to have a big tidy-up, ready for when people come for lunch on Christmas Day.'

Cue another collective groan.

'Who's coming?' said Jennifer.

'Grandma and Granddad *and* Granny and Grandpa, so we need to make it nice for them.'

'And Santa,' said Adam. 'Jordan's mum said there wouldn't be room for Santa to put the presents if he didn't put his toys away.'

'Precisely,' I said.

'But Santa's n ...' began Jennifer.

Dave cut across her with a warning glance. 'That settles it, then. If we all do a bit of tidying this morning while Mum goes to the supermarket, perhaps we can sit and watch a film together this afternoon.'

The supermarket put me in mind of Oxford Street at rush hour. Trolleys were three abreast in most aisles, which meant that negotiating my way around the store took four times longer than usual. According to my (unscientific) survey, trolley jams were caused by two extremes of behaviour: those who became embroiled in a fight to the death over the last packet of sprouts, and those who stopped every ten yards to exchange Christmas greetings with people they'd no doubt been ignoring for the rest of the year. Grrr!

Tuesday 23rd December

I've long suspected that lists beget lists, but it appears doubly true at Christmas. Thought we'd done well in terms of crossing stuff off, but this morning's (revised) list was still twice as long as yesterday's.

Jennifer announced she'd tackle the cake today. Helped her roll out the marzipan and mix the icing, then left her to get on with it. Came downstairs an hour later to find the kitchen looking like an explosion in a sugar factory. A plastic Santa and snowman eyed each other from opposite corners of the cake, and she'd used a tube of writing-icing to put Merry Christmas across the middle. The 'a' and the 's' were squished together, right at the edge.

'D'you like it?' said Jennifer. 'I ran out of space when I was doing the writing.'

'Looks amazing, but I think we'd better get cleaned up in here. It looks like there's been an icing sugar snowstorm.'

Had to risk a return trip to the supermarket as I'd forgotten to buy stuffing yesterday. I'm convinced the same two blokes were still arguing over the same bag of sprouts …

Wednesday 24th December

Jennifer appeared at breakfast shaking her piggy bank.

'I thought you did your shopping weeks ago,' said Dave.

She emptied the contents onto the table. 'All except Laura's. She's my best friend, so I didn't want to rush out and get her any old thing.'

Made a pact with Dave that I would take Jennifer into town while he stayed at home with Ellie and did the hoovering. Adam insisted on coming into town too.

'Are you sure?' I said. 'We're not going to be very long, and it'll be very busy.'

'I want to see if there's anything else for my Christmas list,' said Adam.

'Bit late for that, isn't it?' said Dave. 'Santa'll have everything packed up by now.'

'You could text him,' said Adam, with all the assurance of one who has been brought up in an age of technology.

Braced myself for my last pre-Christmas trip to the supermarket at half-past four (sherry for Mum and Linda) but when I got there, the aisles were deserted and the shelves were half-empty. There were no sprouts left to argue over. The checkout operators were all yawning and checking their watches every other minute.

The girl at the self-service till was passing the time by picking bits off her nail polish.

'I thought it'd be heaving still,' I said.

She stopped messing with her nails long enough to verify I wasn't some spotty fifteen-year-old trying to sneak a bottle of alcohol through when no one was watching. The badge below her left shoulder proclaimed that she was Kylie, and 'happy to help', but I wasn't persuaded.

'Nah,' she said, 'it always goes dead quiet about four on Christmas Eve. Everybody's at home, having a good time, while we're stuck in here.'

'Have you got much time off?'

'Back in on Boxing Day. Hardly worth bothering.'

'Well, at least you get Christmas Day to celebrate with your family.'

Kylie went back to scrutinising her nails.

'Not much of a celebration, is it? Me dad'll have too much to drink, and then he and me mam'll end up having a row. Last year me and me sister just sat in my room and watched rubbish on the telly.'

'Oh.' A more spiritual person than me might have seen this as a perfect evangelistic opportunity, but while I was still dithering about what to say next, the supervisor appeared.

'Kylie, can you go and help restock shelves? Aisle three.'

She grunted and shuffled off. If I was going to say anything, I had about three seconds left in which to do it.

'I'll pray you can have a peaceful time this year,' I called after her.

Kylie paused to check her hair in the mirror next to the cosmetics display. 'Yeah, whatever,' she said.

11.45pm. Why do I do this to myself every year? There's always some good reason why we're sorting stuff at the last minute, but it would be nice to be organised for a change. Still, at least we were inside in the warm this year. Two years ago, we splashed out and bought the kids a fancy climbing frame for Christmas. It seemed like a brilliant idea until we realised we'd have to assemble it after the kids were asleep on Christmas Eve. Building a climbing frame in the cold and the wet at eleven o'clock at night is not my idea of how to whoop it up on Christmas Eve. Didn't help that our neighbour across the road thought we were being burgled, and called the police, although I understand it caused much hilarity down at the local police station.

Thursday 25th December

I have to admit to being like a big kid myself this morning. I never sleep very well on Christmas Eve: I keep imagining the children tiptoeing through, stockings in hand. Jennifer was the first to appear. I'm sure I heard her moving around at half-four, but she didn't poke her head around our door until the (almost) civilised hour of 6.25.

'Mum, Dad, are you awake?'

Poked Dave in the ribs. 'Wake up, darling … it's Christmas.'

Jennifer dumped her stocking on the end of our bed, and rushed off to wake the other two. Adam bounced through a moment later, followed by Ellie, who was still rubbing the sleep from her eyes. I held out my arms and pulled her onto the bed.

'Happy Christmas, everybody,' I said. 'What've you all got?'

Christmas Day at church is the best. Offered up a silent prayer for Kylie when we were singing the first carol. It must be awful to not have anything to look forward to on Christmas Day.

George encourages the children to bring along a new toy to show to everybody. He examined them all with great enthusiasm, particularly when Garfield Robinson, Blessing's oldest boy, produced a remote-controlled car.

'Least you know what to get him for his birthday,' I said to Anita.

Nearly had a bust-up between Ellie and Elijah McKay when it transpired that Elijah had received a toy vacuum cleaner exactly like the one Ellie already has.

'My c'eaner,' said Ellie, elbowing Elijah out of the way.

Elijah looked confused and took a step backwards, allowing Ellie to steer it into the nearest chair.

'No, Ellie, yours is at home. Why don't you find your fire engine to show to Elijah?'

'My engine!' said Ellie, retrieving her smart red sit-and-ride vehicle from the corner where she had parked it.

'Sorry about that,' I said to Helen. 'Ellie has one of those at home, too.'

She gave a nervous laugh. 'Doesn't harm to start them off early, I suppose,' she said. 'I'm sure there's something in Proverbs about teaching your children good habits.'

Not sure my children are familiar with that particular verse.

Christmas dinner passed off peacefully enough, apart from the annual squabbles when I insisted the kids at least try one of the sprouts before deciding they didn't like them. By the time we'd stuffed ourselves full of Christmas pud, my eyelids were drooping, and I was hoping none of the kids would suggest an energetic game of 'Twister'.

Mum started piling plates up next to the sink. 'Why don't you go and sit down, Becky? Your dad and I can do the dishes, can't we, Hugh?'

Dad – whose head had been sagging towards his chest for several minutes – sat up with a start when he heard his name mentioned.

Linda frowned. 'Why don't I do them?' she said. 'Hugh looks as if he's half asleep.' She waited until Mum had moved back towards the table, then made a grab for the rubber gloves.

Mum took it all in her stride. 'It's kind of you to offer,' she said, 'but Hugh won't mind. I was just saying to him on the way here that we ought to offer to help with the washing-up: I'm sure our Becky will have enough on her hands without having to clear up after everybody, too; it's very kind of her and Dave to have us all round, isn't it, Hugh?'

'Aye,' said Dad, 'and a grand job ...'

Linda turned the taps on full-force. 'I can't let you think I'm not doing my bit,' she said, 'and Graham can help me put things away when I've done.'

Graham looked less than thrilled at the prospect, but staggered to his feet dutifully, anyway. 'Just tell me where you want stuff putting,' he mumbled.

Mum shook out a tea towel. 'Why don't you wash, and I'll dry? We'll let the menfolk put the kettle on. I said to Hugh earlier, this is such a special thing to do at Christmas, we are lucky to have somewhere to go at this time of year. One of our neighbours – do you remember Mrs Quinn, Becky? – has three sons, but she never sees them from one year to the next: it's such a shame.'

Linda held a plate up to the light to check it was cleaned to her satisfaction. 'Some people are so ungrateful,' she agreed. 'Graham! Don't put those there, I haven't had chance to wipe the table yet.'

Mum gave the plate she was holding a perfunctory wipe before passing it across to Graham: I could see Linda itching to check whether it was properly dry. 'Hugh, is the kettle on? I'm sure Linda and Graham could do with a cup of tea; I think I might have a coffee, actually, just one sugar. Have you asked Becky and Dave what they'd like?'

The downside of having four senior adults doing the washing-up is that it takes about three times as long as it should do – in this case, mainly due to Linda feeling obligated to check everything was done to a sufficiently high standard. I grabbed two mugs of tea and took refuge in the lounge. Twenty minutes later, Dad and Graham emerged from the kitchen looking somewhat subdued, and promptly went to sleep just in time for the Queen's speech. The bonus is that our kitchen now looks like something out of a rather swish show-home, as Mum and Linda vied for pole position in the tidying-up stakes. Perhaps we should celebrate Christmas more often.

Friday 26th December

Was woken at seven by what sounded like a siren screeching in my ear. Next time I buy Ellie a new sit-and-ride, I'm going to find one that doesn't come with added sound effects.

Spent this morning having coffee with Dave's aunt, then went to my gran's house for tea. Gran's a sweetie, but she thinks the children are all still about three. Jennifer's got used to her now, so when she opened her present and found a plastic food set she still managed to feign enthusiasm. Adam was less than impressed with his nursery rhymes DVD, but fortunately Ellie chose that moment to knock Dave's coffee over.

Saturday 27th December

I'd promised myself a lie-in this morning, but Jennifer had other plans. She's been nagging me since 6.37 on Christmas morning (when she found the pound coin at the bottom of her stocking) about going to spend her Christmas money.

'You won't get much for a pound,' said Dave.

'S'all right,' said Jennifer, with the nonchalant air of one who has learned that grandparents are more reliable than Santa. 'I'll get some more later.'

'Some more' amounted to £26 in total by the time we'd done the round of family visits. Predictably, the volume of nagging was directly proportional to the amount of money accrued.

'Mum, can we go to town today?' were the first words I heard this morning.

I rolled over and glanced at the clock. Ten past eight. Ugh! 'Can't you go and watch a DVD or something?'

Ellie came rushing through. 'My shopping,' she said, swinging a small plastic shopping basket three inches from my nose.

Struggled to focus my eyes on the contents. (Maybe that third glass of prosecco wasn't such a bright idea.)

'What's that you've got there?'

'My got 'nanas.'

Yuck! So she had. Three and a half bananas, to be precise: the other half was smeared around her mouth and down her pyjamas.

Forced myself to sit upright and reached for my dressing gown. 'Come on, pickle-pot, let's get you cleaned up.'

Jennifer spotted her chance. 'So, *can* we go shopping, then?'

Town was vile, full of a zillion other harassed-looking parents and professional sales-goers with half a dozen carrier bags under each arm. Some of the larger department stores had queues snaking out of the doorway, and most of the Christmas decorations were now smothered in *Sale* signs.

'What d'you want to get?' I asked Jennifer.

She shrugged. 'I dunno … I just wanted to look.'

'Oh, great,' muttered Dave. 'Can't think of anything else I'd rather be doing.'

Got home exhausted after three hours going in and out of the same shops several times. Adam had a new Lego model to add to his collection, and Ellie had one of those books where you can press little pictures at the side and get accompanying noises. Jennifer's purchases were as follows:

- Two books (that's OK, I approve of books)
- A craft set (should be all right, as long as she confines the glitter to the paper rather than spreading it throughout the house)
- Some lilac nail polish (cause of an enormous scrap when I said she couldn't buy some mascara 'like the one Megan-at-trampolining always wears')

Oh, and I bought myself a dress. (A dress!) It's a size fourteen, so it's too tight at the moment, but it was massively reduced. (It'll be a good incentive for me to lose weight in the New Year.)

Sunday 28th December

Got chatting to Anita after the service.

'So, have you got any plans for New Year?' she said.

I shook my head. 'I'm not sure I can stay awake that long these days. We'll maybe get a takeout, or something.'

Jennifer and Laura materialised as if by magic.

'Mum!' said Jennifer. 'That's so boring.'

'We ought to go to a party,' said Laura. 'I can easily stay awake till midnight.'

'That's 'cos you haven't got kids,' said Anita. 'Just you wait.'

'We could have a party,' said Jennifer.

'Oh no,' I said, 'it wouldn't be fair on Ellie. Besides, most of our friends have small children, so they might not want to come, anyway.'

'But Laura could come,' said Jennifer, 'and Anita and George and Emily.'

Anita laughed. 'Doesn't sound like much of a party to me. You and Emily and Laura might last till midnight, but the grown-ups would all be snoring by half-ten.'

Once Jennifer has an idea in her head she's like a bloodhound who's picked up the scent of some poor, unsuspecting fox.

'Dad,' she said in the car on the way home, 'don't you think we should have a party for New Year?'

Did my best to head this one off at the pass. 'Jennifer, I've already explained I don't think that's a good idea: it's too late for the little ones.'

'Mmm,' said Dave, and I waited for him to quash the idea. 'I don't think a New Year's Eve party would work ...'

'Aww, Dad!'

'… but maybe we could do something on New Year's Day.'

Could almost hear the cogs whirring in Jennifer's brain.

'Can Laura come?'

'Don't see why not,' said Dave. 'Maybe we'll have a barbecue. I think the weather's supposed to be quite mild this week.'

'Cool!' said Jennifer.

'Party, party, party!' shouted Ellie.

A barbecue? In January? Dave's either completely off his rocker, or it's a stroke of genius.

Monday 29th December

Sent a Facebook invite to everyone in Mums' Group this morning, while Dave rang a few more people who have so far managed to resist the relentless march of technology.

Starting to feel excited about this, especially after several people messaged back to say what a good idea they thought it was. Everybody's volunteered to bring stuff to put on the barbecue, and Anita and Debbie are bringing puddings, so there won't be too much for us to organise, which is *even better*!

Annie rang this evening to ask if we'd mind if John came, too.

'No, that's fine,' I said. 'It's mostly going to be church people, though. Will he be all right with that?'

'He'll be fine, as long as it's not too religious.'

'No, it's just a party.'

'Of course,' said Annie, wistfully, 'it'll be quite nice for him to see that we're not all some sort of weirdo sect.'

Absolutely. Just need to work on my non-threatening-yet-completely-on-fire-for-God look. Oh, and keep him well away from Helen McKay.

Polished off a whole box of chocolate mints this evening on the grounds that I won't be able to eat them once I get stuck into my New Year's diet. Adam wanted me to try this trick he's seen one of the students do where you balance a mint on your cheekbone and then manoeuvre it into your mouth just by wiggling your face. (Who thinks up these things?) Gave up after two attempts, but not before Dave had caught a photo of me with chocolate smeared down the left-hand side of my face. Good job he doesn't do Facebook.

Tuesday 30th December

Mega supermarket shop this morning. Dave offered to go, but wasn't sure I could rely on him not to forget something vital (like charcoal for the barbecue). Left him at home with the kids instead while I filled the trolley with enough food to last a fortnight. (Well, the supermarket is closed on Thursday ...)

Came home to find him looking frazzled. Ellie had been talking at him non-stop.

'Can't imagine where she gets that from,' he said.

Cheek!

Put all the shopping away, then realised I'd forgotten to get ketchup, brown sauce and extra milk.

Dave gave me a condescending pat on the shoulder. 'It's all right,' he said. '*I'll* go this time.'

Wednesday 31st December

Can't believe that's another year gone. Thought perhaps I should spend some time with God, reviewing my spiritual achievements for this year, and setting some resolutions for the next. Found I was struggling to concentrate on the first section, so had a couple of chocolate biscuits to boost my energy.

Messed around on the internet and found a spiritual checklist to help me:

Average daily quiet time: .... hours
No of Christian books read: ....
No of converts: ....
Most powerful sermon you've heard: ....
Most inspiring conference attended: ....

Boy, that's depressing.
Started on the second list (think positive):

Lose some weight.
Tidy/clear out my wardrobe.
Learn to play the guitar (Why not? I could be a real asset to Mums' Group).
Get to church (and school) on time.
Try not to shout at the kids so much.
Try not to moan at Dave so much, either.
Spend more time with God.
Tell lots of people about Him.

Realised after I'd written it that I ought to rearrange it so it looks more spiritual, ie put the last two items at the top, just in case I get some mad, impulsive urge to show it to someone else.

Roped the kids in after lunch to do a family tidy-up time, which basically means that they return to their bedrooms all the items that have migrated downstairs since the last time we all tidied together.

'Mum,' said Jennifer, 'can I stay up till midnight, anyway?'

Made a deal with that she could stay up to see the New Year in as long as she promised not to be grumpy in the morning. After some debate, it was agreed that Laura could come and sleep over. George dropped her off at teatime.

'See you tomorrow,' he said, ruffling her hair. He winked at me and Dave. 'Laura likes to be in bed by eight o'clock.'

'Dad!' said Laura, scowling. 'You're not funny.'

Packed the younger two off to bed by half-eight, then put a film on for Jennifer and Laura once they were in their pyjamas. Opened the tin of chocolate biscuits that Linda and Graham brought round on Christmas Day (because I won't be able to have any after tomorrow, and I want to be able to tell Linda honestly how nice they were). Dave and I had a glass of wine each, and the girls had some of that fizzy non-alcoholic stuff.

'Cheers!' said Laura, clinking her glass against Jennifer's.

Jennifer giggled. 'This is very soficated, isn't it, Mum?'

Soficated?

'D'you mean sophisticated?' said Dave.

Oh. Not surprising I didn't recognise it, then. The last time I was accused of being sophisticated was when one of the older ladies at church commented on my new lipstick; which means it's at least ten years ago. (I do remember feeling quite flattered, until I realised she wasn't wearing her glasses.)

The next half-hour was punctuated by rhythmic clinks, as it appeared it was necessary for them to bump glasses every time they took another sip. It sounded like we had been transported to an Alpine meadow. (Maybe we should have gone for the *Sound of Music* instead.)

By the time the film had finished, it was quarter to eleven.

I stifled a yawn. 'Well, girls, did you like that?'

'Shh!' Dave pointed across the room.

Jennifer's head was tipped back against the sofa, while Laura was leaning in an awkward position against Jennifer's shoulder. They were both fast asleep.

Woke Jennifer and Laura at ten to midnight so they could watch the Big Ben countdown. After that we opened the curtains and watched other people's fireworks. Our house is near the top of a hill, so if it's a clear night you can see for miles, including getting a good view of a series of massive rockets streaking across the midnight sky. Dave stood behind me with his arms around my waist and his chin resting on my shoulder.

'Happy New Year, darling,' he whispered. 'Hope it's a good one.'

Chapter Nine

Thursday 1st January

9am. So, here it is: another new year. It's a bit like when you're at school and you get given a brand-new exercise book. No blemishes, no mistakes, no grumpy offspring telling me I'm the world's worst mum. Haven't even shouted at the kids yet, although Ellie did rather try my patience by coming through at half-past six.

Plonked her in front of her favourite DVD so that I could grab a few minutes to pray. I am so determined to stick with that list of resolutions. Was painfully aware after a few minutes that my prayer time had turned into a shopping-list of requests. Remembered Anita's pre-Christmas challenge about giving something back to God. Mmm.

Dear Jesus, I know I'm waffling on here, but I do really want to serve You this year and not let You down so often. I promise I'm not going to shout at the kids as much, and I'll try not to moan when Dave leaves his dirty socks on the bedroom floor. Much love, Becky. Sorry, I mean Amen.

PS Please could the party go OK ... and if You could keep the weather fine, that would be a big help.

There, that's resolution number one ticked off for today. Now I just have to keep it up for another 364 days.

11am. Helen's just rung to say that Brendan's mum has turned up unexpectedly, so she was sorry, but they wouldn't be able to come after all.

Yes!

5pm. Well, I think Dave may have started a new tradition among our church friends.

'Fab idea,' said Blessing, wrestling to remove the tomato ketchup from around WG's mouth. '*Garfield!* Sit down while you're eating that sausage.'

George raised his coffee mug in a gesture of appreciation. 'Are you open again next year?'

'Ooh, can we?' said Jennifer. 'And can Laura sleep over again?'

Dave laughed. 'We'll have to see. I think I ought to plan some lessons first before I start organising next year's New Year party.'

John – Annie's husband – turned out to be easy to talk to. He could almost have been one of us ... (*Sorry, Jesus, that sounds far too cliquey.*)

Caught Adam sneaking his new Lego model downstairs at one point.

'Can you help me build this, Mum?'

'I thought I told you to leave that in your bedroom.'

Adam's lower lip wobbled. 'But I want to build it now, Mummy. You said you'd help me when I got it.'

John cleared a space on the coffee table. 'Can I help you? I need some practice for when Ben's a bit bigger.' He glanced at me. 'As long as your mum doesn't mind.'

Didn't want to appear like no-fun mum in front of John. 'That's very kind of you. Adam, can you just make sure you keep the little bits away from the babies?'

Adam was already tipping coloured pieces onto the table. 'Yeah.' He jabbed at the instruction leaflet with his forefinger. 'Can we do this one?'

Annie stood in the doorway, watching. 'Two big boys together. It'll do John good, this. He and Ben had a whale of a time on Christmas morning.'

'Did he get lots of goodies, then?'

'Enough to fill a toy shop. Mostly big, expensive stuff from John's mum: he won't be able to play with it for at least another six months.'

'I bet he liked the paper, though.'

Annie nodded. 'Especially eating it. We got him one of those sets of stacking cups. They only cost a fiver, but they were brilliant. John spent two hours on Christmas Day building towers so that Ben could knock them down again. I'm not sure who was laughing the most.'

Seized my opportunity to talk to John when he offered to help with the washing-up.

'So, how long have you been going to the church?' said John.

Did a quick mental calculation. 'We joined about a year before I had Jennifer, so it must be getting on for eleven years.'

'Boy, you take it seriously.'

Felt a bit flustered. Resolution number two, and I didn't want to muck it up.

'We … we try to. It's something that's important to us.'

He grimaced. 'Seems like Annie's taking it pretty seriously, too. Didn't bargain on her signing up for the God Squad when we got married.'

'Do you mind?'

His face reddened. 'If you want my honest opinion, it's all a load of rubbish. Can't quite work out how she fell for it. I thought perhaps it would all blow over when her hormones got back to normal, but she seems more committed than ever.'

'Maybe that's because she's found something worth committing to.'

'Well …'

John rubbed the plate he was drying with extra vigour, and I sensed an opening.

'You could always come and try it for yourself.'

John snorted. 'Think it'll take more than that to convert me. Ten out of ten for effort, though.' My disappointment must have been more obvious than I thought, because he continued: 'Sorry, wasn't trying to be rude. I've just no interest in getting involved with some mythical being who's completely irrelevant to modern life.'

'Then why the hesitation?'

'Because …'

He tilted a glass towards the light to check it was dry. 'Because … firstly, it's none of my business to tell Annie what she should think.'

'And?'

He paused, and I turned to face him.

'Because what is worth committing to is a bunch of loyal friends. I know she's appreciated being part of that women's group you both go to.' He reached out and touched my shoulder. 'She's had a tough few months. Thanks for being there for her.'

Hadn't seen this one coming. 'Well, I hope we've made her feel welcome.'

'No ... I mean, yes. What I meant was thank *you*: she thinks the world of you, Becky.'

Dear Jesus, that wasn't quite the conversation I had planned. So, is that a good thing, or a bad thing?

Tried talking it through with Dave after they'd all gone home.

'The thing is,' I said, 'I'm touched by what John said, and it's great that Annie's found the group so helpful.'

'Well, that was one of the reasons it was set up, wasn't it?'

'Yes, I just don't want her to put me on some sort of pedestal.'

'Mum!' yelled Jennifer. 'Why didn't you tell me *So You Wanna Be a Dance Star?* was on tonight? I've missed half of it now.'

'I shouldn't worry,' said Dave, 'you won't be up there for long.'

Friday 2nd January

Opened our emails this morning to find a message from Liz:

Hi Becky, just wanted to wish you all a Happy New Year. Hope you've had a good break. Please would you pray for us as we plan out the next few months? There's loads of things we'd like to do with the centre, but we're asking God to show us what to prioritise. You're in our prayers, too! Liz xx

Had what I thought was a great idea. Rang George.

'Hi, it's Becky. Just been in touch with Liz Strachan. She was wanting people to pray for them and the community centre they run in Guatemala. I was wondering if we could have a slot in the service on Sunday to spend time praying for them?'

George was only too happy to agree (he's always keen to get us thinking globally). 'We'll do it straight after the children go out to Sunday school. Why don't you introduce it?'

Me? I mumbled something along the lines of that being the sort of thing he was good at.

'No, no, I'm sure people get fed up of listening to me all the time,' said George. 'Besides, Anita was telling me how passionately you talked about them at Mums' Group the other week.'

Not sure how I got myself into this. I mean, as anyone who knows me will testify, I love talking. It's one of my favourite things to do; as long as it's one-to-one, or in a small group. There are around 100 people at our Sunday morning service: that's still between sixty and seventy after the children go out. (Funny, Dave says he's much more intimidated by small groups, whereas he can talk to 200 teenagers in assembly no problem.)

Had to eat a chocolate biscuit or two to calm my nerves. I know I'm supposed to be on a diet, but surely the odd biscuit won't hurt?

Saturday 3rd January

Got up at seven so I could try to plan what to say tomorrow. Covered two sides of A4, then asked Dave's advice.

'How long is this supposed to last?'

'George said about ten minutes.'

'It'll take you ten minutes just to read that.'

Brevity has never been my strong point, but I managed to whittle it down to three bullet points.

'Much better,' said Dave. 'You'll be good at this.'

'Are you sure you don't want to do it?'

'Certainly not. It was your idea, after all.'

'Yeah, but I didn't realise George would expect me to *talk* about it.'

'He must recognise your expertise.'

Rolled the paper up so I could hit him over the head. 'Cheek!'

Went to bed with a slight sniffle.

Sunday 4th January

Woke up half-hoping that the sniffle would have developed into mild influenza overnight so I'd have a good excuse to stay at home. No such luck: in fact, even the sniffle had disappeared.

'That's because I prayed you'd feel better this morning,' said Dave when I 'fessed up. Erm, thanks for your support … I think?

Felt too nervous to eat much breakfast. (At least that should compensate for the chocolate biscuits.)

Thought (hoped) church might be quite empty given that we're still technically in the school holidays, but people must have got bored of too much telly and too little exercise, and had made the effort to turn up.

Pulled Debbie aside in the foyer. 'I don't think I can do this. George has asked me to talk about the Strachans, and then I've got to lead prayers for them.'

Debbie was trying to wrestle Sophie out of her coat, which looked as if she'd rolled in a convenient puddle on the way to church. 'Stop it, Sophie, I don't want you wiping mud all over the chairs.' She broke off to give me a quick hug. 'You'll be fine, won't you?'

'But what if I say the wrong thing, or nobody prays?'

'They will. And you'll be grand. Just look at me and pretend there's no one else here.'

Suspected she was right. And I'm sure it's ridiculous getting so worked up over something like this at my age. I just don't like speaking in public. The thought of being watched by an audience of more than ten turns me into a gibbering wreck.

Couldn't focus through the first few songs: I just wanted to get my bit over and done with.

'And now,' said George, 'I'd like you all to sit down and listen …' (Oh no!) 'as Anita's going to come and talk to the children.' (Phew!)

Took a surreptitious peek at my list while Anita was talking. Maybe I should have had more bullet points? Or fewer?

Tuned back in to hear Anita asking the kids about school. 'Who's looking forward to going back to school tomorrow?'

Jennifer's hand shot up, as did Laura's. After some deliberation, Adam raised his finger to just above his shoulder. Ellie followed suit (she likes to be included in these things).

Anita pressed on. 'Anybody *not* looking forward to school?'

Dave's hand moved even faster than Jennifer's.

Anita's very good with the children. (Even the forty-one-year-olds.) She got them to describe the things they liked doing, and the stuff they found difficult.

'Year Ten, set five,' muttered Dave.

'When I'm scared, or worried about something,' said Anita, 'there's this verse that really helps me.' She opened her Bible. 'Here it is. It says that I can do all things through Christ who makes me strong.'

Drifted back to my list. Should I make a joke first, to get people listening? Mmm: that sort of thing is more Dave's skill than mine. Felt someone nudge me. No, not a physical nudge: something deep inside me. 'That verse isn't just for the children, you know.'

Wondered at first if Anita had spoken to me directly, but when I looked up, she was guiding the children back to their seats.

But I don't know if I can do this, I thought.

'Yes, you can. Just stop trying to do it in your own strength.'

Oh. Realised it didn't matter too much what people thought of me as long as they got down to some serious prayer on Liz and Rupert's behalf. Did I feel any less nervous? Well … maybe a teensy-weensy bit. But my being scared didn't seem like such a big deal any more.

Monday 5th January

9.15am. Hurrah! Jennifer, Adam and Dave are all safely back at school. Of the three of them, Jennifer was the keenest. Adam grumbled when I said he needed to wear his hat and gloves.

'Why, Mummy?'

'Because it's January, and it's cold.'

'And foggy,' said Jennifer. 'I can't even see across the street.'

'My see frogs?' said Ellie.

Dave brightened up a bit. 'Good job you pointed it out,' he said, 'otherwise we might have *mist* it.'

'Da-aad!' said Jennifer.

'Huh,' said Adam.

Time to undecorate the Christmas tree (or whatever the correct term is).

'My help,' said Ellie. She yanked at a strand of gold tinsel, and a shower of pine needles scattered across the carpet.

'Oh dear,' said Ellie, frowning at the floor, 'my broken it.'

Every December, I am tempted by the nostalgia-value of a real tree. Every January, I promise myself that next year we will have an artificial tree. It always takes me till June to get all the needles out of the carpet; a fact that has not gone unnoticed by Linda.

Let Ellie play with the knitted Santa and Mr Snowman off the tree while I did the rest. Santa and Mr Snowman had a happy half-hour going to the supermarket, eating plastic pizza and building a den with the sofa cushions. Santa in particular must have been having a great time, as when I came to put the decorations back in the loft, he was nowhere to be seen. Now, that could cause a serious crisis in eleven-and-a-half months' time.

Popped into the (real) supermarket after I'd collected the older two from school. Felt myself flushing as I noticed Kylie staring at me across the checkouts. Why couldn't I have said something intelligent to her on Christmas Eve?

Jennifer pointed at the newly restocked shelves. 'Hey, look, Mum: Easter eggs!'

I know they say time speeds up as you get older, but that's ridiculous.

Tuesday 6th January

Back to Jelly-Tots today. Ellie was ecstatic, and spent the first five minutes greeting all the cars in turn. Annie texted to say she wasn't coming as Ben had a bit of a cold, but Carly was there with Maisie.

'Good Christmas?' said Carly.

'Lovely, thanks, although it's more peaceful now they've all gone back to school.'

'You're telling me! For some reason, my mum thought it would be nice to give Ethan a drum for Christmas. He thinks it's a good idea to practise at seven o'clock in the morning.'

I grimaced in sympathy. 'He should join forces with Jennifer. I thought we might get a break from her recorder once Christmas was over, but now they're rehearsing for some charity event.'

George appeared in time for tea and biscuits. 'Thanks for Sunday, Becky. It went well, I thought.'

'Ugh! I was so nervous.'

'You didn't sound it. And people joined in, which was good.'

'Yeah. I'm sure Liz will be pleased when I tell her.'

'Well, thanks again. I'll know who to ask next time.'

Next time?

He wandered off to say 'hello' to a new dad who had the alarmed expression of someone who realises he's outnumbered twenty to one.

'What've you been up to?' said Carly.

Uh-oh. Resolution number two again (and the first attempt wasn't an astounding success). Tried to explain in words that:

a) A non-Christian would understand
b) Would make me come across as sincere, but not a complete fruitcake

'You're really into this God stuff, aren't you?' said Carly.

'I guess so.'

What kind of an answer is that?

'Strange,' said Carly. 'You seem pretty normal.'

Started gabbling like that auctioneer off the telly who talks at twice the speed of sound. 'I like to think I'm fairly down-to-earth, but then I hope it makes a difference to the way I live … my faith's really important to me.'

Yes!

'Mmm.' She scooped an extra dollop of sugar into her tea. 'So how important is "really important"?'

'Well …' Dug around the recesses of my brain in the hope of turning up a concrete example.

Carly stirred her tea absent-mindedly. 'I mean, take this couple you were talking about …'

'Liz and Rupert?'

'Yeah, them. I don't know what I think about God and all that, but I can see it must matter to them.'

I nodded. 'It's been hard for Liz in particular, but they're convinced it's the right thing for them to be doing.'

Carly waved her spoon at me. 'So: put yourself in their position. What would you do if you felt God was telling you to go off to Guatemala?'

I laughed, and reached for another biscuit. (I know, I know, but they were Anita's home-made ginger snaps, and it would be a shame to cause offence.)

'I don't think that's going to happen,' I said.

'Maybe not, but hypothetically?'

'Well … I dunno. It'd be quite difficult at the moment, with the kids being so young.'

'So: your faith matters, but there are limits?'

'No, that's not what I meant to say …' My voice trailed off as I realised I'd made a hash of things yet again.

Carly winked at me. 'Sorry, didn't mean to put you on the spot. I'm just fascinated by what makes people tick.'

I was still trying to formulate an intelligent response when Ellie dashed up.

'Need a wee, Mummy.'

Great! Another chance to share my faith, and I'd blown it. Wondered (not for the first time) why my life couldn't be more like that of the early Church. I'm not necessarily asking for major miracles: I'd just like to be able to talk about my faith coherently without turning into a babbling idiot who sounds like she's put her false teeth in back to front.

Wednesday 7th January

Didn't sleep well last night as my conversation with Carly kept looping round in my head. Felt all hot and cold just thinking about it. Wish I was one of those people who always know the right thing to say.

'You all right, love?' said Dave through a mouthful of toast.

'Tired.' Explained about my chat at Jelly-Tots.

He gave me a quick hug. 'At least you tried. Mark Davies in the history department keeps trying to engage me in a debate about science and religion. Once I hid in the toilets so I wouldn't have to speak to him. How pathetic is that?'

'Yeah, but he doesn't want to know what you think, he just wants a scrap.' I had met Mark at a staff social. 'He makes Nietzsche look like Mother Teresa.'

'Fair point, but it doesn't excuse me trying to avoid him.'

'Tell you what,' I said. 'I'll pray for you to be brave with Mark, and you can pray for me to have a chance to put things right with Carly.'

'It's a deal. Although I think you're being too hard on yourself. I bet Carly'd rather you were honest than pretending to be someone who's got all the answers off pat.'

11.30am. Decided I'd give Maggie a ring, anyway. She listened while I ran through the conversation with her.

'Don't you think you're being too hard on yourself?' she said.

'Huh. That's what Dave said.'

'I'm inclined to agree with him.'

'I just feel like I've let God down – again.'

'It's not our job to convince people of their need for salvation,' said Maggie. 'That's what the Holy Spirit does.'

'Mmm ... but what if that was Carly's chance to accept Jesus, and I messed it up?'

Maggie laughed. 'I think God's bigger than that, don't you?'

Dear Jesus, I'm sure Maggie's right, it's just that I can't help feeling that I'm a disappointment to You sometimes.

Thursday 8th January

Hadn't realised how much I'd missed Mums' Group until I got there. Maggie produced leftover mince pies ('cos they needed eating up), and Helen had brought a huge, sticky chocolate cake (she'd treated herself to a new mixer in the sales).

Helen's cakes really are to die for: she ought to enter that baking competition on the telly, except it wouldn't be very fair on the other contestants. For several minutes, there was a reverent silence as between us we polished off most of the cake and a dozen mince pies.

'Yummy!' said Anita. 'Now, I thought it would be good if we could share some of our hopes and dreams for this year. Anyone got any big plans, or made some exciting resolutions?'

I chased the last few crumbs around my plate with my finger. 'I was hoping to lose a bit of weight, but I'm a sucker for a nice bit of cake.'

'I'd just like Ben to sleep,' said Annie. 'He's better than he was, but I still feel like I'm permanently exhausted.'

Gillian sighed. 'I'd like to find a new job. Three nights a week on the checkouts does fit in well with the kids, but it's so tedious.'

'I've got this bizarre notion of teaching my kids some manners this year,' said Blessing. 'WG, take your fingers out of that juice!' She smiled an apology. 'As you can see, it's been an underwhelming success so far.'

Helen rearranged her features into what Dave calls her super-saintly look. 'I'm just praying for lots of opportunities to share the gospel with my unbelieving neighbours. After all, we know neither the day nor the hour ...'

Blessing interrupted her with an impish smile. 'I think you'll find it's a Thursday, and it's about quarter to eleven. Would you like to borrow my watch?'

Helen flushed. 'No, no, I meant we don't know when the Lord Jesus is going to return. We need to remain in a state of constant readiness.'

'Oh, good point,' said Blessing, as though this was news to her.

I could feel the corners of my mouth twitching, and had to pretend I was wiping chocolate off my face with a tissue.

'Any other thoughts?' said Maggie.

Debbie coughed and pulled herself up straight. 'I'd like to do a parachute jump.'

We all turned to stare at her.

She held our gaze for a few seconds. Then: 'Not really,' she said. 'I just thought it'd be fun to make something up. I feel completely uninspired when it comes to New Year's resolutions.'

'Well,' said Maggie, once the laughter had subsided, 'I think maybe we should take a leaf out of your book, Debbie. Not that we should be doing parachute jumps ...' (phew!) '... but we could ask God to give us something big to do for Him this year.'

'Something that'll take us outside our comfort zone,' said Anita.

'Something challenging?' said Gillian.

'Something scary?' said Blessing.

'What like?' said Annie.

'Dunno,' said Maggie. 'All these things we've been sharing are good things to pray about ...'

'Except the parachute jump,' said Annie.

'Well, maybe not that,' said Maggie, 'but I think it would be good to ask God what plans He has for us this year.'

'There's our challenge for this week,' said Anita. 'Perhaps next week we can spend some time sharing what we think God's been saying to us.'

Mmm. Wish I was better at listening to God. When I try to do anything like that I end up falling asleep, or else I get sidetracked into worrying about whether those eggs I've got in the fridge that are four days out of date will still be fit to eat. Shared my concerns with Debbie as we were washing up the cups for Maggie at the end of the meeting.

She thought for a moment. 'OK,' she said, 'here's the plan: we'll persuade Helen to go first, and then by the time she's finished talking it'll be too late for anyone else to have a turn.'

Sorted.

Friday 9th January

Emailed Liz this morning to see whether they felt any more settled about things in Guatemala.

She wrote back: It was hard being away from family and friends at Christmas, but I'm sure this is where God wants us to be at the moment, and it feels like we can make a difference to people's lives. We've been praying about how we can make the centre a more welcoming environment – it's pretty rundown, and the toilets are like something out of the Victorian era – but God has provided a solution. There's a church in Leicester who've

190

been very supportive of us, and now they've offered to send a team of young people out for a week to rebuild the toilet block and do some basic repair stuff. They've even planned some fundraising events to raise money for paint and other materials. Isn't God good!

I emailed back: Sounds great – you'll have to send us some pictures when it's all done. I'll mention it to George – we might be able to ask for donations at church, too.

Liz: That would be fantastic – and if you could get people to pray for this team, I'd be grateful. They're coming out at the end of March, so we'll have to put up with the crumbling walls for a bit longer.

Saturday 10th January

George was delighted when I rang to ask if we could have an extra collection to help Liz and Rupert out.

'Good idea, while it's still fresh in people's minds,' he said. 'You can introduce it, if you like?'

Ha! No chance.

Chapter Ten

Sunday 11th January

George (thank goodness) didn't drag me up to the front again to talk about the Strachans (although I kept my gaze fixed on the floor, just in case he tried to catch my eye). Interesting talk, too, on how meditating on Scripture can help us to grow in our faith.

Would have liked to stop and talk to him afterwards, but Jennifer had other ideas.

'Mum, do you know where my new bracelet is?'

'The one Laura gave you?'

'Yeah. I can't find it anywhere.'

Stupidly, I didn't think to ask her when she'd last had it until we'd spent the best part of half an hour hunting about church.

She wrinkled her nose in concentration. 'I wore it when we had the barbecue.'

'But didn't you have it on this morning?'

Jennifer shrugged. 'Dunno. I was going to wear it, but I can't remember if I did or not.'

Sighed. 'Well, perhaps you could spend this afternoon searching your bedroom. You could tidy up at the same time.'

She gave me one of her looks. 'Stop fussing, Mum: it's not that bad. It's not my fault if I can't find it.'

Monday 12th January

Wrote out Proverbs 3:5 and 6 on a sticky note this morning while the kids were squabbling over breakfast.

Jennifer squinted across the table in an effort to read upside down. 'What're you doing?'

'It's my favourite Bible verse. I'm going to stick it up on the fridge to remind me to trust God more.'

Dave leaned over to see what I had put. 'Good idea; and you've found a really *cool* place to put it.'

Jennifer groaned and rested her head in her hands. 'Dad, d'you even know what cool means?'

Tuesday 13th January

Whizzed off a quick email to Liz after breakfast:
Hi Liz, just wanted you to know there's an extra £235 here towards your renovations. Hope all the plans are coming together. Becky xx

Hi Becky, that's amazing! People have been so kind. There's quite a lot needs doing, so I hope this group won't feel too overwhelmed when they get here. We've been planning out where to accommodate everybody, and I think we should have a couple of beds to spare, so it should be all right. They're mostly quite young – although there's a few adults coming to supervise and deal with the plumbing and electrics – so I don't suppose they'll mind if the accommodation is a bit basic. Love to all, and thanks again for the gift. Liz.

PS Rupert says to ask Dave what he thinks of England's chances in the World Cup?

Wednesday 14th January

Realised this evening that I'd forgotten to pass on Liz's message. Dave was in the middle of a marking marathon; an exercise which was accompanied by a crescendo of sighs and the corners of his mouth drooping ever closer towards his chest. Read him Liz's email in the hope that it might cheer him up.

'And,' I added, 'Rupert wanted to know what chance you thought England had in the World Cup.'

Dave scrawled across the page he was marking, then tossed it onto the pile with the other books. 'About as much chance as Alice Winterbottom has of passing GCSE physics next year,' he said.

'I take it that's not good, then?'

Thursday 15th January

Took a copy of Liz's email to Mums' Group.

'It sounds so exciting,' said Annie. 'I wish I'd been brave enough to do something like that when I was younger.'

'Liz must be mad,' said Blessing. 'Not sure I'd trust a bunch of teenagers to sort out my house.'

'She sent me a picture of the centre,' I said. 'It looks pretty grotty at the moment, so I don't suppose Liz and Rupert'll be too fussed if it's not as posh as it could be. And I think there's a few adults going as well, to help with the plumbing and electrics.'

'Well, we'll keep them on the prayer list,' said Maggie. 'Now, has anyone else got anything they want us to pray for?'

Can't help feeling a bit discouraged sometimes after Mums' Group. Anita did a study on Samuel: the bit where he's asleep in the temple, and then keeps waking up 'cos God's calling him. I must have been woken up zillions of times over the last nine-and-a-half years, but only by hungry/poorly/grumpy children.

This led onto a conversation about how God speaks to us today.

'I find God speaks to me all the time,' said Helen.

'I wouldn't say He speaks to me all the time,' said Blessing, 'but there have been occasions ...'

Debbie nudged me. 'That'll be why I never seem to hear Him, then,' she said, *sotto voce*. 'It's because He's too busy talking to Helen.'

Friday 16th January

Still mulling over this puzzle of how God speaks to us. I mean, I'm 99.99 per cent sure that He does, but there seems to be a fault on the line sometimes. Wish I was more like Helen: then I'd live in a permanent state of spiritual ecstasy *and* I've have a house that didn't look as though it should feature on one of those television programmes about serial hoarders.

Met up with Debbie this afternoon at our local soft-play barn. It's our (well-earned) treat: we do it on the pretext that it's a chance for Ellie and Sophie to let off steam; but it's really an excuse to indulge in their yummy coffee cake and have a good natter. (I haven't forgotten about the diet, but I didn't want to make Debbie feel guilty.)

We agreed that we'd like to hear God speaking to us more (as long as it wasn't to ask us to do anything too scary, of course), but that this wasn't always as easy as it sounds.

Debbie leaned back in her chair and licked the last smidgen of icing off her fork.

'I wonder ...'

'What?'

'Maybe sometimes we don't notice when God is speaking to us 'cos we're looking for something big and dramatic instead of expecting Him to prompt us in more subtle ways.'

'Ooh ... like Elijah and the still, small voice? Or was it Elisha?'

'Elijah, I think. But yes. Maybe it's about listening for the gentle whisper rather than looking for the writing on the wall.'

I'm sure Debbie has a point, but given the usual noise levels in our house, it's going to be pretty hard to hear anything below shouting volume.

Saturday 17th January

Aren't children disgusting?

Thought I'd cheat at teatime and use a packet mix for the cheese sauce to go with our pasta.

Jennifer prodded at it, frowning. 'What's this?'

'Macaroni cheese. You've had it lots of times before.'

She leaned over to sniff at her plate. 'It smells funny.'

197

I dipped the end of my finger in the sauce. 'It's only cheese sauce. I think it's got a bit of parmesan in it.'

She took a cautious mouthful. 'Yuck! It smells like sick.'

'Jennifer!'

Adam had been munching away. Now he put his fork down. 'Jordan was sick at school yesterday,' he announced. 'It went everywhere. His mum had to come and get him.'

'Poor Jordan,' I said, 'but I don't think …'

But there was no stopping Adam. 'There was a huge pile of it on the carpet. You could see bits of baked beans in it.'

Jennifer's face had gone grey, and she pushed her plate away. 'I think I might go and sit upstairs,' she whispered. Couldn't say I blamed her.

For some unfathomable reason, nobody (apart from Ellie) seemed very hungry after that. Ended up throwing most of it away, then making tons of toast at suppertime.

Sunday 18th January

It's fourteen years today since Dave and I first met (at a local ecumenical planning meeting). He was tall, slim, dark and handsome, and I was short, slimmish and talked enough for both of us. I'd like to say it was love at first sight, but the truth is we only really got to know each other when we both helped on a community project clearing rubbish from a children's play facility in a rundown area of Leeds. This last detail is a tremendous disappointment to Jennifer, who thinks we should have fallen in love on some sun-drenched Caribbean island.

Yet another instance where I've failed to live up to her expectations.

Given that babysitters are hard to come by, Dave offered to cook a romantic dinner at home instead. So, that's carrot and coriander soup, followed by roast pork with all the trimmings, and then sticky toffee pudding for afters. Yum!

'Will there be any for us?' said Jennifer.

Dave was busy peeling potatoes. 'Nope. This is for me and Mum. You'll be in bed.'

'I could stay up late,' said Jennifer. 'I did at New Year.'

Dave tipped the potatoes into a pan. 'Not a chance ... but if you're extra-good, I might make it again sometime.'

Managed to get all three kids in bed by eight, with a proviso for Jennifer that she could read for half an hour. By five past eight, we were sitting down with a bowl of soup.

Dave clinked his wine glass against mine. 'Here's to us.'

'To us.' I took a sip. 'This is wonderful, thank you.'

We gazed into each other's eyes across the table – in that soppy way that Adam hates – for several seconds. Then Dave lifted his spoon.

'Well, let's tuck in.'

We had almost finished the first course when we heard a voice from upstairs.

'Mum. Mum? I'm too hot.'

Went to investigate while Dave carved the pork. Adam was standing at the top of the stairs, peering over the banister. His thick, dark hair – which to date had resisted all my attempts to tame it – was plastered to his scalp.

I felt his forehead. 'Shall I get you a drink?'

Tucked him back up with a promise that I would go and check on him later.

Dave was piling food onto our plates when I got back downstairs. 'Problem?'

I slid back onto my chair. 'Adam complaining he's too hot. He looked pretty dopey, though.'

'I expect he wanted an excuse to be nosy.'

'Sounds about par for the course. Still, it wouldn't do for us to have an evening free of interruptions.'

As it happened, we were well into the pudding course before we heard the next summons.

'Mum! Can you come here?'

Dave pushed me back into my seat. 'I'll go this time.'

I could hear a muttered conversation from upstairs, followed by a louder parting shot from Dave as he came back down.

'No more getting up. I don't want to have to get cross.'

I raised my eyebrows. 'Adam?'

Dave nodded. 'Says he can't get to sleep. He still seems a bit hot.'

'Must be all that jumping in and out of bed. He'll be grumpy in the morning when he's too tired.'

Dave topped up my wine glass. 'I'll be grumpy if he doesn't settle down soon.'

Half an hour later, we were snuggling on the sofa, and Adam wasn't the only one who was feeling hot.

Tap, tap, tap.

Dave sat bolt upright. 'What was that?'

'Mummy!' Adam's voice trembled in the hallway.

Dave flung the door open. 'I thought I told you to stay ...' He stopped.

Adam – ashen-faced – was clutching at his stomach. 'Sorry, Mummy,' he whimpered. 'I don't feel very ...'

I suppose I should look on the bright side: at least he didn't throw up all over his bed. (That came later, at around 2.45am.) Romantic dates are never the same once you have children.

Monday 19th January

Jennifer was most indignant that Adam got to have two days off school. Ellie did her best to play nursemaid by piling teddies on top of him, a gesture that was not entirely appreciated by Adam. By mid-afternoon, they were both fed up: Adam because he was starting to feel hungry again and I would only let him eat toast to begin with, and Ellie because Adam kept tipping the teddies onto the floor.

Tuesday 20th January

Adam came running downstairs first thing this morning. 'Am I going to school today?'

Tried to ignore Jennifer's baleful glances. 'Tomorrow. School say you need to have two days off if you've been sick.'

Adam paused to digest this bit of information. 'So, can we go to the park?'

'I don't think so. You've been poorly.'

'Acksherly, I'm better now.'

Started setting out the breakfast things. 'I'm glad to hear it, but I don't think Mrs Baxter would be very impressed if she thought you were playing in the park when we've told them you're not well.'

'Why not, Mummy?'

I was still feeling the effects of having been up half of Sunday night changing bedding. 'Because I say not, that's why.'

Ellie joined in. 'Park, Mummy?'

Dave checked his watch and stood up. 'I'm off. Hope your sanity's still intact at the end of the day.'

Huh! Not much chance of that. Going on today's performance, I'd say my sanity evaporated some time ago ... about ten minutes after we decided to stop using contraceptives.

Wednesday 21st January

Cruel, heartless mother that I am, I ignored Adam's protestations that he was feeling 'still a little bit poorly, Mummy', and bundled him off to school with Jennifer.

Now all I need to do is clear up the debris that accumulates whenever I have a sickly child at home. Found my Bible buried underneath Ellie's teddies in the lounge. So much for listening to God more. I've been so bogged down with washing vomit-covered bedding and trying to keep Adam entertained that my average quiet time over the last few days has lasted approximately 53.2 seconds.

Thursday 22nd January

Helen had volunteered to lead the Bible study at Mums' Group this morning.

'God's really placed the story of Abraham on my heart,' she said. 'There's so much we can learn from his example.'

'Not sure I could cope with the idea of setting out not knowing where I was going,' said Blessing. 'No satnav, either.'

'What about when he was asked to sacrifice Isaac?' said Gillian.

'Yeah,' said Debbie. 'It's all right for us: we know the story has a happy ending. Imagine being in Abraham's shoes.'

'Or sandals,' said Maggie.

'Well, I'm sure we'd all be willing to do it if God asked us to,' said Helen. 'That is, if we're serious about our commitment to Him.'

There was an awkward silence as we all wrestled with the concept of dragging our offspring up the nearest mountain for sacrificial purposes. Annie looked puzzled, so I pointed to the relevant passage in my Bible.

'I don't think I could do it,' said Blessing, 'although – come to think of it – I could have murdered Garfield last night when he kicked his football at the light fitting and showered us all with minute particles of glass. I was still picking bits out of the carpet at breakfast this morning.'

'Blessing!' said Helen in a shocked voice. 'You don't mean to say you let your children play football in the house?'

'Not exactly,' said Blessing, 'but I was just trying to chase the twins up to bed.'

'Don't think I'll tell John that bit about Abraham almost sacrificing Isaac,' said Annie. 'He asks enough tricky questions as it is.'

Could sense Helen getting frustrated by the lack of spiritual depth among our group.

'But shouldn't we all aspire to be like Abraham?' she said. 'After all, he's one of the great heroes of our faith.'

Maggie stepped in. 'I think there's a lot we can learn from Abraham,' she said. 'It's unlikely that we'll be asked to make the same sacrifices that he did, but it would be quite surprising if God never asked us to do anything difficult.'

'We're back to that trust thing again,' said Anita. 'Abraham had to learn to trust God, even when it didn't make sense.'

Kept my mouth closed. Sometimes I have trouble trusting God even when it does make sense.

'It would be nice to do something significant for God, though,' said Debbie.

'Like Liz and Rupert,' said Annie. 'That's a sort of sacrifice, isn't it?'

'Exactly,' said Anita.

Maggie stopped me on the way out. 'You OK, Becky?' she said.

'I still feel I've a lot to learn when it comes to trusting God.'

'You and me both. Maybe we should both ask God for an adventure.'

'Don't think I'm up to that: I've got enough on, running round after three kids.'

Realised that this wasn't exactly going to get me into the spiritual League of Champions, so I added: 'Of course, if I felt God was calling me to do something specific ...'

'You never know. It doesn't have to be something big and dramatic. He might ask you to take a new role in church, or to get involved in something in the community.'

'As long as he doesn't want me to emigrate somewhere obscure where you can't buy proper teabags and the spiders are the size of dinner plates.'

'Yuck!' Maggie pulled a face. 'Sounds horrendous. What about doing something short term, like that thing the Strachans are organising?'

Felt all twitchy, like I needed to get outside for some fresh air. 'That's a bit too far-fetched,' I said. 'Anyway, it's aimed at young people.'

'Fair point,' said Maggie, 'but I bet God's got something special lined up for you at some stage.'

Friday 23rd January

Debbie's volunteered to help me in crèche this Sunday, so we met up to do some planning. We're doing the story of the lost sheep, so shamelessly prevailed upon her to draw an outline for our sticking activity. (She's much better at drawing than me.)

She passed it over for my inspection. 'What d'you think?'

'That looks great. A big improvement on my attempt, anyway.' Retrieved my paper from the bottom of the wastepaper basket. 'Here: looks like the unfortunate love child of a cloud and a particularly skinny sausage dog.'

Debbie giggled. 'Maybe that's why it wandered off – couldn't stand being teased about its bizarre appearance.'

'Mmm, not sure that's quite the message I was hoping to give to the children.'

'We might get a few complaints, I suppose.' She passed the deformed sheep back to me. 'Just as well you're good at other stuff.'

'Like shouting at the kids and messing things up?'

'Huh! We've all got A levels in those. No, I meant stuff like … like talking to people, and helping them out.'

Talking? I thought that was something that just happened when I'm awake. Opened my mouth to argue, but Debbie hadn't finished.

'I mean it, Becks. You're fantastic at engaging with people, knowing what to say. And you like helping people, too. When I needed someone to look after Sophie the other week, you just did it without fussing. My mum gets in a terrible flap if I don't give her at least two weeks' notice.'

'Isn't that what friends are for?'

'I guess, but I still think you have a particular gift for putting people at ease. Some of us find that sort of thing much harder.'

'Not sure I remember talking being on that list of spiritual gifts George was reading out the other week.'

Debbie nodded. 'Not as such, but then there is that bit somewhere about using our words to build others up.'

Tossed my rejected sheep back in the wastepaper basket. 'I guess.'

'Church needs people like you just as much as it needs the people who can preach or lead worship. You're a good team player, Becks.' She paused, frowning. 'You know what you'd be good at? Going to Guatemala with that team Liz Strachan's got together.'

I laughed. 'Now you're being ridiculous. Just when I was starting to believe your little pep talk, too.'

She blushed. 'Sorry, don't know where that came from.'

'Anyway, what about you? You've got lots of gifts to offer church.'

Debbie held out her picture at arms' length and studied it, her head tipped to one side. 'Oh sure,' she said. 'At least I can draw a sheep that looks like a sheep.'

Saturday 24th January

Sometimes I feel like my husband doesn't understand me.

Came back from doing the Saturday shop to find Dave had landed me with an extra task for Sunday morning.

'I had George on the phone while you were out,' he said. 'He said he'd tried your mobile, but you didn't answer.'

Rummaged around in my handbag. 'Blow, I must have left it in my other coat pocket. Did he say what he wanted?'

'He was just talking about the Strachans, and how it would be good to spend some more time praying for them.'

This sounded ominous. 'And?'

'He wanted to know if we'd be there tomorrow, and if so, could you do another short slot to bring people up to speed?'

'I'd rather not. I'm still shaking from the last time.'

'But you were fine. People found it really helpful.'

'I still ...' Noticed the expression on Dave's face. 'What? You haven't told him I'll do it, have you?'

Dave edged backwards towards the kitchen door. 'I thought you wouldn't mind. You're always banging on about how good it is when people pray for them.'

'Dave!'

'I'm sorry, darling, I didn't think ...'

'No,' I snapped. 'That's the problem: you never do think.'

Dave grabbed the phone. 'I'll ring him back, tell him I made a mistake.'

'You'll do no such thing. He'll think I'm pathetic.'

Dear Jesus, I know it's good to pray for others, but are You sure You know what You're doing here?

Sunday 25th January

Had a good moan at Debbie before the service.

'Don't know why George keeps asking me to do it,' I said. 'Being upfront has never appealed to me.'

Debbie looked thoughtful. Then she said: 'Isn't it a bit like Abraham? Maybe this is God's way of calling you out of your comfort zone.'

'Well, He's certainly done that. Goodness knows what I'd be like if He called me to do something really sacrificial.'

Dave hugged me as we sat down. 'Look, darling, I am sorry if I've landed you in it, but you'll be great, I know you will.'

Huh! Wish I felt so confident.

George sidled up to me after the service. 'Thanks for that. You have a real heart for what they're doing, don't you?'

'I guess.'

He grinned. 'Have you thought about going out with this team from Leicester?'

'Stop winding me up,' I said. 'Debbie'll tell you my creative skills are non-existent.'

'Yes, but it's not exactly designer living, is it?' said George. 'You're not telling me you can't slosh a bit of paint on?'

'You're not serious? Most of them are lots younger than me.'

'Liz would love it if you went with them.'

'I dare say she would, but it's not practical at the moment.'

George shrugged. 'Just a thought.'

Monday 26th January

Found my New Year's resolutions list when I was changing the bed this morning. It had fallen down the gap between the side of the bed and the bedside table. Whoops! Thought I'd do a quick assessment on how I was doing so far. Sat down with a large cup of tea and a piece of chocolate cake to sustain me.

Ten minutes later, I was beginning to wish I hadn't bothered. My ambition to tell lots of people about Jesus had fizzled out after the discouragement of my conversation with Carly. My dream of learning the guitar had been hampered by the fact that I hadn't yet got around to buying one. And my plan to be a calm and laid-back mum had lasted all the way to 2nd January, when Jennifer managed to empty her pink glitter into the basket of ironing I had just completed. As for losing weight ... I studied the crumbs on my plate and decided that another small slice wouldn't make that much difference.

Glanced at the verse on my fridge. I can pretty well recite it from memory now, but I feel disappointed by the lack of impact it's had. Thought that God would have given me some amazing revelation by now, or at least the confidence to share my faith without making a complete hash of it.

Was rescued from the temptation of a third piece of cake by the phone ringing. Maggie (of course). I sometimes think God must have her on speed dial.

'You OK, Becky?'

'Sure.'

Don't know why I bother pretending, as she never believes me.

'I was just praying about Mums' Group and you came to mind, so I thought I'd better ring you.'

'Well ...'

Had a good whinge for several minutes about how I'd failed at all my resolutions, and that I'd tried to trust God and listen to Him, but it didn't seem to make any difference.

'D'you think God loves you any less because you didn't keep your resolutions?'

Wish she wouldn't ask things like that. 'Well, no ... I ...'

'Exactly. So maybe for you, trust is about believing what God says: that He loves you loads, and that He delights in you.'

'I guess.'

Felt more peaceful after she'd prayed for me. Still can't quite get rid of the sense that I'm somehow missing something.

Chapter Eleven

Tuesday 27th January

Carly arrived late at Jelly-Tots.

'You OK?' I asked.

'Oh yes.' She smiled. 'We've just been booking our summer holiday.'

'Going anywhere nice?'

'Two weeks in Portugal: I'm so excited.'

'Wow, good for you. You're very organised.'

She nodded. 'I hate leaving it till the last minute – and we got a special deal.'

I fetched her a cup of tea.

'So,' said Carly, 'have you made any plans for the summer?'

I shook my head. 'We're always a bit last-minute. Last year we went to Filey for a fortnight. Not quite as glamorous as you, I'm afraid.'

'I like the east coast,' said Carly, 'but it will be nice to go somewhere a bit warmer.'

'Mmm, we might venture down to Cornwall this year. I've heard it's beautiful there.'

'Not planning to go off to see those friends of yours in Guatemala, then?'

Still can't explain what happened next. Had one of those surreal moments when your brain thinks one thing, but when you open your mouth, something quite different comes out. In my mind, I was already lolling on an idyllic and somehow deserted beach in Cornwall. Dave was helping the older two build a sandcastle, while Ellie pottered around near my deckchair, collecting seashells in a red plastic bucket. I smiled in anticipation.

'Actually,' I said, 'I *am* thinking about going to Guatemala. There's a group going out for a week in late March, and Liz said there's still a couple of spaces available.'

It would be fair to say that Carly was almost as taken aback by this statement as I was, but she recovered it well.

'Good for you,' she said. 'I bet you'll have a great time.'

Back-pedalled as fast as I could. 'I'm only *thinking* about it at the moment,' I said. 'I mean, there's a lot of stuff to consider ...'

'What's the problem? A week, you said?'

'Yeah. I just ...'

Wouldn't you know it, George walked in. I'm sure that guy has a built-in tea and biscuits detector. Either that, or he loiters outside the door until he hears the cups rattling.

Carly gestured towards George. 'Does he know about your trip?'

Wondered if I could get away with hiding under the table until the end of the session. Lowered my voice to a whisper. 'Erm, not yet. After all, I haven't quite decided ...'

'Oh, I think you should go,' said Carly, in tones that resonated across the hall.

George headed towards us like a hawk moving in on its prey. 'Am I missing something?' he said. 'What are you planning, Becky?'

Gulped. 'Nothing much … I mean, it's just an idea. I need to think it through a bit more.'

Carly filled in the gaps. 'Becky was just telling me she wants to go and see that missionary couple you both know. She's going to do some building work or something.'

George did a little jig. 'I knew it wasn't just me,' he said. 'As soon as they mentioned this team business, I thought of you.'

'But …' I hesitated.

George checked his watch. 'Tell you what, Anita had to pop into work this morning, but she should be home by half-twelve. Why don't you join us for lunch? We can have a chat about it then, if you like.'

'Don't let her back out,' said Carly.

'Don't worry,' said George. 'I'll make sure she signs on the dotted line.'

Hmph. Ever felt like you're being stitched up?

So, at lunchtime, I found myself sitting at Anita and George's kitchen table, wondering what on earth I was getting myself into.

'Tell us all about it, then,' said Anita as she passed me a plate of sandwiches.

Felt good to be able to talk. Explained what had happened with Carly.

'The thing is,' I said, 'up till this morning I was sure it would be ridiculous for me to go to Guatemala. Now I'm all confused.'

George leaned forward in his chair. 'Have you talked to anyone else about it?'

'A bit. Debbie and Maggie both suggested I should consider going, but I thought they were just winding me up. Oh, and then you said something similar on Sunday.'

'Well,' said Anita, 'that could be a rather large coincidence ... or maybe God is trying to tell you something.'

'I know I keep saying this,' said George, 'but you do come across as very passionate about the work that they're doing.'

'But I don't know why God would want me to go,' I said. 'I'm sure there are other people who would be much better suited.'

George scratched his head. 'Maybe,' he said, 'and maybe not. If we understood everything that God was doing, there would be no room for faith.'

'A bit like when Abraham set out from Haran,' said Anita.

'But I haven't talked to Dave yet. I don't know if he and the kids would manage without me. He's got a lot on at work.'

'That's stuff you'll need to talk about,' said George, 'but in my experience, if God wants you to do something, the practicalities will fall into place.'

'Becky,' said Anita, 'just try to let go of the logistics for a minute. If you knew that all that was going to be OK, and there was nothing stopping you from being part of this team – how would you feel?'

Good question. If Anita had asked me at breakfast time, before Carly started posing awkward questions, I'd have laughed out loud at the suggestion. But now ... now I was aware of a delicious tingling sensation stirring deep inside me. For the second time in twenty-four hours, my response took me by surprise.

'I'd feel excited,' I said.

Wasn't sure how Dave would react to my proposal. (I'm sure I wouldn't be best pleased if he disappeared for a week and left me to cope with the kids on my own.) Waited till he was settled in an armchair with a cup of tea after he got in from work.

'Darling,' I said, 'you know that group thing the Strachans are organising?'

He raised his mug to his lips. 'Mmm?'

'Well ... I don't know how to put this ...'

'But you'd like to go, too?'

Almost dropped my tea. 'How do you know? Has Carly been talking to you?'

'Carly?'

'The one who joined us at Halloween.'

'Oh, her. No, haven't seen her since.'

'So how ...?'

Dave grinned. 'Well – just to prove that people do take you seriously when you're up at the front – I've been praying for Liz and Rupert quite a lot over the last few weeks.'

'And?'

'Well, every time I've prayed about this trip, I kept thinking of you.'

'So why didn't you tell me?'

'Wasn't certain, so I kept chickening out. Thought I'd wait for you to make the first move.'

'But I had no idea, up until today.'

Told him about my recent conversations with Debbie, Maggie, George and Carly.

'Seems pretty convincing to me,' said Dave.

Still couldn't quite get my head around it. 'Are you sure you don't mind?'

'What, a week's peace and quiet?'

'Cheek! Anyway, you won't get much peace with three kids to run around after.'

Dave pretended to be horrified. 'You mean you're not taking them with you?'

'I'm sure they'd have a great time ... but no. Wouldn't want to deprive you of their company. And I'll ask Debbie if she'd be willing to look after Ellie.'

He leaned over to plant a kiss on my forehead. 'It'll be odd without you – and I'd like us to pray together some more – but if this is God's idea, then I'll support you 100 per cent.'

Emailed Liz before I lost my nerve.

Dear Liz,

How are you both? I've been thinking and praying about that team that's coming out to tart up the community centre. Just wondering if there are any places left? I sort of have this feeling that God might want me to be part of it. What do you and Rupert think?

Love, B. xx

Wednesday 28th January

Checked the emails about twenty times between getting up and going out to school.

Nothing.

Maybe she doesn't want me.

Had to take Ellie to a party at our local soft-play barn at twelve. The phone signal's rubbish in there, which meant I didn't look at the emails till I got home just before two. No answer.

Maybe she doesn't know how to tell me.

Decided cleaning the bathroom might take my mind off it. (Bit desperate, I know.) My mood was not enhanced by the discovery of a mould-infested mug hidden behind the curtains.

Was almost late for school as the emails were taking forever to load up. Still no reply.

Dear Jesus, have I just made a total mess of things again?

Anita rang just before tea to see how I was getting on.

'I don't know,' I said. 'I emailed Liz yesterday ...'

'Brilliant!'

'... but she still hasn't replied.'

'I don't think I'd worry too much.'

'But what if she doesn't think I'm suitable, and she's just trying to work out how to say so? What if God wasn't telling me to go to Guatemala, and I've just made myself look like a donkey? What if ...?'

'What if,' said Anita, 'she's been busy, and hasn't seen it yet?'

'I suppose ...'

9.30pm. Finally got a reply:

Hi Becky,

Yes, yes, yes! I think it's a fantastic idea – it would be so nice to see you, and you could help me keep all those teenagers in order. Consider yourself booked in!

Love, Liz x

PS Knew God had something special lined up for you.

PPS Sorry I didn't reply earlier – our internet's been playing up again.

Thursday 29th January

Wondered what Mums' Group would make of my adventure. Didn't want them to think I was having a mid-life crisis.

'Any prayer requests?' said Maggie.

Swallowed two or three times. 'Well …'

'I have,' said Blessing. 'My mum's going in for a minor op next week, and she's feeling anxious about it.'

'OK,' said Maggie. 'Anyone else?'

Tried again. 'I'd like to …'

'Can we pray for John, please,' said Annie. 'He's got the chance to go for promotion at work, but it'll mean longer hours, so he's a bit undecided.'

'Does he know we're praying for him?' said Blessing.

'Oh, yes. He said we're all deluded, but if it made us feel better, we might as well: it wasn't going to do him any harm.'

Debbie asked if we could pray for her neighbour, who was in hospital with a broken leg, and Gillian wanted us to pray for a new job for her.

'Shall we pray, then?' said Maggie.

Felt myself flushing. It was now or never, but I couldn't frame my thoughts into a coherent sentence. Helen had already closed her eyes, with her hands clasped together in a perfect Albrecht Dürer pose, and she was sighing earnestly. Blessing was balancing a twin on each knee, pointing out pictures in a book, while Annie was discreetly adjusting her top so that Ben could suckle while we prayed.

Dear Jesus, have I got the wrong end of the stick (again)? Are You sure You don't want Helen to go instead? Or maybe Blessing – working alongside a group of teenagers should be a doddle compared to managing her brood. Perhaps I shouldn't say anything, just in case ...

Glanced around the room in desperation, and caught Anita winking at me.

'Actually,' she said, 'I think Becky might have something to share.'

Friday 30th January

Can't get over how nice people have been about my suggested trip. Maggie and Debbie jumped up to hug me, while Annie gave me the thumbs-up.

'Wow!' said Blessing. 'Sounds like a huge adventure.'

'Glad it wasn't just my daft idea,' said Maggie. 'I bet Liz is chuffed to bits.'

'I wasn't sure what she'd say,' I admitted, 'but she seems dead keen.'

Helen reached over and grasped my hands. 'You're such an example to us all, Becky,' she said. 'I'm sure you'll be a real blessing to all those people Liz and Rupert work with.'

Sat down with Dave this evening to go through the numbers.

'Are you sure we can afford this?' I said. 'We got through most of our savings when we replaced the car.'

Dave frowned. 'Things are a bit tight at the moment – but the more I think about this, the more settled I am about you going. How much do you need?'

'About £1,000 altogether, I think: there's flights and transport their end, plus accommodation and stuff. Oh, and I'll need to get down to Heathrow, so maybe a little bit more.'

He flicked around the computer screen. 'There. We've got just over £900 left in our savings, but I reckon we can find the rest of it before the end of March. D'you need to pay it all now?'

'No, I think I can pay £100 now, and the rest two weeks before I go.'

'You'd better start packing, then.'

'Mmm.' Leaned across to kiss him. 'Love you, darling. Are you sure you don't mind?'

'I'll be fine, although if Adam doesn't stop saying "Why?" every five minutes, you might find him stuffed in your suitcase.'

Saturday 31st January

Debbie rang this morning to say that she'd be happy to pick the kids up from school as well as looking after Ellie while I was away.

Jennifer appeared just as I was hanging up. 'Who was that, Mum?'

'Debbie.'

'What did she want?'

'She was just offering to help me with something.'

'What?'

'Just something I was talking to her about the other day.'

Jennifer's eyes narrowed. 'Is it something to do with us?'

'We'll talk about it later,' I said.

Jennifer folded her arms across her chest. 'It is about us, isn't it?'

'Yes … well, sort of.'

A triumphant gleam shone in her eyes. 'I knew it, Mum. You're so rubbish at secrets.'

At present, Jennifer's intention is to either be a dance teacher or to work in a pet shop when she grows up. Personally, I think she'd be better off working for the Crown Prosecution Service.

Made her wait till we were all sitting down to lunch before I shared my news.

'Can't we all come?' said Adam.

'No, you'll be at school.'

'We could just miss it for a few days,' said Jennifer. 'Miss Slater wouldn't mind.'

'I think she would,' said Dave.

Jennifer pouted. 'That's not fair. Megan-at-trampolining had two weeks off school when she went to Florida. And anyway, I thought you said there were some older children going from that other church.'

'You'll have to move to Leicester,' I said. 'Their school holidays are earlier than ours.'

'But who's going to look after us?' said Adam.

'Debbie'll drop you off at school and pick you up afterwards,' I said. 'That's what the phone call was about.'

'What about tea?' said Jennifer.

'Daddy'll be in charge, so you'll all have to help him.'

Dave rubbed his hands together in anticipation. 'Just you wait,' he said. 'We'll have crisp sandwiches and beans on toast for a week.'

'Cool!' said Adam.

'My have c'isps?' said Ellie.

Sunday 1st February

Felt blessed to be part of such a supportive fellowship this morning. (News travels fast in church circles.) A number of people came to say what a good idea they thought it was, and that they'd be praying for me.

Had a completely different response this afternoon. We'd just finished lunch when the phone rang.

'I'll get it,' said Jennifer, dashing through to the hall. She always assumes it'll be for her, on the grounds that Dave and I are far too decrepit to have a social life. Moments later I could hear her chattering away at someone.

'That'll be Laura,' said Dave. 'You'd never think they'd only seen each other a couple of hours ago.'

'Wonder what they're plotting this time?' I said.

Jennifer reappeared, holding out the receiver. 'Mum, Grandma wants to talk to you.'

'Hello, Linda, how are you?' I said.

Linda has no time for social niceties if she has something on her mind. 'I just had a rather worrying conversation with Jennifer,' she said.

It's a good job phone lines don't transmit temperature, or I'd have had an ear full of ice.

'Oh?'

'She tells me you're going on holiday – on your own.'

'It's not exactly a holiday,' I said. 'It's a mission trip.'

Linda tutted. 'I'm not sure that makes any difference,' she said. 'It still seems rather irresponsible to me.'

'I'm only going for a week.'

'But have you thought about how the family will manage without you? Does David know you're going?'

Was tempted to say that no, I was planning to sneak off while he was at work, but realised that this might not help matters.

'We've had a good chat about it,' I said. 'It's something that we both want to support, and one of my friends is going to help with the children.'

'I do think you need to be careful about this,' said Linda. 'Perhaps I'll just have a quick chat with David, if he's there.'

Dave reappeared twenty minutes later, rubbing his ear.

I poured him a fresh cup of tea. 'How was that?'

He wrapped both hands around his mug. 'Well, I don't like to jump to conclusions ... but I'd say she's not impressed.'

Pulled my chair closer to his. 'I'm sorry, darling. Have I made the wrong decision?'

Dave snorted. 'I'd be more worried if she did approve.'

Monday 2nd February

Got a rather different reaction from Mum when I rang to tell her the news.

Spent the first quarter of an hour listening to a blow-by-blow account of their next-door neighbour's fracas with the local car mechanic, and how Mrs Quinn-across-the-road's son – you know, the one with bright red hair that went to live in Australia – was getting married for the third time, only this time it was bound to last as she was a doctor and therefore the epitome of respectability. I mumbled along in the background, trying hard to smother my simmering sense of frustration. Eventually, she said: 'You're very quiet today, dear. Is everything OK?'

'I'm fine, Mum. I just wanted ...'

'As long as you're OK. I thought perhaps you were coming down with something. You're sure you haven't caught a bug off one of the children?'

'No, they're all fine, too. It's just ...'

'And how's Dave doing? Is he very busy at work, still?'

Gritted my teeth. 'Dave's fine, too, Mum. Can you please listen to me for a minute?'

Explained about my trip, and why I was going.

'But it's OK,' I added, "'cos Dave says he's happy to look after things at home for a week, and Debbie's going to do the school run and look after Ellie during the day.'

There was a pause of at least two seconds while Mum digested this bit of news. Then: 'That's nice, dear,' she said. 'You will make sure you pack plenty of sun cream, won't you?'

'Yes, I'm perfectly capable of ...'

But Mum was back into her stride now. 'Have you heard what Katie's doing this summer? They're going for a fortnight somewhere in Brittany.'

'That's ...'

'I'm sure it'll be lovely once they get there, but it does seem a terribly long way to go with two small children. I said to your dad, I hope they've thought this through properly, it'll be awful on the ferry if they all get seasick, and none of them speak French either.'

I've often thought Mum ought to take up freediving now that she's retired. Given that she can talk non-stop for ten minutes without appearing to draw breath, she should be a natural.

Tuesday 3rd February

Can't believe how well everything's falling into place for my trip. (Apart from being in Linda's bad books, but then that's par for the course.) Funny how God's plans work out: this time last month I'd never have dreamed I'd soon be setting off for Guatemala with a group of complete strangers.

Feels like other parts of my life are coming together, too: we've been on time for school every day the last couple of weeks, and Ellie has at long last worked out that she needs to sit on the potty rather than next to it.

Anyway, good, efficient day today. Spent the morning at Jelly-Tots, then nipped to the shops to get more milk and bread. Remembered to stick a load of towels in the wash after lunch, then spent the afternoon playing shops with Ellie, and catching up on a bit of tidying before it was time to go to school.

'Can I have a glass of milk?' said Adam when we got home.

'Sure,' I said. 'Jennifer, would you mind reaching him a glass down while I sort Ellie out?'

Jennifer reappeared minus the glass. 'Mum, why is there a load of water on the kitchen floor?'

'What?'

'The kitchen floor's covered in water.'

Rushed through to see what was going on. When she said *covered*, it was only a slight exaggeration.

'Puggle!' shouted Ellie, dragging her wellies through from the hall.

If I believed in reincarnation, I think I'd come back as a plumber. The one I eventually got hold of charged an exorbitant amount just to come and admire the mess. He shuffled through to the kitchen and scratched his head.

'Ee, there's a lot o' watter there.'

Yes, thank you, I had noticed …

He ambled round the kitchen, turned the taps on and off a few times and then fiddled with the stopcock. More head scratching.

'It'll likely be washin' machine.'

Oh, great!

'Can you fix it?' I asked.

He shook his head, clearly surprised at the notion that he might be required to mend something. 'Nah,' he said. 'Need to get repair man to tek a look.'

Well, don't strain yourself …

'What are we going to do now, Mum?' said Jennifer.

'Looks like it's time for a mopping party.'

Ellie stamped her foot in the edge of the water. 'Party, party!'

Wednesday 4th February

Texted Debbie first thing so I could get the number of the washing machine repair firm she used last time.

'Is it urgent?' said the woman who answered. Don't know why they ask that: can't imagine anybody saying no, they'll be fine without it for the next fortnight.

Booked a visit for this afternoon. At least this bloke was more cheerful than the plumber.

'Right, let's get this sorted.' He opened an enormous set of tools. 'Might make a bit more mess, I'm afraid.'

'I don't mind that; I just need to get it fixed. I've got three children.'

'Goodness, you've got your hands full. I'd best crack on, then.' He prised the door open, provoking a small deluge.

As the afternoon wore on, the corners of his mouth gradually turned downwards. After two and a half hours he stood up, wiping his hands on my last remaining clean tea towel. 'It's not good news, I'm afraid.'

'Can't you do it?'

He held up a twisted piece of metal. I'm no engineer, but even I could tell it wasn't supposed to be that shape. 'See, this mechanism should operate that bit there.'

'Can you get a spare part?'

'Hmm.' He rubbed the side of his nose with a grubby finger. 'Possibly, although I think they've stopped making this model. And it might well go again – it's quite an old machine.'

'So isn't there anything you can do?'

'I think you'd be best off getting a new one, love. Sorry.'

Spent an unhappy couple of hours on the internet looking at washing machines after the kids had gone to bed.

Dave tried to be positive. 'C'mon, darling, I'm sure we can work something out.'

Put my head in my hands. 'But they're so expensive. And I'm supposed to be saving for Guatemala.'

He reached across and closed the laptop lid. 'Don't worry. I'm sure your trip won't be a complete washout.'

I groaned. 'Do me a favour?'

'What?'

'Save your jokes for the children. I'm not in the mood right now.'

Chapter Twelve

Thursday 5th February

Related my sob story at Mums' Group.

'Sounds expensive,' said Annie.

I nodded. 'By the time we've paid for the call-outs plus a new machine, we'll be lucky to have change from £400.'

'Ouch!' said Debbie.

'I had to wash a load of undies in the sink last night,' I said. 'Makes you grateful to be living in the twenty-first century.'

'You can bring some washing round to mine, if you want,' said Blessing.

'Are you sure? You must have more than enough to do.'

Blessing shrugged. 'I've decided it must be my spiritual anointing,' she said. 'Some people preach to thousands, some arrange soup-runs for the homeless. I just operate the washing machine that never sleeps.'

Friday 6th February

Dave strode into the kitchen this morning, frowning. 'Have you seen the car keys?'

I pointed to the worktop. 'Sorry. I think they're in my handbag. I must have left them there last night after I took that washing to Blessing's.'

Dave grabbed my bag and felt around inside, while I returned my attention to the cereal I was trying to chisel off Ellie's high chair tray.

'Whereabouts?'

'D'you want me to have a look?'

'It's all right.' He turned the bag over and shook the contents onto the table.

'Dave!'

'Got them.' He dumped the bag on a chair. 'Why on earth do you have so much stuff in there, anyway?'

'Because I have three children. The day I gave birth to Jennifer was the day I swapped my perfectly serviceable clutch bag for a bottomless sack that would have put Mary Poppins to shame.'

He grunted. 'I'm sorry. Are you OK to put it all back again? I'm running late.'

Left the bag until I got back from school, so I could have a proper sort-out.

Arranged the items into three categories: handbag (purse, tissues, phone, a spare nappy and a small packet of wet wipes), to keep elsewhere (half a dozen paperclips, three hairpins, a Lego figure, two felt-tips and the scarf from Ellie's beloved giraffe), and bin (three out of date money-off coupons, a spare programme from Adam's Christmas performance, a packet of cough sweets that had gone sticky and horrible, and an odd sock). I don't need a handbag: I need a filing cabinet.

Saturday 7th February

The good news in our house is that Jennifer has moved on from the glitter stage. The bad news is that her new favourite pastime is designing things with beads; the ones you can build into a pattern and then fuse together with an iron. (It's not that I object to her being creative: quite the reverse. I have to say I don't know where she got it from. Between us, Dave and I have the combined creativity of an amoeba.)

What bothers me is the resultant mess. I can always tell what medium she's been working with just by glancing at the floor. We'd no sooner cleared away the breakfast things this morning than she was spreading her equipment across the kitchen table.

I feigned enthusiasm. 'What are you going to make today?'

Jennifer was wrestling with the lid of a large jar full of beads. 'I haven't quite decided yet. I might do some Easter presents.'

'That sounds good.' I noticed the angle of the jar. 'You will be careful, won't ...'

Well, I can now say with some authority that the sound of a full jar of beads being tipped onto a wooden floor is almost identical to the noise a hailstorm makes on a caravan roof.

'Oops!' Jennifer set the jar down and started to work with the few beads that remained on the table.

'Jennifer! You can't just leave them all on the floor.'

She pushed her chair back with unnecessary force. 'OK, OK. I was gonna pick them up later, anyway.'

'Pick them up now, please!' I pushed the beads nearest to me into a small pile. 'Otherwise, they'll end up in the bin.'

Ellie toddled into the kitchen and stared, fascinated, at the rainbow of colours scattered across the floor.

'Oh dear, Mummy.' She picked up a bead and offered it to her sister. 'Here, Je'fer.'

I took it from her and put it back in the jar. 'I think they're a bit small for you to play with. Why don't you come shopping with me?'

Ellie shrieked with delight, and ran off to find her wellies. I know how to spoil my children.

Sunday 8th February

Why are Sundays always so stressful? By the time I've nagged the kids into getting ready for church (including a ten-minute fashion debate with Jennifer), I'm exhausted. And it was my turn in crèche this morning (which I love doing) so I was wrecked by the time we got home. I might even have dropped off for a few minutes after lunch.

Came to with a start when Ellie tugged at my jumper. 'Mummy, Mummy. Wake up!'

I lifted her onto my lap. 'What's up?'

She pointed to her face, which was paler than a Narnian winter.

'Stuck, Mummy.'

'What d'you mean, stuck?'

She rubbed at the side of her face, then tried to poke her finger inside her ear. 'It's stuck.'

I pulled her hand away. 'Don't do that. Here, let me have a look.'

Didn't take me long to discover that Jennifer's promise that she had cleared up all the beads she had spilled was not as watertight as I had hoped.

Ellie was sobbing by now. 'Don' like it, Mummy.'

Why do these things always happen to me? Or – to be more precise – to my children? It took the A and E nurse a mere two minutes to remove the bead from Ellie's left ear, but Ellie was clingy and fractious for the rest of the day, and Jennifer showed her appreciation of my lecture on the importance of putting things away properly by sulking in her room for most of the evening.

Dear Jesus, why is it always me who ends up in the doghouse? Anyone'd think it was me who shoved the bead in Ellie's ear.

Monday 9th February

Ellie had recovered enough this morning to decide it was time we revisited the 'hide the shoes' game (under her duvet on this occasion).

'Ellie!' I plonked her on the bottom stair so that I could do them up. 'You mustn't do that. You've made us late.'

'Sor-ree, Mummy!' She tried to put her arms round my neck, hampering my attempts to tie her laces.

'Ellie! Stop it.'

Her face crumpled, and two oversized tears ran down her cheeks and plopped onto the carpet. 'But my sor-ree, Mummy.'

Great! Not only am I late; I've also regained my Meanie-Mummy-of-the-Year title. Serves me right for thinking I was getting on top of things.

Was just locking the door when my phone rang. I set off at a march down the drive, trying my best to steer the buggy with one hand so that I could operate my phone with the other.

'Hello, darling.'

Dave's voice wobbled like an operatic tenor practising his vibrato. 'Sorry to disturb you,' he said, 'it's just …'

'Are you OK?'

'Yes … no … well, a bit shaky.'

Transpired that Dave had managed to scrape another car in the staff car park.

'Badly?'

'It looks a bit of a mess. What's worse, it was Mark Davies' car.'

'Whoops! That'll cheer him up.'

'He just made some comment about us holy Joes getting it wrong, too.'

'Won't the insurance cover it?'

'Yes … but there's £100 excess.'

Dear Jesus, this isn't funny. I know it was an accident – and I promise I'm gonna try extra-hard not to get mad at Dave – but my Guatemala fund is getting seriously depleted. This isn't so much of a straight path as a scenic detour with multiple stop-offs. It'd be nice if You could make my life a little less complicated at times.

Tuesday 10th February

I'm sure the man at the garage rubs his hands together when he sees us coming. If things carry on like this, we'll be entitled to our own private parking space on his forecourt. I tried not to check my watch while he paced around the vehicle, making whistling noises through his teeth and pausing every now and then to prod at the dent.

'What 'appened here, then, love?'

'My husband. He bumped another car at work.'

This information elicited another protracted whistle. 'Bet he's in your bad books.'

Didn't want to appear too disloyal. 'It was an accident. D'you know how long it'll take to sort it?'

'Erm ...' He gazed into the distance, as if hoping to find inspiration among the chimney pots of the adjacent street. 'Mebbe Monday? But I can get you fixed up with a courtesy car.'

There must be an insurance rule-book somewhere that states that cars can only be offered to people in our situation if they've first been retrieved from the nearest scrapyard and then driven through a swamp. Ended up with a battered old vehicle with a stodgy gearbox, and more dimples than a golf ball. Still, at least Jennifer was pleased.

'Hey, Mum, can we keep this one?' She loitered on the driveway to admire the (somewhat tatty) silver paintwork. 'Anything's better than orange.'

Wednesday 11th February

It could be argued that this has not been a good couple of weeks. First the washing machine, then the car. Just goes to show how much we rely on modern gadgetry. Trying not to think about the dent this'll make in our savings.

Decided I'd do a roast dinner tonight, to cheer us all up: it's one of the few things all the kids can be guaranteed to eat.

'Roast chicken tonight?' I said, as we walked to school.

'With roast potatoes?' said Adam.

'Yep. *And* carrots and peas, and lots of gravy.'

Jennifer narrowed her eyes at me. 'Have we got people coming round or something?'

'No – I just thought it'd be a nice family thing to do. Why?'

'Nothing – it's just that we only have nice meals when we've got visitors.'

Huh! Nice to know my culinary efforts are so appreciated.

Needed to return our library books after school, so made sure I had everything prepared before I went to pick the children up. Praised the Lord (not for the first time) for oven timers. By the time they'd all dawdled over making their selections, I was salivating.

Adam was in a whingey mood. 'I'm cold,' he said.

'Never mind, 'I said. 'I'll do hot chocolate when we get home, and then there's chicken dinner to look forward to.'

'Yay!' said Adam. 'Can I have a bit with the bone in?'

The house felt warm and cosy when we got in. Brewed three mugs of not-too-hot chocolate for the kids, and a cup of tea for myself. Fifteen minutes later the children were all sporting chocolate moustaches. (That's another photo I can save to embarrass them when they grow up.)

Jennifer compounded the mess by using her finger to wipe the last bits of chocolate out of her mug. 'What time's tea?' she said.

'About half five – I just need …'

I realised what had been niggling at the back of my mind since we got home. The chicken should have been cooking since about 3.15, but the only thing I could smell was the lingering aroma of warm milk.

'What's up, Mum?' said Jennifer.

'Think I might have forgotten to turn the oven on.'

My spirits plummeted like a skydiver in freefall as I ran from the lounge into the kitchen. The oven was colder than the atmosphere in Linda's house when Ellie spilled blackcurrant juice on their new carpet. Typical!

'Sorry, guys,' I called. 'Looks like we'll be a bit late with tea.'

There was a disgruntled chorus of: 'Oh, Mum!'

Fiddled with the timer, then the temperature knob, then the timer again. Nothing happened. Twisted a few other switches, just for good measure. Didn't work. Even tried that trick you do with computers where you turn it off and on at the wall, and it magically fixes itself. Nope: our oven knows nothing of computer folklore. Kicked it a few times for good measure, earning myself a stern telling-off from Ellie in the process.

'Why don't you pray about it?' said Jennifer. 'Losing your temper won't make any difference.'

Felt more like crying. Why is it that when I want everything to be perfect, it all goes wrong? And how come even my nine-year is more spiritual than I am?

Dear Jesus, are you sure about this Guatemala thing? Maybe Jennifer should go instead. In fact, she and Adam and Ellie

*could all go, and I could hide in a corner and stop pretending
that I can make any difference.*

Couldn't let Jennifer think that prayer wasn't an option,
though.

'Good idea,' I said. 'D'you want to join in?'

9.30pm. Our cooker has no soul. If I'd been on the
receiving end of Jennifer's prayers, I'd have apologised
profusely and got on with cooking the dinner. Instead, it
just sat there and refused to cooperate. Ended up with a
sumptuous feast of (microwaved) beans on toast, which
would have been more bearable if Jennifer and Adam
hadn't insisted on counting them to check who had the
most.

Thursday 12th February

Our house deserves its own special listing in the local
trades' press. First the plumber, then the washing
machine repair bloke and now someone to sort the oven
out. They must have developed some sort of script
between them, as the latest engineer only took half an
hour to decide that the cooker was beyond redemption,
and should be consigned to the appliances graveyard at
the local tip.

'Does that mean we're getting a new cooker?' said
Jennifer.

'Yes, but they can't deliver it till next Wednesday. Not
sure what we're going to eat for the next few days.'

Adam's eyes brightened. 'We could have fish and
chips every day.'

Huh! The amount of money we've shelled out on unforeseen expenses, he'll be lucky to get bread and jam. The only way we could afford the new cooker was by using the credit card, which Dave prefers to keep for emergency use only.

'It is sort of an emergency,' I pointed out, 'and we can pay it off at the end of the month when your salary comes in.'

He grimaced. 'If we use the bit that would normally go into our savings account plus what's already in there, that should about cover it. As long as I pay the bill straight away when it comes, we shouldn't get hit with interest charges.'

Put my arm through his. 'We'll be all right, won't we? Not sure we've got much left that can go wrong now, anyway.'

Friday 13th February

Wondered if I'd somehow woken up too early this morning: the noise from the cars going past our house seemed more muted than usual. Two minutes later, Jennifer came dashing through.

'It's snowing, it's snowing!' she yelled, dancing past our bed so she could yank the curtains open. 'Look, Mum, look, Dad. D'you think we'll have a snow day?'

Even from the bed I could see that the sky was a dull, leaden grey colour. Large flakes of snow were hurtling past the window.

I staggered to my feet. 'Maybe. We'd better check the website.'

'Can we build a snowman?'

'Not till we've found out whether school's open or not.'

'But it's snowing – it ought to be closed.'

Adam came to find out what all the commotion was about, his eyes widening as he took in the view. 'I'm going to make an igloo,' he said.

Dave joined us by the window. 'I don't think it's deep enough for that yet,' he said.

'But you did when you were little.'

'Yeah – but that was after it had snowed non-stop for about three days,' said Dave.

'I'll go and find out what school are saying,' I said.

Jennifer clenched her fists and hopped from one foot to the other. 'I hope it's closed, I hope it's closed.'

'Then Mrs Baxter could play in the snow, too,' said Adam.

Mrs Baxter is a rather large lady of mature years: she reminds me of a Beryl Cook painting. Couldn't quite get my head round the idea of her shooting downhill on a sledge.

Dave yawned and then stretched. 'Can you check the high school, too?' he said. 'I'd better get in the shower.'

'Won't your school be closed?' said Jennifer. 'It's not fair if they say you've got to go in to work.'

'They'll keep it open if they can,' said Dave, 'and I'm not sure I fancy taking the car out when it's like this: I'll have to walk.'

'Poor Dad!' said Jennifer.

Ellie toddled through, dragging Ginger Giraffe by one leg, and I lifted her up so she could see out. She stared, fascinated. 'Wha' is it, Mummy?'

'Look, Ellie, it's snowing,' said Jennifer. 'Would you like to help me build a snowman?'

'No-man, no-man,' said Ellie, twisting her neck so she could peer at the sky. 'My make no-man, Mummy?'

Hoped she wouldn't be too disappointed when it didn't fly off like the one on her DVD. 'Sure,' I said, 'but not in your pyjamas. And I need to find out whether Jennifer and Adam have to go to school today.'

Took several goes to load the website as it kept crashing. No doubt hopeful children all over town were nagging their parents to find out if they'd gained an extra day's holiday. Not sure whether the parents were quite so thrilled at the prospect.

'Yay!' said Jennifer. 'School's closed, school's closed.'

'Looks like Dad's got to go in, though.'

'That's not fair,' said Jennifer.

'He should ring the head teacher,' said Adam, 'and tell him to close the school.'

Mmm – not sure that's quite how it works.

Dave came in dressed as if for an Arctic expedition.

'They shouldn't make you walk to school when it's like this,' said Adam.

Dave leaned over to plant a kiss on my cheek. 'Well,' he said, 'there's *snow* way I can get the car out today.'

'Da-ad!' said Jennifer.

'See you later, darling,' I said. 'Watch out for those polar bears.'

Adam ran over to the window and peered out. 'Will you really see a polar bear?' he asked.

'Don't be silly,' said Jennifer. 'Mum's trying to be funny.'

Got through breakfast in record time. (Shame it doesn't snow every morning.) Getting dressed was an equally speedy operation, although Ellie had to be persuaded not to wear the Hawaiian skirt from the dressing-up box.

'Can we build a snowman now?' said Jennifer.

'Can we go sledging?' said Adam.

'Let's go sledging first,' I said. 'Then if Ellie gets too cold, I can bring her inside while you two play in the garden.'

Unearthed the sledges from the back of the garage, and came out to find the older two teaching Ellie how to do snow angels.

'Look, Mummy!' she shouted. 'My can do it.'

'So you can.'

'Yours do it, Mummy?' She took my hand and pulled me across the lawn to an unblemished patch of white. 'There, Mummy.'

Winced as a layer of snow found a gap between my scarf and my hat. Hoped none of the neighbours were watching as I thrashed my arms up and down. Couldn't help marvelling at the relentless flurry of swirling flakes above me – until I was interrupted by a lump of snow being deposited on my chest.

'Right, you two ...'

I struggled to my feet, but Adam and Jennifer had taken refuge behind an azalea bush, and were shrieking with laughter. Adam grabbed fistfuls of snow and started hurling them towards me. Fortunately, his aim's pretty rubbish: it must have been a pure fluke that he got me the first time.

The field behind our house slopes gently away from the garden, and there were already several children taking turns to launch themselves down the hill. Wedged Ellie between my legs before pushing off. She was enchanted.

''Gain, 'gain, Mummy,' she said, as we slithered to a halt.

'Come on, then – help me pull the sledge back.'

When we got to the top, Jennifer and Adam were squabbling.

Jennifer yanked on the rope. 'It's my turn to go in front.'

Adam tried to push her out of the way. 'I don't like going at the back – I can't see anything.'

'It's not my fault if I'm taller than you.'

Adam scuffed at a heap of snow with his boot, showering the sledge with its own personal snowstorm. 'S'not fair!'

'Hey, you two!' I lifted Ellie off the spare sledge. 'Why don't you have one each? Ellie and I can watch for a few minutes.'

Adam clambered onto our sledge and waited just long enough to stick his tongue out at Jennifer before pushing off down the hill. Jennifer – turning from obnoxious older sibling to caring big sister in the blink of an eye – held out a hand to Ellie.

'You can come on my sledge, if you want.'

Ellie didn't need to be asked twice, and I found myself abandoned at the top of the hill, along with several other adults who had found themselves surplus to requirements. Soon got chatting with another mum I recognised from the school playground. I was so deep in conversation that I only gradually became aware of someone calling me.

'Mum. *Mum?* Mum!'

I turned. Jennifer was scrambling up the slope as fast as she could manage. She was carrying Ellie, who was sobbing. There was no sign of their sledge.

'Jennifer?'

On hearing my voice, Ellie reached out towards me, and I lifted her onto my hip.

'What's the matter? What have you done with the sledge?'

Jennifer's voice trembled as she pointed back down the hill. 'It's Adam. He's covered in blood.'

Chapter Thirteen

Saturday 14th February

Well, once again, any notion I might have had regarding a romantic Valentine's Day were – literally, on this occasion – knocked on the head.

Spent most of yesterday afternoon at the hospital, waiting for Adam to be seen to. His was the fifth sledging-related injury they'd had in, and there were several more arrivals after us. As far as we could make out, Adam had veered off course at the bottom of the hill and hit a partially buried pile of rocks from a collapsed wall. He'd scraped his face along a rock – which accounted for the fact that he looked as though he was preparing to be an extra in a low-budget horror movie – and he'd broken his left arm.

'You're very lucky, young man,' said the nurse, cleaning his face up as best she could. 'Any faster and you'd have knocked half your teeth out.'

Sunday 15th February

Suggested to Adam he might like to stay at home this morning.

'Aksherly, I want to go to church.' He lifted his coat off its hook, then glanced at his damaged arm. 'I've got to show them this.'

Dave helped Adam with his zip. 'Can't see any 'arm in that,' he said.

Monday 16th February

Thought I'd coped quite well with our escapades over the weekend, but had a bit of a wobble today. What if Adam had been seriously injured? Was it my fault for letting him use the sledge on his own? Should we take the sledges to the tip? And (most persistent of all) should I really be thinking of leaving the kids for a week while I go off to Guatemala?

Dear Jesus, am I being thick here? Maybe I shouldn't go to Guatemala. Perhaps all these setbacks – financial or otherwise – are Your way of telling me to stay at home.

Asked Dave if he thought I should back out.
He snorted. 'Don't be ridiculous.'
Still wasn't convinced.

Tuesday 17th February

Dear Jesus, I'm confused – a little nudge in the right direction would be much appreciated.

Arranged to meet Carly at the soft-play barn as there was no Jelly-Tots at church today because of it being half-term.

'How're your plans?' she said. 'I'm dead excited for you.'

I shook my head. 'Don't know if we can afford it any more. Our finances have taken a few hits.'

'You're not going to let that stop you? Don't you want to go any more?'

'It's not that I don't want to go: I'm just not sure where the money's going to come from.'

'But isn't that ...' She stopped.

'Go on.'

She set her mug down on the table. 'Listen, I don't pretend to understand this God business, but you gave me the impression He wanted you to go to Guatemala?'

'That's what I thought.'

'So won't He help you get the money sorted?'

'Mmm.'

''Cos otherwise, it'd be a bit like me telling the kids they could come to Portugal with us, but then not giving them a lift to the airport.'

Oh! I could feel my face burning.

Carly lowered her gaze. 'Take no notice of me. I'm sure you know much more about this faith business than I do.'

Gulped. 'No, that's helpful. You seem understand God better than a lot of Christians I've come across.'

Carly shrugged and picked up her mug. 'Whatever,' she said.

Dear Jesus, when I said I'd like a little nudge, did You have to make it so embarrassing? Now even my non-Christian friends have more faith than I do.

Wednesday 18th February

Praise the Lord, we have a new cooker! Thought perhaps we could celebrate our return to normality by having a treat at teatime. It fell to Adam – as house invalid – to make the decision.

'What would you like for tea today? Anything special?'

He screwed up his face as if I'd just shown him one of Dave's A level physics questions. 'I fink ... beef burgers and chips would be nice.'

Given the chance, Adam would eat chips with every meal. Hope he's not planning to be a dietician when he's older.

Gave Maggie a lift to the supermarket, as her car had gone for its MOT. Halfway down the cereals aisle – in the middle of a delicate negotiation where I argued for cheap and healthy, and the kids pressed for expensive and sugary – I realised that Kylie was standing next to us, arms folded tightly across her ample chest.

'Hey!' she said, in a manner reminiscent of a detective about to solve a particularly tricky case. 'Did you say you were gonna pray for me?'

For a split second, I wondered whether I should claim to have forgotten. Wasn't sure I could face another scolding over my lack of faith.

'Well ... I ... um ...'

The corners of her mouth twitched ever so slightly upwards, as if somewhere deep inside her, a smile was making a desperate bid for freedom.

'Thought so,' she said. 'Me dad said he was fed up with getting ratted every year. Took us all out for Christmas dinner instead, didn't he?'

She turned and marched away, leaving me spluttering and staring wildly after her.

'Well,' said Maggie, raising an eyebrow. 'What was it you were saying the other week about not being very good at sharing your faith?'

Thursday 19th February

Wondered if Mums' Group might be cancelled, seeing as it was half-term, but Maggie bravely insisted she was still happy to host us along with all the extra children.

'I haven't organised a Bible study as such,' said Anita, 'but I've been reading this book on simplicity, and I wondered whether that would be a good topic for discussion this morning.'

'Huh!' said Blessing. 'Not sure having five kids and simplicity go together.'

'Depends how you define simplicity,' said Maggie.

'It's a bit weird,' said Debbie. 'All these mod cons, and yet we seem to be busier than ever.'

'Speaking of appliances,' said Annie, 'have you got your washing machine sorted, Becky?'

'Coming on Saturday, all being well,' I said, 'although that's not the only thing I've had to contend with this week.'

'That's tough,' said Gillian, after I had recounted our latest disaster.

'What're you going to do?' said Annie. 'You're not going to back out, are you?'

'Liz'll be gutted,' said Anita.

'That was my first thought,' I admitted, 'but I think God has other ideas.' Told them about my conversation with Carly.

'Good for Carly,' said Anita. 'Although she certainly knows how to put you on the spot.'

'We could have a whip-round,' said Blessing, 'just to get you started off.'

'No, no – please don't do that,' I said. 'You've all got plenty of other calls on your finances.'

'But we'd like to help,' said Debbie, delving into her handbag.

Maggie came to my rescue. 'Let's not embarrass Becky,' she said, 'but I'm sure she won't mind if we pray for her?'

Was struck once again by the depth of my friends' faith – and the paucity of my own. 'I'd like that,' I said.

'We'd better get praying, then,' said Anita.

Went home feeling more settled about the idea of going to Guatemala; although I still have no idea where on earth I'm going to find £946 (and thirty-two pence).

Friday 20th February

Left Dave at home with the kids while I went to the supermarket. (It's amazing how much less I spend when I haven't got three nagging children to assist me.)

Got back to find a huge bunch of flowers on the kitchen table, and two empty coffee mugs next to the sink. One of them had a faint smudge of lipstick on the rim.

'Wow, these are beautiful!' I picked the bouquet up for a closer look.

'They're from Anita. Said she thought you could do with cheering up.'

'That's very sweet of her. Was she OK?'

Dave plonked the mugs in the sink. 'She's fine. Said could she grab a quick coffee as she was just on her way out somewhere.'

'So, while I was slogging my way around the supermarket, you were sitting here entertaining another woman?'

Dave's cheeks turned a peculiar shade of deep pink (not dissimilar to the lipstick mark on Anita's cup).

'We were only chatting ... honest!' he said.

'Hey!' I put down the flowers so I could give him a hug. 'I'm only teasing. What were you chatting about?'

He grabbed a couple of tins out of the nearest bag. 'Nothing much. D'you want a hand putting the shopping away?'

Saturday 21st February

Rang Anita to thank her for the flowers. 'I gather you and Dave had a nice chat,' I added.

There was a pause.

'Oh, well, we weren't chatting about anything in particular,' she said.

I laughed. 'That's what Dave said. Can't have been a very inspiring conversation.'

'Mmm, perhaps not,' said Anita. 'Anyway, I'd better go and get on with some jobs.'

Felt a bit uncomfortable after I came off the phone. Anita's not normally that abrupt. Couldn't help wondering if I'd upset her somehow … but then, she's not really the type to take offence easily. Strange.

Sunday 22nd February

Still haven't caught up with the backlog of washing, so Dave was reduced to wearing one of Linda's sweaters to church this morning; the one that looks like it's escaped from a Jackson Pollock gallery.

'Where's Daddy?' said Ellie, when we came out from crèche. I pointed across the room. Even from behind he was instantly recognisable. He was deep in conversation with Maggie.

'What are you two plotting and planning?' I said, hoping he might have remembered to get me a drink.

Dave jumped like a jack-in-the-box, dribbling coffee down his jumper. Fortunately, the mark was camouflaged by all the other splashes and splodges of colour.

'You'll give the poor man a heart attack, sneaking up on him like that,' said Maggie.

'Sorry. Did you get me a cup of tea?'

'Here.' Dave reached over to grab a mug off the windowsill.

'You were both looking very serious,' I said.

Maggie seemed a bit flustered. 'Sorry,' she said. 'I was just telling Dave about our discussion on Thursday.'

'Oh … yeah,' said Dave. 'You've certainly got me thinking.'

Monday 23rd February

For once, Adam was excited about going back to school. He needs to keep the cast on his arm for another two weeks, so that's plenty of time for him to go around and show all his teachers – not to mention embroidering his story as much as possible. I overheard him telling Keziah yesterday that he shot off his sledge 'at a hunjred miles an hour'.

'Mrs Baxter will be s'prised when she sees this.' He pointed to the cast, which had been lovingly decorated by his sisters.

'I'm sure she will. Maybe you can talk about it in circle-time.'

Adam used his good hand to pat at the scar on his jaw. 'I can tell them about all the blood.'

'Maybe, but you need to be careful. Some people are a bit funny about blood.'

'Oh.' He thought for a moment. 'Did you get any photos of me when the blood was all running down?'

I shuddered as I recalled the state of Adam's face as he lay in the snow. 'No, sorry. I was too busy calling the ambulance.'

Jennifer grabbed the opportunity with both hands. 'You should get me a phone, Mum. Then I can take pictures of stuff like that.'

When I was young (not all that long ago), a phone was something attached to the wall, and you used it to talk to other people. Now it's for taking gory pictures that could double as an advert for the nearest abattoir.

Tuesday 24th February

George's internal tea-detector must have been on the blink this morning, because he appeared a good quarter of an hour before drinks were served. Credit where it's due, though: he's very good at going round and engaging with people.

'George seems very sociable this morning,' I said to Anita, who was busy manoeuvring the urn into position.

'Saves him from having to do any proper work,' said Anita. 'Hey, would you mind giving me a hand bringing some more cups through from the kitchen?'

George had worked his way as far as Carly and Annie by the time we got back with the cups. They were both smiling and nodding at him.

'Great idea,' I heard Carly say. 'You can count …'

'George!' said Anita – rather sharply, I thought. 'Can you just help Becky with this tray?'

He leaped to attention. 'Sorry, ladies – duty calls.'

Carly called after him: 'Just let me know, won't you?'

'Know what?' I said, plonking myself down next to her. 'Hope you and George haven't been planning any more adventures for me.'

Annie spluttered, and Carly jumped up to help her. 'Hey, are you OK? Sorry, Becky – could you just go and find some tissues?'

Wednesday 25th February

Wasn't till I got home yesterday that I realised that Carly never did tell me what she and George were talking about. Not that it's any of my business, of course, but I can't help being nosy sometimes.

Thursday 26th February

Rather hoped we'd be able to continue last week's discussion on simplicity: it'd be nice to work out how my life could be a bit more God-focused, and a little less possessions-dependent.

Maggie and Anita had other plans, however: we're going to do a series on 'Inspiring Women of the Bible'.

'I like that idea,' said Blessing, 'as long as you're not planning to include that irritating woman in Proverbs 31.'

Helen's jaw dropped. 'But I *love* that passage,' she said. 'She's such an example to us all.'

'To you, maybe,' said Blessing. 'She always makes me feel like a complete no-hoper.'

I was inclined to agree with Blessing, although experience has taught me it's wiser not to get drawn into a theological debate with Helen. I kept quiet, and hoped that nobody would ask for my opinion.

Maggie was more honest. 'I used to avoid that passage,' she said, 'but then I tried looking at the attitudes behind her actions.'

I was intrigued, despite myself. 'How d'you mean?'

'Well ...' Maggie paused to gather her thoughts. 'It talks about how she fears God; which I took to mean that she listened to God and tried to honour him. Then there's the bits about her caring for her family, and reaching out to people who are in need. And I realised that all of that was stuff I could aspire to.'

Helen nodded smugly, but Blessing frowned. 'Well, maybe,' she said, 'although most days, my aspirations don't stretch any further than getting through to bedtime without having a nervous breakdown.'

Friday 27th February

Dear Jesus, I'm with Blessing on this one … so is it true what Maggie was saying?

Felt almost serene today, which is not often a word I'd pick to describe myself. I've promised myself that there'll be no more flapping in this family about keeping on top of the housework. Hurrah!

Saturday 28th February

Hmph! What was I saying?

Think Dave got out of bed on the wrong side this morning. Obviously, our house is never going to feature in one of those magazines devoted to designer living. Still, Dave doesn't seem to notice until it's got to the point where he needs an ice axe and crampons to negotiate the washing mountain.

This morning he was upstairs stomping about in the bedroom almost as soon as breakfast was over. When I went to investigate, he was tipping piles of clothes onto the bed.

'What are you doing?' I asked.

'Isn't it obvious? I'm having a sort-out.'

'What brought this on?'

He gestured at a pile of Linda's birthday offerings. 'I've got far too much stuff – and some of it I'll never wear.'

I picked up the nearest jumper, turning it this way and that. 'I dunno – you might get invited to a modern art for the gullible convention.'

He snatched the jumper off me and returned it to its rightful place. 'I thought I'd bag a load of stuff up for the charity shop.'

'Good plan – I can drop it off later this week.'

He hesitated. 'Might be wise to wait until we've finished sorting – no point in making lots of separate trips.'

'Goodness – you're making it sound like a military operation.'

'Well – I did think you might want to have a clear-out, too.'

'Me?'

'Yeah – you must have loads of things you don't wear any more.'

'All feels a bit energetic for first thing on a Saturday morning.'

Dave marched across the room, flung open my wardrobe doors, and grabbed two fistfuls of hangers off the rail. 'There. Why don't you have a look through that lot? Bet your pile'll be bigger than mine.'

'Don't be so sure. At least my mother hasn't been buying me psychedelic jumpers for the past fifteen years.'

Felt quite satisfying, I have to admit – even if my pile did end up about eighteen inches taller than Dave's.

'What're you doing?' said Jennifer, who hates to think she might be missing out on something.

'Having a clear-out,' said Dave. 'You can join in, if you want.'

'I'm sure you've got too many clothes,' I said. 'Why don't you see what you can get rid of?'

Jennifer stared at us, her lips pressed into a thin line. 'Funny!' she said.

Sunday 1st March

Bit anxious that Dave's having some sort of mid-life crisis. Anyone would think he was nesting or something.

'Right,' he said, when we got back from church, 'why don't we sort out the under-stairs cupboard?'

'You what?'

'It's full of rubbish – I thought we could empty it out while we're in the mood for sorting.'

'*In the mood?* That's stretching it a bit.'

'Come on.' He pulled the vacuum cleaner out of the way. 'I'll pass things out, and you can decide whether to keep them or not.'

The cupboard did look better by the time we'd finished. Ellie thought it was great, and promptly showed her appreciation by granting Ginger Giraffe squatters' rights in the furthest corner.

Maggie had posted on the Mums' Group Facebook page:

I keep coming back to this idea of simplicity – I've discovered things in the back of the wardrobe I haven't worn for ten years.

Tell me about it, I replied. Dave's been like a man on a mission since he heard about our discussion – you should see how many bags we've got to go to the charity shop.

She texted me later: There's something I need to talk to you about regarding Mums' Group. Are you free Wednesday evening?

Me: Sure – sounds all mysterious!

Maggie: No – just a bit complicated to explain by text. Shall I pick you up? We could go out for a drink somewhere.

Me: Lovely! Would after seven be OK? Then I can get Ellie into bed first.

Maggie: Pick you up at 7.15.

Monday 2nd March

Almost broke my neck this morning tripping over the charity shop bags in the hall. Hope Dave doesn't take it into his head to do any more sorting, or we won't be able to get through the front door.

'Sorry,' he said when I moaned to him at teatime. 'Can you put up with them till the weekend? I don't think I'll have chance to go to the charity shop before then.'

'D'you want me to take them?'

He shook his head. 'No. Please don't … they're far too heavy.'

'OK – but I don't want them sitting there till Christmas.'

Tuesday 3rd March

I think I must have offended Carly. Every time I went near her today, she clammed up. Funny, she's not one to keep her opinions to herself – although come to think of it, one or two of the other mums were a bit quiet when I was around. I was so concerned I even nipped off to the loo at one point so I could sniff my under-arms, just in case I'd forgotten to use deodorant this morning … but all was well.

Then there's this odd meeting Maggie's set up. What's that all about? Have I been upsetting people, and she doesn't know how to tell me?

Dear Jesus, have I made a mess of things again? I didn't mean to upset Carly, and now she'll be more convinced than ever that Christians are a bunch of hypocrites. And I don't know what to think about going out with Maggie. Is she really being a bit strange with me, or am I just making things up?

Chapter Fourteen

Wednesday 4th March

For once, Ellie was in a cooperative mood, so I even had time to pull a brush through my hair and put on a clean jumper before Maggie tapped on the door at fourteen minutes past seven.

'Did you get Ellie settled?'

'Yep. All set.'

'Have you got those bags for the charity shop?'

'They're just here – but it won't be open now.'

Maggie grabbed the bags. 'Just thinking I could put them in my car and then drop them off next time I'm passing.'

'Well, if you're sure.'

Maggie's normally pretty chilled, but she seemed preoccupied. I was so busy trying to puzzle it out that I didn't notice where we were going until we swung into the end of Cowper Street.

'Hey, Maggie, I thought we were going to the pub?'

Maggie manoeuvred into a space between two other cars. 'I just need to pop into church for a minute. Can you give me a hand?'

'Sure. Hey, isn't that Anita's car?'

'Oh, yes – can't keep her away from the place.' She opened the rear door in order to retrieve my bags.

'What are you doing with those?' I said.

Maggie looked at the bag as if trying to figure out what had happened. 'It'd be a shame if they got nicked.'

I was starting to get worried now. Who would steal a few bags of tatty clothes, especially if it meant breaking into the car first? 'Maggie, are you feeling all right?'

'I'm fine,' said Maggie. 'Come on, let's get inside, out of the cold.'

I was hit by a blaze of light as we opened the door, and I stopped, dazzled. The church hall was full of people: Annie, Helen, Debbie and the rest from Mums' Group. Carly was there, along with several other faces I recognised from Jelly-Tots. Along either side of the hall was a row of trestle tables, laden with clothes and other goods.

Debbie rushed across. 'Surprise!' she said.

'I don't understand,' I said. 'What's going on?'

'It was Maggie's idea,' said Debbie.

Annie joined us. 'We wanted to do something to help you,' she said. 'You know, with funding for your trip.'

'But what are all these people doing here?'

'It's a clothes-swap sale,' said Debbie. 'You know when we were having that conversation about simplicity at Mums' Group?'

'We thought we could all clear out our cupboards,' said Maggie. 'Then we invited as many people as we could think of to come and buy things; and what we don't sell can go to the charity shop.'

'Everybody wins!' said Annie.

'Dave was in on it too,' said Debbie. 'That's why he kept nagging you to sort through your things.'

Shook my head. 'I thought he was just being extra-grumpy.' I paused. Kylie was standing behind the furthest table, arranging a selection of toiletries. She waved shyly when she saw me.

Debbie followed my gaze. 'That's Carly's cousin,' she said. 'I wouldn't have thought this would really be her thing, but Carly said she was desperate to come and help.'

Waved back. 'Good for her,' I said.

Had such a fabulous evening – once I'd got over the shock – although I've told Maggie I'll never trust her again. Altogether we raised £413.26. Amazing!

Dear Jesus, thank you for giving me such wonderful friends – I feel quite humbled. Oh, and thank you for my fantastic nearly new winter coat that cost me all of £20 – can't believe that Carly didn't want it any more.

Thursday 5th March

Dear Jesus, how am I going to find the other £533?

Not that I'm trying to complain: I'm still stunned by my friends' generosity.

Blessing arrived at Mums' Group at the same time as I did. 'You should've seen the look on your face,' she said. 'Shame no one thought to take a picture.'

''Cos that would've been so flattering,' I said. 'Goldfish is so not my best look.'

There was a loud cheer as we walked into Maggie's front room.

I pretended to curtsy. 'It's not often I'm speechless,' I said, 'but you lot managed it last night. How on earth did you plan all that without me finding out?'

'It was a bit tricky,' said Annie, 'especially when Carly almost blurted it out after George had been talking to us.'

'She'd never hack it as a secret agent,' I said. 'She can't resist sharing whatever's on her mind: that's probably why we get on so well.'

'How much do you need to raise now?' said Gillian.

Gulped. '£533.'

Anita passed me a large mug of tea. 'You're nearly halfway there, then. Better start packing.'

Friday 6th March

Edith Mason rang this morning to ask if I could get her a few things from the supermarket.

'You can stop and have a cup of tea with me, if you're not too busy,' she added.

Borrowed a leaf out of Adam's book and persuaded Ellie to pretend that the trolley was a racing car, so that we made it round the supermarket in record time. I love visiting Edith: her house makes me feel like I'm stepping back into a bygone era. There's a huge grandfather clock in the hall which belonged to her mother, but still keeps perfect time. She always serves tea in proper china cups, and arranges the biscuits on a plate with one of those paper doilies: I didn't even know you could still get them.

I also suspect she's been single-handedly responsible for shoring up the British souvenir trade for the past fifty years. She has an assortment of snowstorms and paperweights, several wooden lighthouses decorated in vibrant primary colours, and a plethora of miniature vases; in fact, every bit of available space has some trinket or other to adorn it. There's a brass handbell in the shape of a Welsh lady on the hearth, which is Ellie's favourite plaything when we go to visit.

Edith reached up to the mantelpiece and took down a gaudily painted wooden box with the words *A present from Skegness* engraved across the front.

She caressed the box with tender fingers.

'Me and Harold had our honeymoon there,' she said, her eyes misting over. 'We only got the two days. He was in the Forces, you know.'

I picked up the wedding portrait that stood on the occasional table next to me. Harold was stiffly smart in his regimental uniform, while, beside him, Edith's eyes shone as though she would burst with pride.

'He was very good-looking,' I said. 'You look so happy together.'

Edith sat down and rested the box on her lap. 'He was such a gentleman.' She pulled out a dainty lace handkerchief and dabbed at her face. 'Never had eyes for no one else once I met 'im.'

Maggie told me once that Harold had died relatively young, and that he and Edith never had any children. Most of the time you'd never guess, because she's so full of life and vitality, but every now and then she gets all dewy-eyed. I busied myself with pouring the tea while she replayed her memories.

'Anyway ...' Her voice became brisk. 'I was 'aving me quiet time this morning, and me 20p box came to mind.' She opened the wooden box, which was full of coins. Edith pushed them around with the tip of her finger. 'I don't know how much is there – happen it's not that much – but I'd like you to have it. For that trip of yours.'

'Edith!' Felt almost as dumbstruck as when my friends had surprised me earlier in the week. 'That's so sweet of you.'

A smile danced on Edith's lips, and for a moment she could have been the young woman in the photograph again. 'I just collect all my 20p pieces in this box. Then when it's full, me and God have a chat about what He wants me to do with it. I hope you have a grand time in wherever it is you're going.'

'Guatemala.' I transferred the money to the inner pocket of my bag. 'I'll come and show you all my photos when I get back.'

Felt quite misty-eyed myself as I left. I know it's only £14.60, but it was so sweet of her to give it to me.

Saturday 7th March

Had a long, chatty email from today from the lady who's in charge of the Guatemala trip. Between them, she and Liz have got the itinerary planned down to the last millisecond. (I do so admire people who are organised.)

Dave whistled as he read over my shoulder. 'Looks like you'll need a fortnight's holiday afterwards to recover.'

'Is that an offer?'

'Not unless we come into some money.'

I pointed to the PS at the bottom: Please could those of you who haven't paid the balance do so by next Saturday?

Dave removed his glasses and rubbed his eyes. 'Well, that gives us something to focus on this week. I'll check the credit card balance later.'

Started to feel nauseous. I'm sure we could work something out with the credit card if necessary, but I know Dave would prefer not to. Somehow, I need to find £518.46 pronto.

Sunday 8th March

Make that £500.46.

Annie thrust Ben at me as I went to queue for tea after the service.

'Here, would you mind taking him for a minute?'

'I'd love to.'

I know he can still wail like a banshee at night, but when he's in a good mood Ben is gorgeous. He gave a deep chuckle as I rubbed my nose against his.

Annie rummaged in her purse. 'You see, John and me have got into the habit of having a takeaway on a Friday night.'

'Sounds good to me.'

She scooped out a note, along with a fistful of change. 'Well, we decided that this week we'd do without. Then you can put the money towards your trip.'

Almost dropped Ben as I reached across to hug her. 'Are you sure? Didn't John mind?'

Annie stuffed her purse back in her bag. 'It was his idea. He said he didn't want you thinking that heathens like him have no moral compass.'

'As if I would!'

Annie lifted Ben back onto her shoulder. 'His idea of a joke. I think he's secretly rather impressed with what you're doing.'

Monday 9th March

Just in case I started feeling too positive …

Linda phoned this morning to see 'if you're still planning to go on this ridiculous trip of yours'.

I know she's Dave's mum, but some days I find it hard to be civil with her. Made sure I counted to ten before I spoke. 'I'm only going away for a week. Dave and I have talked about it lots, and he's very supportive of me.'

Linda harrumphed in a way that would have put any Grand National winner to shame. 'I still think it's very irresponsible of you. Isn't it very expensive?'

Didn't like where this was heading. 'Mmm … it's not too bad. And people have been very generous.'

'I don't think you should be relying on hand-outs from other people.'

Counted to twenty this time. 'It's not like that. And I'm sure it'll all come together before I go.'

There was a pregnant pause.

Then: 'I do hope you know what you're doing,' she said.

Felt pleased when I came off the phone that I'd stood my ground. Half an hour later, I was less sure. Linda's accusations had wriggled their way into my subconscious. Was I being irresponsible? And – on reflection – my friends have been more than generous, but it would be unfair to expect them to stump up any more cash. Which means that there's still a dizzying chasm between the amount I've raised and what I actually need to pay out.

Tuesday 10th March

Dear Jesus, I need £500 by next weekend – help!

Wednesday 11th March

Dear Jesus, I'm starting to panic a little bit – OK, a lot. It's Wednesday evening, and I'm supposed to have the money into the Leicester church's bank account by Saturday. I thought this was Your idea – have I got it wrong, after all? I know it says something in the Bible about it being a wicked and adulterous generation that asks for a sign, but it'd be nice to know that I haven't completely messed up here.

Thursday 12th March

Shared with Mums' Group this morning about the £500. Felt a bit awkward about it – didn't want people to think I was begging for money. They've all been so generous already.

'Please Jesus, can You show Becky the way through this?' said Blessing.

'Thank You, God, for calling Becky to go to Guatemala,' said Gillian, 'and please can You help her to get the money she needs?'

'Jesus, we want to leave this with You – we know You're in control,' said Debbie.

Quite touching, really; although it did leave me with the sense that somebody else should be going instead. They all seem to have so much more faith than I do.

Annie looked thoughtful after we'd finished praying.

'Maggie,' she said, 'd'you remember that verse you told us about ages ago? The one about trusting God instead of thinking that we know best?'

'Oh yes,' said Maggie, 'it's one of my favourite verses.'

'I can't get it out of my head,' said Annie. 'All the time we were praying, it was just going round and round in my brain.'

Anita was thumbing through her Bible. 'It's in Proverbs 3,' she said, 'shall I read it out?'

Trust in the LORD with all your heart and lean not on your own understanding; in all your ways acknowledge him, and he will make your paths straight.

Annie nodded. 'That's the one.' She turned to me. 'I think that God wants to remind you of that verse this morning – but it might be just me.'

I was starting to feel all goose-pimply. 'Mmm,' I said. 'Actually, I have the same verses stuck to my fridge.'

Stayed behind for a chat after the others had gone. Maggie obviously felt the need to exercise her knack for asking awkward questions.

'So, what do you make of that verse?' she said.

Gulped. 'I guess it means I've got to trust God more.'

Maggie grinned. 'You and me both,' she said. 'What about the second bit?'

'Well, I've got to acknowledge God – whatever that means.'

Maggie considered for a moment. 'I think it's about believing who God says He is – and trying to live in a way that shows we believe it. Then He'll show us what to do.'

'But what does that mean for *me*?'

'Dunno exactly – except that you're already showing what you believe by listening to God when He asked you to go on this trip.'

'I suppose ...'

'So we can trust that God will fulfil His side of the bargain. He'll sort it out.'

I can see what she means. Just wish I could accept it as easily as she does.

Dear Jesus, I could do with an extra dollop of faith right now. Not to mention £500.

Friday 13th March

Lots of supportive texts and messages from my friends this morning.

Debbie: Prayers and a big hug. xx
Annie: Keep thinking of that verse! Hope God helps you find a way.
Maggie: Don't worry, God'll sort it!
Helen: Prayed extra hard for you this morning. Would it be OK if I popped in this afternoon?

Gulp. Hope that's not for one of her God-can-do-anything-if-you-just-believe homilies. (I know He can in theory; it just always seems more complex than that in real life.)

Texted back: Sure – about 1.30?

6pm. Just sent Dave out to get fish and chips as I'm still too shell-shocked to make tea.

Helen rang the doorbell at twenty-five past one. (She'd never dream of being late.) Moved Ellie's teddies off the sofa so she could sit down.

'Tea?'

She shook her head. 'I'm all right, I just wanted to chat about something.'

I took the seat next to her. 'No problem. I've been reliably informed on a number of occasions that chatting is one of my greatest skills.'

Given that it was Helen, I hadn't expected her to roll around on the floor laughing at this – but then I hadn't expected her to burst into tears, either.

'Helen, I'm so sorry. I didn't mean to offend you.'

She sobbed even louder.

'Please forgive me, Helen, I just say the first thing that comes into my head.'

Helen pulled a (beautifully ironed) handkerchief from her pocket, and blew her nose noisily in a most un-Helen-like manner. 'It's … it's not you,' she wailed.

'What is it, then? What's happened?'

Helen started dabbing at the corners of her eyes. 'I wish I was more like you.'

Pardon?

'I'm sorry, I think I misheard you,' I said. 'What did you say?'

She snivelled. 'I wish I was more like you.'

Didn't know how on earth to respond to this. My ability to talk for England had deserted me. 'But Helen …'

'I mean it, Becky. You're always so kind and thoughtful. You always know the right thing to say to people, and I just seem to rub them up the wrong way.'

'Hey, that's not true.' (Well, maybe the last bit.) 'Don't knock yourself. You're so efficient and organised. Whereas me, I'm always Mrs Always-on-the-last-minute.'

'Yes, but you're good at the things that matter. What's the point of a clean house if people don't feel welcome?'

I gestured at the mound of toys in the corner. 'I wouldn't mind my house being a bit tidier: almost broke my neck this morning falling over a car that Ellie had left on the stairs.'

Helen sighed. 'You see? If that'd been me I'd have got so mad. You just take everything in your stride.'

'I'm not sure I can picture you getting mad, Helen. You always look so in control.'

A tear trickled down her cheek. 'I do get cross – furious, sometimes – but I try not to show it because I don't want to set the children a bad example.'

'But your kids are great,' I said, 'and they're all developing their own relationship with Jesus.'

This provoked another torrent. Her hanky was sopping wet by now, and I passed her the tissue box. Three coloured beads and a small plastic elephant clattered onto the coffee table as she pulled out a fresh tissue.

'I just feel such a hypocrite,' she said. 'I try to be a good mum, but inside I'm just a seething mass of resentment and anger.'

'But Helen …'

'You don't have to try to make it better,' she said. 'I've been so busy trying to have everything perfect that I've missed out the things that matter most.'

'What d'you mean?'

'I mean stuff like being a good friend, and showing people that I care. All those women at Mums' Group yesterday, saying nice things about you and praying for you – that's because they know you care about *them*.'

'But you care too, Helen. I'm sure you've been praying for me lots.'

'Yes, I know I have – but I find it difficult to say the right thing to encourage people. I think sometimes I just intimidate them.'

'Well …'

She pulled herself up straight and looked me in the eye. 'It's all right. You don't have to pretend.'

Didn't want to upset her any more than she already was. Fumbled around for the right words. *(Dear Jesus, how can I say this?)* 'Well, maybe you do a bit, sometimes. You're mega-organised, you're very creative. You know lots about the Bible, and you always pray so passionately.'

'I don't mean to scare people off, though.'

'No. And all those things are good things. It's just … maybe you need to let people see when you're struggling, too.'

She crumpled again. 'I'm not very good at that. I'd just despise myself for being weak, when I know there are others who have much more important stuff to worry about.'

'Hey, give yourself a break! Your needs matter just as much to God as anyone else's.'

'I suppose. But aren't we meant to be strong in our faith?'

'I think that's one of those paradox thingies: when it comes to faith, we can't be strong until we admit how weak we are.'

'"*When I am weak, then I am strong*",' said Helen. 'It's in 2 Corinthians.'

'There you go,' I said. 'You're much better than me when it comes to finding your way around the Bible.'

Helen gave a wan smile. 'Now I just need to do it. I mean, stop pretending I'm strong all the time.' She took my hands. 'Becky, I'm so sorry if I've intimidated you in any way – you will forgive me, won't you?'

Let go of her hands so I could give her a hug. 'Course I will. I think you're brave for sharing all this stuff. I'm glad you came round.'

Helen squeezed me back: a proper squeeze, not one of her usual genteel affairs. 'Thanks for listening. You're a good friend.'

'You're welcome. Now, how about that cuppa?'

9pm. Another text – Helen again.

Hi Becky, thanks again for this afternoon. I've just had a good chat with Brendan about it. Please pray for me – I'm going to try to live out that verse. I've written it out and stuck it on the fridge. God is good. xx. PS Still praying about the money.

11pm. Couldn't sleep as I was still thinking about Helen. Came downstairs to get a glass of milk. Felt tired but awake all at the same time. Had that itch in my brain that you get when you know there's something simmering away, but you can't quite work out what it is.

'So, what are you going to do about your verse, Becky?'

The words swam into focus; a kaleidoscope of letters forming a perfect pattern.

'Erm ... well ... I suppose I have to try to live it out, too.'

The words persisted: 'And how can you do that?'

Oh. All of a sudden, it seemed very simple. I knelt beside the sofa.

Dear Jesus, I know You have plans for me, and I'm pretty sure they include going to Guatemala. So, I'm gonna keep trusting You, even when things feel a bit muddled. If You want me to go, I'll trust You to provide. Amen.

Felt an enormous sense of peace, like being cocooned in a fluffy blanket. Was also pretty sure that somewhere, Father, Son and Holy Spirit were smiling.

Chapter Fifteen

Saturday 14th March

Must have drifted off on the sofa last night. Crawled into bed at half-past two.

'Wha' you been doin'?' muttered Dave.

'Talking to Jesus – but I think I fell asleep.'

'Tha's nice ...' His voice trailed off into silence. I snuggled into the space next to him and kissed the top of his head.

'Night-night, darling. I think it's all going to be OK.'

9.30am. Huh! Wish I felt as confident in the cold light of day as I did at 2am. Tried to hold onto my verse by singing it aloud while washing up the breakfast things – it fits quite nicely to the tune of *I Had a Little Nut-tree*.

In all your ways acknowledge Him, and He will make a way.
In all your ways acknowledge Him, and He will make a way.
In all your ways ...

Ellie cackled. 'Funny Mummy!'

'Couldn't agree more,' said Dave. 'Sorry to interrupt your musical routine – Mum's just texted to say they'd like to call in this morning. Around ten-ish.'

Stopped mid-sentence. Oh no! Never got around to vacuuming yesterday, what with Helen coming to see me. Could do without Linda reminding me how incompetent I am. Could feel my remaining confidence seeping away: time for a pity party.

Trudged through to check the state of the lounge. Ellie had constructed herself a nest of teddy bears on the sofa, with her blanket draped across the top. She tried to push me away as I scooped them up and deposited them in the corner.

'Sorry, darling, but we need to make sure there's somewhere for Grandma and Granddad to sit. Why don't you build a den in the corner?'

Ellie was not to be placated. 'Gan-ma on floor,' she said, trying to reclaim her place on the sofa.

Hmm, don't think that would go down too well. Yanked at the cushions to straighten them up, and caught a flash of white next to the arm of the sofa. Helen's handkerchief.

Wonder how she's doing today, I thought. *Dear Jesus, please help Helen with her verse.*

Oh. I sat down with a bump. Bit dopey of me praying for Helen and her verse, and then ignoring mine.

OK, God – if You're asking me to trust you, then I'll go for it.

Started humming again. In all your ways …

Linda and Graham were prompt (as always). Steered them into the lounge, to find Ellie dragging her blanket across the floor. There was a huge pile of teddies next to the coffee table, with Ginger Giraffe in pride of place at the top of the heap.

'Ellie!' I said. 'I thought you were going to make a den in the corner? Grandma and Granddad need somewhere to sit down.'

Ellie launched herself on top of the pile. 'My den here,' she said.

'It's not the most helpful place …'

Graham came to her defence. 'Can I help you?' he said. 'I used to be quite good at making dens when I was little.'

Ellie cocked her head on one side, trying to work out whether Granddad was up to the task. Then – the ultimate honour – she held out her blanket. 'Yours do it,' she said. 'My help.'

'That's grand,' said Graham. 'I tell you what, Daddy and I can help you make a den, and Grandma can go and put the kettle on.'

'What a good idea,' said Linda. 'Re … Becky, would you come and show me which are the right cups?'

'I got everything out ready,' I said, trailing behind her into the kitchen. 'There's tea in the pot – it's just brewing.'

'Lovely,' said Linda. 'Why don't you and I sit in here and have a little chat? We'll leave the boys to play dens with Ellie.'

'Er, OK.'

Didn't feel OK. Wondered whether Linda had somehow engineered things so that she could give me one of her little lectures about the best way to clean the grouting in the bathroom. But she was quiet. Too quiet.

'Is everything OK, Linda?' I said. 'You look a bit pale.'

'Yes, yes – I'm fine. Just wanted to come and see you about something.'

Thought as much. 'I'm all yours,' I said.

Linda opened and closed her mouth several times. She's not one to hold back on expressing her views. I was starting to feel panicky. Whatever I'd done, it must be bad news.

'It's not easy to say this, Rebec … Becky.'

I'd already worked that out. (And why was she calling me Becky?)

'Can I help?'

'No, it's all right.' She took a most un-Linda-like swig of her tea. 'No, I just need to tell you what happened on Thursday morning.'

'Nothing serious, I hope?'

'I went out for coffee with two of my friends – do you remember Jane and Louisa?'

My memory of Linda's friends was that they were even more into competitive cleaning than she was. I nodded.

'Well, we were talking about our families, and what you were all doing. Jane's son has just got some huge promotion, and his wife is on the town council. Louisa's daughter runs her own business, and jets off to the south of France every other weekend to see her boyfriend. They were both going on about what big mortgages they had, and how they all deserved a nice lifestyle because they worked so hard.'

She paused to top up her cup. 'Anyway, they started asking about you and David, and I was telling them about this trip of yours.'

'Oh?' My spirits wilted, and I braced myself for another barrage of criticism.

She banged her cup into the saucer. 'Do you know, I felt quite cross with them. They pretended to be interested for about five seconds, but then they just started talking about whether Louisa's daughter should paint her lounge *blush rose* or *peach melba*, and how Jane's son was getting a top-of-the-range Mercedes as part of his new job package.'

Had to bite my lip as she added: 'I can't bear it when people make so much fuss about keeping up appearances.'

'I can see how that was frustrating,' I said, 'but please don't worry about me – I don't mind what they think.'

'But I do,' said Linda, 'and the more I thought about it, the more I minded.'

The colour had come back to her cheeks, and she was sounding more like her usual feisty self.

'Well, it's very kind of you to be so concerned,' I said, 'but there's really ...'

But Linda was going full steam ahead now. 'It was going round and round in my head all Thursday afternoon,' she said. 'I couldn't even concentrate properly at bridge yesterday. How could they be so shallow?'

Hoped this was rhetorical, as I wasn't at all sure how to answer it otherwise.

A note of hesitation crept back into Linda's voice. 'I know I wasn't at all enthusiastic about the idea to begin with,' she said, 'but I had an epiphany yesterday teatime. You're doing this because you believe in it – and it's much more important than trivial stuff like getting your lounge walls the perfect shade of pink.'

'I suppose it takes all sorts,' I said.

Linda grabbed her handbag from beside her chair, and began flicking through the contents.

'Yes, but you're committed to helping other people rather than just yourself,' she said. 'I shall remind my friends next time I see them that there's more to life than interior design.'

Well, absolutely.

She flourished a pale pink envelope in front of me. 'Anyway, I just wanted to bring you a card to say all the best.' She stood up and tucked it behind a plant pot on the windowsill. 'I'll leave it there and you can open it later.'

'Thank you – that's very kind.'

'No, no, not at all.' She leaned over and gave me an awkward hug. 'Now, shall we see how the boys are getting on? I expect building dens is thirsty work.'

'Well, that was bizarre,' I said, as Dave and I watched their car pull out of the drive half an hour later.

'You're telling me. I think Dad was lying about building lots of dens when he was younger. Either that, or he's more forgetful than I thought.'

'Don't s'pose Ellie minded.'

Dave chortled. 'She kept saying "No, Gan-dad, not like that!" – but he just did as he was told.'

'I guess he's learned from experience.'

'Probably. Is there any tea left in the pot?'

'I'll make some more. Darling, d'you think your mum's OK?'

'Seemed all right to me. Why?'

I was trying to analyse our conversation. 'I dunno, she just seemed less imperious than usual.'

'I'm sure she'll make up for it next time she's here.'

'And she kept calling me Becky.'

Dave followed me through to the kitchen and grabbed two fresh mugs off the drainer. 'Now that is a worry. Maybe they're both coming down with something. What did she want to chat about?'

I smiled at the recollection. 'She was complaining about her friends being obsessed with how their houses looked, or something.'

'That's a bit rich.'

'Yeah. Oh, and she wanted to give me a card.'

I retrieved the envelope and slid my finger under the flap. A slip of paper fell to the floor. The inside of the card was covered with Linda's precise, neat handwriting.

Dear Becky,

I wasn't quite sure how to say this, so I thought it might be better if I wrote it down.

I hope you can forgive any negative comments I might have made regarding your trip to Guatemala. Graham and I are very impressed with what you're doing, and we're very proud of the fact that we have a daughter-in-law who stands up for what she believes in.

I'm not sure I'd ever have the confidence to do what you're doing, but I would still like to do my bit to make a difference.

Please would you accept the enclosed towards your trip?

With love, Linda

I bent down to pick the paper up from the floor, then held it out to Dave. My legs had turned to jelly. Dave scanned the cheque and whistled

'*Five hundred pounds!*' He wiped his glasses carefully before taking another look. 'Well, you know what they say about God working in mysterious ways?'

Sunday 15th March

George's sermon – appropriately enough – was on God providing for our needs. Felt very grateful (in a still-slightly-stunned sort of way) as I reflected on the events of the past couple of weeks.

Although, if I was inclined to be picky, I'd have to point out that I'm still forty-six pence down. I guess that's the difference between books and real life: in all the books, when people pray they get the right amount of money, down to the last farthing.

Monday 16th March

God had the last laugh.

Jennifer came bounding through to the kitchen while I was getting tea ready.

'I've found my bracelet; I've found my bracelet.'

I swung to face her, scattering frozen peas across the floor as I did so.

'I told you it'd turn up. Where was it?'

'Down the side of the sofa. I dropped my pencil down there, so I was just trying to get it out and I found my bracelet.'

'See? It must have fallen off when you weren't looking.'

Jennifer looked indignant. 'It's not my fault!'

'Well ...' I started picking peas off the floor. 'Did you find any more missing treasures down there?'

She dumped her bracelet on the worktop (right next to the potato peelings that were about to be thrown in the bin). 'I'm just going to have another look.'

Jennifer and Adam reappeared five minutes later, each clutching a fistful of goodies. There were three felt-tips (one with no lid), five hair clips, several biscuit wrappers and enough Lego to build a small mansion.

Oh, and an assortment of coins, totalling 46p.

Tuesday 17th March

That means it's real.

Wednesday 18th March

Still can't quite believe this is happening to *me*.

Thursday 19th March

Didn't want to embarrass Linda by saying where the money had come from, so just shared with Mums' Group the gist of what had happened the previous Saturday.

'Thank you all so much for praying,' I said. 'I still can't quite believe that it's all come together like that.'

'You'd better start packing,' said Maggie. 'Will you have any space to take a few goodies out for Liz and Rupert?'

'I thought I'd take some teabags – they're not very easy to get hold of over there.'

'How's Dave feeling about it?' said Maggie. 'D'you think he'll cope OK without you?'

'It'll be funny being apart for a week,' I said, 'but I'm sure he'll be fine.'

'Hope his cooking skills are up to scratch,' said Debbie.

'I think he'll get through half a ton of oven chips,' I said, 'but I don't suppose the kids will object. He's threatened to do some other stuff around the house, too; although I did think perhaps I ought to warn him that Tallulah-the-Toilet-Roll-Fairy and Wendy-the-Washing-Fairy don't actually exist.'

Friday 20th March

One week to go! Had a big panic this afternoon. What if Debbie's poorly, and can't pick the kids up? What if Linda changes her mind and demands her £500 back? What if I meet a ginormous spider while we're away, and I frighten all the teenagers by screaming at the top of my voice?

Texted Dave at lunchtime to ask if he thought I should back out.

Don't you dare! he replied, I've just managed to negotiate leaving the staff meeting early on Tuesday so I can sort the kids out.

Saturday 21st March

This time next week I'll be in Guatemala.

Did a mammoth-sized shop at the supermarket this morning. Dave stared in amazement as I dumped bag after bag on the kitchen floor.

'Are we preparing for a siege?' he asked.

'I just want to make sure you've got enough stuff in while I'm away.'

'But you're only going for a week.'

I stood back to survey my purchases. 'You'll still have to go and pick up things like bread and milk,' I said, 'unless you want me to do an order online?'

'I'm sure we can manage.'

I pulled the crumpled list out of my jeans pocket and began checking things off. 'I just want everything to be organised – pasta, tomatoes, rice …'

Dave reached over my shoulder and prised the list out of my hand. 'Just chill, Becky – I do know where the supermarket is, as it happens.'

Suddenly saw the funny side. 'Oh, yeah?' I said. 'Next, you'll be telling me you know how to work the washing machine.'

Sunday 22nd March

(Five days to go.)

George took great delight in embarrassing me this morning. As soon as the children were out of the way he turned and beckoned to me.

'I think most of you know that Becky's off to Guatemala on Friday,' he announced, 'so I think it'd be good if we could all pray for her before she goes.'

Crept up to the front, half-hoping that the Second Coming would happen before I got there.

'Come on, Becky, don't be shy,' said George, waving the microphone under my nose. 'Would you mind just telling us a bit about what you'll be doing?' He winked at me and lowered the microphone. 'I know how much you hate being upfront,' he whispered, 'so I thought I'd just surprise you.'

I worry about George sometimes: for a pastor, he has a very naughty streak.

Still, it was nice being prayed for by everyone – once I'd stuttered my way through a rather convoluted description of why I was abandoning my family for a week.

'Well done,' said Anita, after the service. She handed me a carrier bag. 'I bought some teabags for you to pass on to Liz, and there's a few things that Laura's grown out of that I thought she might find useful.'

Edith waved at me as I joined the tea and coffee queue.

'Would you like me to get you a drink, Edith?' I said.

'Ooh, yes, please, dearie – that'd be grand.' She rummaged in her handbag. 'And would you like to take these with you – for that lovely couple you're going to see?'

'Liz and Rupert,' I said, dropping the teabags in with Anita's gifts. 'That's very kind of you.'

'Ooh, it's my pleasure. If I was ten years younger, I think I'd be coming with you.'

Had a rather lovely picture of Edith, propping herself up on her walking stick while she sloshed paint around with her free hand and kept an eye on the younger generation all at the same time.

'I think you'd be great,' I said. 'Maybe next time?'

'What's all that stuff?' said Jennifer, when we got home.

'Things people have given me to take to Guatemala.'

She peered inside one of the bags. 'There's well loads of tea in here.'

'Mmm.'

Emptied the bags onto the table. It's very good of people to be so generous – but I now have to work out how to fit 840 teabags plus an assortment of children's clothes into my suitcase. Looks like I'll be travelling light.

Monday 23rd March

(Four days.)

Climbed into the loft this morning to find a bigger suitcase. Even with the teabags and the extra clothes, there's still plenty of room for my stuff. Wrote myself a list:

- Clothes
- Toiletries
- Towel
- Bible
- Passport/travel insurance

Went back into the bedroom to find Ellie filling the remaining space with an assortment of soft toys, and plastic food from her toy kitchen.

'My helping, Mummy,' she said.

'That's very kind, Ellie, but I expect your giraffe would prefer to stay here and help you look after Daddy.'

Retrieved my passport and travel insurance from the filing cabinet and tucked them into the pocket inside the suitcase so I won't forget them.

Tuesday 24th March

(Three days.)

Carly waved me over when I got to Jelly-Tots. 'Are you all packed, then?' she said.

I shook my head. 'Not yet – but I've made a start.'

Carly thrust a carrier bag at me. 'That's OK, then – I've dug out a few things that Maisie's grown out of – thought that friend of yours might be able to use them.'

'Er – thank you.' More clothes! The bag was filled to the point where it looked like it might explode at any point.

Dear Jesus, people are being very kind, but at this rate You're gonna have to provide me with a private jet to transport all the extra stuff.

Wednesday 25th March

(Two days. *Two days!*)

Had a mega-washing session today. Thought I might get a bit of packing done after lunch, but Mum decided to ring me up for a pre-holiday catch-up.

She managed to keep going for a full forty-five minutes, during which period she reminded me at least half a dozen times to be careful and told me to make sure not to accept any packages from strangers.

'Well,' she said, eventually, 'I mustn't keep you, I'm sure you've got lots to do. Make sure you let us know you've got there safely, won't you, only your dad and I will feel a bit anxious if we don't hear from you.'

Thursday 26th March

I am going to Guatemala tomorrow!

Wasn't sure whether to go to Mums' Group, but Maggie texted to say it'd be nice to have me there so that they could all pray for me. Came home afterwards feeling very appreciative of all the prayers that had been uttered on my behalf. Was less appreciative of the extra 160 teabags, and the five jumpers that Helen had knitted herself 'in case Liz knows anyone who needs them'. (Although, being Helen's handiwork, they are exquisite – shame they're all too small for me.)

Laid all Liz's goodies out on the bed after lunch, then made a separate pile of my own things. It was a bit like the first time we took Jennifer away on holiday: her stuff took up about three times as much room as Dave's and mine put together. Hmm. Decided that seeing as this was supposed to be a working holiday, I could go for the minimalist approach. Allowed myself clean undies for each day (even I have some standards), but discarded three T-shirts and a dress that I had planned to take 'just in case'.

Meanwhile, Ellie was having great fun using the empty suitcase as a boat.

'My rowing, Mummy,' she said, rocking back and forth with a vigour that would have made most people seasick.

Left her to play while I grabbed an old beach towel from the airing cupboard. It's not the poshest towel I've ever seen: in fact, it's rather scruffy. It does, however, have the advantage of being big enough to preserve my modesty – something I'm feeling quite anxious about, given that I'm twenty-plus years older than most members of the team.

'Come on, Ellie, Mummy needs to pack now.' I scooped her out of the suitcase and onto the floor.

'No!' shouted Ellie. 'My boat.'

Had a sudden brainwave. 'Why don't you pack a little case for Ginger Giraffe? He could come with you to Debbie's in the morning.'

Ellie was miraculously appeased. (Must be all that prayer earlier.) She ran off, then reappeared with her giraffe. I fished around in the bottom of my wardrobe and found an old vanity case for her to put things in. Ginger's packing list was rather more eclectic than mine. It seems that a well-travelled giraffe needs four green wooden bricks, two slices of plastic pizza and a pair of toy sunglasses with sparkly blue frames. Oh, and a wind-up musical box that plays *My Bonnie Lies Over the Ocean* at top speed – bet Debbie's going to love that.

Managed to squash everything into my case, then forced the zip closed by sitting on the lid. Hurrah! There was just time for a quick cuppa before I needed to pick the older two up from school.

'All sorted?' said Dave, after tea.

'Surprisingly, yes. The suitcase is all packed, and I've laid out my clothes for the morning.'

'You managed to fit all those teabags in?'

'Including the extra ones I got given this morning. Goodness knows what Security'll make of it if they decide to open my case.'

'Money? Just in case you need something at the airport.'

'In my handbag – although I don't suppose there'll be much I want to spend it on.'

'Tickets?'

'The group leader from the church in Leicester has got them all with her – I'm meeting them all when I get to Heathrow.'

'Good stuff. Got your passport?'

'I put it in the inside pocket of the suitcase.'

'But you'll need it with you.'

'I left it in there so I didn't forget it. Maybe I ought to put it in my handbag.'

Dave prised my mug out of my hands. 'Go and do it now, otherwise you'll wake up in the middle of the night flapping about it.'

Felt ever-so-slightly smug as I climbed the stairs. For once in my life, I was on top of things. Yanked at the zip on the suitcase, hoping that I wouldn't get buried in an avalanche of teabags. Forced my hand through the narrow opening, and felt around for the pocket. Found my travel insurance almost straight away, but – wouldn't you know it – the passport must have dropped right down to bottom, because my straining fingertips couldn't find it.

There was nothing for it but to open the case properly and hope that I could get everything back in again afterwards.

'Dave!' I yelled. 'Have you seen my passport?'

I could hear him moving through to the hall. 'What?'

'My passport. I can't find it.'

He bounded up the stairs. 'I thought you said it was in the suitcase.'

'I put it there on Monday – but it's not there now.'

'It'll have fallen out and got mixed up with the other stuff.'

He grabbed the case and scattered the contents across the bed.

'Dave! It took me ages to get everything in there.'

'I'll help you sort it in a minute.' He began shaking out the clothes I had so neatly folded. 'Are you sure you put it in here?'

'I know I did: I'm not completely stupid.'

'Well, I can't see it now. I'll go and check in the filing cabinet.'

Sank onto the bed, wondering if I'd ever manage to get everything back in the case. Not that there'd be much point, if my passport didn't turn up.

Dear Jesus, is this Your idea of a joke?

Dave strode back in, followed by the older two children hoping to find the cause of the commotion.

'Can we help?' said Jennifer. 'I'm good at finding things.'

'Be my guest,' said Dave, 'and get praying that it turns up quickly.'

Jennifer dropped to the floor and tried to peer under the bed. Adam frowned and gazed into the middle distance, as though he expected it to materialise out of thin air. Dave started chucking clothes back into the case. A green brick tumbled to the floor as he lifted Helen's handiwork off the bed. Reminded me of earlier in the day.

Oh! Pushed past Adam and Jennifer to the bedroom doorway.

'Ellie!' I yelled. 'Have you seen Mummy's passport?'

Epilogue

Friday 15th May

The spiritual high of Guatemala seems to be wearing off. Either that, or I'm coming down with something: I struggled to get out of bed this morning.

'Are you all right, love?' said Dave, as I staggered into the kitchen.

'I don't feel brilliant,' I said. 'Is there any tea in the pot?'

Dave passed me a steaming mug. 'Here. Maybe this'll make you feel better. There's been a lot of bugs going round at school – hope you haven't caught something.'

Took a satisfying slurp of tea. 'I'll be OK. I can't be ill, anyway – I promised Helen I'd help out at Elijah's birthday party tomorrow.'

He leaned over and kissed the top of my head. 'Well, try to take it steady.'

There was a biting wind blowing up our road as we walked to school. By the time we got home my legs were aching, but at least my head was less groggy. Ignored Dave's advice and got on with cleaning the bathroom, then made a mountain of buns for Elijah's party. (Just shows that miracles do happen – this time last year I'd never have dared to bake anything for Helen.) Ellie had great fun helping me decorate the buns, although a large number of the sweets I had bought to go on top found their way into her mouth instead.

'Think we'll have to go to the shops on the way to school,' I said, 'otherwise some of these buns won't have any sweeties to go on the top.'

'Oh dear!' said Ellie, who appeared surprised that we'd run out.

Grabbed a notebook. 'Let's make a list,' I said. 'We could do with some more bananas – somebody keeps eating them.'

'Me!' shouted Ellie, jumping up and down on her chair.

'Yes, you.' I was starting to feel a bit odd again. 'Why don't we go and put the telly on while I'm writing my list?'

I think I must have nodded off for a few minutes, because I came to with a start when Ellie kicked the remote off the sofa. My notebook had disappeared down the side of the cushion, so scribbled on the back of an envelope instead: Sweets, bananas, chicken, mushrooms, sanitary towels, eggs …

'Wha's matter, Mummy?' said Ellie.

Snapped back into the present. 'Nothing, darling – I was just thinking about something.' Glanced at the clock. 'Come on, if we go out now we should have time to go to the shops before we have to get Adam and Jennifer.'

But Ellie was not in a cooperative mood, and we only just made it round the supermarket via the chemists before arriving at school two minutes late. Not that it mattered too much: Adam dawdled out five minutes after most of his class, and Jennifer was later still. I sometimes think she'd move into school on a permanent basis if it was allowed.

Dave tries to get home a bit earlier on a Friday – that's if he doesn't get caught by his head of department on the way out. Today he'd obviously been unlucky.

'Sorry I'm a bit late,' he called. 'My head of department was in a talkative mood.' He dropped two carrier bags full of marking on the kitchen floor, right where people would trip over them. 'How are you doing?'

'Mmm, not too bad. I ...'

Ellie came charging down the stairs, waving a small white plastic stick.

'Daddy, Daddy, my got a wand.' She twirled across the room, flapping her arms in a futile attempt to become airborne.

'Hey, that's cool,' said Dave. 'Where did you get that?'

'My found it ... Mummy's cupboard. Look, Daddy!'

She held it out for inspection. Dave studied it, puzzled, and then turned it over. The thin, blue line was visible from across the room. He looked at the line, and then at me, his face registering confusion followed by understanding followed by delight.

I reached out my arms and pulled him close so that I could whisper in his ear: 'Y'know that early night we had after I got back from Guatemala?'

Beside me, Ellie tugged at my trouser leg. 'Wha's happen, Mummy?'

Dave reached down to ruffle her curls. 'Everything's fine, Ellie. Tell you what, why don't you and I go to the shops and get you a proper wand?'

She tugged at my hand. 'Yours coming, Mummy?'

Dave shook his head. 'This is a Daddy and Ellie adventure. We'll let Mummy sit down and have a nice cup of tea.'

Acknowledgements

I've been writing this book for longer than I care to think about, and I couldn't have made it this far without the encouragement of others along the way. My thanks to Jane Clamp, Kimm Brook, Deborah Jenkins and Helen Murray for taking time to read what I had written and to offer helpful advice, and to Angela Hobday and Bridget Plass for their generous endorsements. I'm grateful to Instant Apostle for being willing to take a chance on a new author, and in particular to Nicki Copeland and Sheila Jacobs for their guidance through the editing process. And – last but not least – thanks to Andy, Jonathan, Lizzie, Sarah and Catherine, for all your love and support.